'You have admitted to me that you do not expect to receive any proposals of marriage,' Captain Fawley ploughed on with brutal candour.

'And that at the end of the season, because of your straitened circumstances, you will have to seek paid employment. You will be quite miserable.'

Deborah's heart was pounding hard. She could not remember any man ever insulting her so comprehensively. Even though all he had said was true, it was cruel of him to fling it in her face. How dared he taunt her with her wish to marry, having told her she stood no chance of snaring a man?

'I do not think I wish to continue with this conversation,' she said, rising to her feet and turning her back on him.

'Miss Gillies, do not turn me down before you hear the whole.'

Turn him down? She froze. What was he trying to say?

'The…the whole?' Reluctantly, she looked at him over her shoulder.

'Yes.' He got to his feet, reached for her upper arm, and spun her to face him. 'I thought you, of all women, might overcome your revulsion for such a man as I am in return for lifelong security.'

'You are asking me to marry you?'

Annie Burrows has been making up stories for her own amusement since she first went to school. As soon as she got the hang of using a pencil she began to write them down. Her love of books meant she had to do a degree in English literature. And her love of writing meant she could never take on a job where she didn't have time to jot down notes when inspiration for a new plot struck her. She still wants the heroines of her stories to wear beautiful floaty dresses, and triumph over all that life can throw at them. But when she got married she discovered that finding a hero is an essential ingredient to arriving at 'happy ever after'.

Recent novels by Annie Burrows:

HIS CINDERELLA BRIDE
MY LADY INNOCENT
THE EARL'S UNTOUCHED BRIDE

CAPTAIN FAWLEY'S INNOCENT BRIDE

Annie Burrows

MILLS & BOON®

Pure reading pleasure™

First published in Great Britain 2008
Large Print edition 2009
Harlequin Mills & Boon Limited,
Eton House, 18-24 Paradise Road, Richmond, Surrey TW9 1SR

© Annie Burrows 2008

ISBN: 978 0 263 20660 9

Set in Times Roman 16 on 18½ pt.
42-0409-79584

Printed and bound in Great Britain
by CPI Antony Rowe, Chippenham, Wiltshire

CAPTAIN FAWLEY'S INNOCENT BRIDE

To Viv
For introducing me to the works of
Georgette Heyer

Chapter One

'Oh, no,' Susannah grumbled to her friend, Miss Deborah Gillies, snapping open her fan and raising it to conceal the lower part of her face. 'Here comes Captain Fawley, hobbling over to ask me to dance again. And I cannot. I simply cannot.'

Deborah compressed her lips to hide her own revulsion—oh, not at Captain Fawley. The poor man could not help the way he looked. He had lost the lower part of one leg, and his left hand in the same explosion which had so badly disfigured his face. His left eyelid would for ever droop into the scarring that covered his whole cheek, twisting his mouth into a permanently cynical expression. No, she could feel nothing but compassion for him.

It was Susannah's behaviour that upset her.

Captain Fawley bowed over her friend's hand, his dark eyes raised to hers with dogged determination.

'Good evening, Miss Hullworthy, Miss Gillies.' Though he included Deborah in his greeting, he shot her only the briefest glance. 'I was hoping I might prevail upon you to dance with me this evening.'

'Oh, dear,' said Susannah, with just the right amount of regret in her voice to sound convincing. 'I am afraid my dance card is already full. And here comes my partner for the quadrille.' She looked over Captain Fawley's shoulder, a smile stretching her lips into a pretty pink bow as Baron Dunning came to claim her hand.

Deborah supposed it was not Susannah's fault that the rules of conduct required a lady to repress her true feelings under a cloak of civility. But surely it would be kinder to Captain Fawley if she could just tell him how he made her feel. Then he wouldn't keep on approaching her, and being rebuffed so prettily that he had no idea that the very thought of him touching her made Susannah feel nauseous.

She flicked him a soulful glance as he watched Susannah walk to the dance floor on the arm of her portly young partner. Captain Fawley must have been strikingly handsome once, she sighed wistfully. Dark haired, as well as dark eyed, with features that were still discernibly pleasing, even under that horribly reddened and puckered skin.

Whereas there was nothing handsome about Baron Dunning. He had a weak chin, made more noticeable by a mouth full of prominent teeth, and his skin was a greasy broth of suppurating pustules.

'Many people suffer from spots,' Susannah had remonstrated when Deborah had pointed out that Baron Dunning's complexion was no better than Captain Fawley's. 'He cannot help that!'

Besides which, he had a title. All the poor Captain had to offer was his devotion. And Susannah might protest that she would hate to look ridiculous hobbling about the dance floor with a man who had a false leg, but she never worried what it looked like to dance with the doddery Earl of Caxton. The *on-dit* was that the cadaverous widower was on the lookout for wife number three, and Susannah was plainly ready to stifle her squeamishness for the sake of a coronet.

The impecunious Captain Fawley could expect no such consideration.

'How could I let him touch me, with that false hand?' Susannah had whined only the previous night, when they had been preparing for bed at the end of an arduous day of husband hunting. It had occurred to Deborah, as her friend applied pineapple water to her skin, that it was most apt to refer to the early weeks of spring as 'the Season'. Débutantes stalked their prey as ruthlessly as sportsmen on a grouse shoot, flushing unsuspecting bachelors from their covers with a swirl of silken skirts, then bagging them with a volley fired from a pair of sparkling eyes. Or lured them into traps baited with honeyed smiles and coaxing words.

'It is very hard to tell it is a false hand, it has been so well made,' Deborah had pointed out. 'It looks just like any other gentleman's hand, covered with an evening glove.'

'I would know it was a dead thing, resting on my arm.' Susannah had shuddered. 'Eeugh!'

As the orchestra began to play, Captain Fawley came back to himself. Turning to Deborah, he inclined his head and held out his arm. His right arm. She had noticed on previous occasions that if he offered a lady his arm, it was never what remained of the left one.

'Shall we take a turn about the room?'

Deborah smiled, and laid her hand upon his sleeve. As she glanced up, it occurred to her that placing her on his right side also had the effect of presenting the unblemished side of his face to her scrutiny. A pang of sympathy smote her. He was sensitive enough to his appearance, without girls like Susannah rubbing his nose in it. He had even grown his hair longer than was fashionable, sweeping part of his fringe over the left side of his forehead, in an effort to conceal the worst of the scarring.

They set out along the edge of the room, in the area behind the pillars that marked the boundaries of the dance floor. Captain Fawley's gait was a little uneven, she had to admit in fairness to Susannah. But by no means did he hobble! And though she had never danced with him, she was certain he would look no worse than many of the men here tonight, lumbering about with straining waistcoats and florid faces.

'I can see you would much rather be on the dance floor,' said Captain Fawley, noticing the direction of her gaze, 'than bearing me company. I shall escort you to your mother, and—'

'Oh, please do not!'

He eyed her curiously.

'I would m…much rather be promenading, than left to wilt on the sidelines.'

Her dance card, unlike that of her friend, bore very few names. If Captain Fawley abandoned her, it would be humiliatingly obvious that she had no partner.

She felt as though the only time she ever got to

dance lately was when one of Susannah's admirers took pity on her, as Captain Fawley was doing now.

And unlike some of those gentlemen, Captain Fawley was invariably attentive and polite, almost managing to make her believe he was enjoying talking to her.

And what was more, she was sure he would never take part in the kind of conversation she had overheard not half an hour since. Not that she could blame Baron Dunning for comparing her unfavourably with Susannah. Although both of them had dark hair, Deborah's curls would have gone limp by the end of the evening. Her eyes, though as brown, were more often lowered bashfully than sparkling with wit. Her complexion, thanks to an inflammation of the lungs she had suffered over the winter months, might, she accepted, by candle-light look somewhat sallow. And when she stood next to the shorter, shapelier Susannah, she supposed she could see why Mr Jay had scathingly likened her to a beanpole.

Not that knowing they had said nothing untrue made their comments any less hurtful, which was why she felt so grateful that Captain Fawley was deigning to spend these few moments with her.

When she thought of the adventures he must

have had, in his soldiering days, she was amazed he could talk to her so kindly about the trivial concerns of a plain, provincial miss like her.

He gave her his wry, lopsided smile, which somehow always managed to make her own lips want to rise in imitation.

'Then let us go and sample the refreshments,' he suggested, turning her towards a door at the far side of the room from where the orchestra was playing.

'Thank you, I should like that.'

She hoped very much that he would linger while she drank a glass of lemonade. Conversation would be limited, for after her initial burst of pleasure in securing his attention, she would doubtlessly become tongue-tied. He had experienced so much, when she had scarcely set foot outside her father's parish before this trip to London. Not that he had personally related how he had fought his way across the Peninsula before suffering the horrific injuries at Salamanca that had left him hovering between life and death for months. No, that information had been gleaned from her mother's friends, who made it their business to know everything about everyone.

They had shaken their heads, expressing pity as they related what they knew of his history, but she could only admire the determination with which he had clawed his way back to his present state. He did everything an able-bodied man did, though it must take him twice the effort. Why, he had even learned to ride a horse. She had glimpsed him on a couple of occasions, cantering through the park in the early morning, before many other people were about. He seemed to her to be so much more manly than the fashionable fops who lounged their languid way through London's drawing rooms. He had overcome whatever life had thrown at him, which you could see, just by looking at him, had been a great deal.

She felt that first betraying blush sweep up her cheeks, which always assailed her at about this point in their meetings. For what could she say that might be of interest to a man like him, a man who had really lived? Though she knew that, whatever she said, he would never give her one of those condescending looks, which so many eligible bachelors seemed to have got down to a fine art. He was so kind, so magnanimous, so…

'Tell me,' he said, as they sauntered towards the table on which a large punch bowl sat, 'just what a man has to do to secure a dance with your friend?'

Deborah's flight of fancy exploded in mid-air,

plummeting to earth like a spent rocket. He had not sought out her company because he wished for it. She was only a means by which he might be able to approach Susannah. Of course a man like him would not willingly spend time with a drab, nondescript, foolish, ignorant, penniless, plain… and let us not forget shy, awkward, dull…

She pulled herself together with effort, and pasted a polite social smile upon her face, as Captain Fawley continued, 'I purposely arrived early tonight, and still her dance card seems to be full.'

'It was full before ever we arrived,' Deborah temporised. It was not her place to tell him that, no matter what he did, Susannah would rebuff him. Not only did she find him physically repulsive, but she had her sights set on a title. Forming an attachment with an impecunious commoner was not part of Susannah's plan at all.

'Before you arrived?' Captain Fawley signalled a waiter to pour Deborah a glass of lemonade.

'Yes,' she confirmed, her heart plummeting as the waiter handed her a drink in a tall glass. It would take for ever to drink it down, and, for some reason, she no longer wanted to spend a moment longer with Captain Fawley than she had to. There was an acid heaviness in her stomach, her throat ached, and, to her annoyance, her eyes had begun to prickle with what she was afraid were burgeoning tears. She did not want him to see her cry. Lord, she did not want anyone to see her cry! What kind of ninny burst into tears at a ball because every man there wanted to dance with her friend and not her!

She took a gulp of the drink, appalled when the glass rattled against her teeth. Her hands were shaking.

'Are you quite well, Miss Gillies?' Captain Fawley looked concerned.

Her heart performed a peculiar lurch as she thought how like him it was to be so observant. 'I…' Lying was a sin. She would not do it. And yet, she desperately wanted to escape. If she was to twist the truth, just a little…there could be no harm in that, could there? 'I think I would like to return to my mother, and sit beside her after all, if you do not mind?'

'Of course.' Captain Fawley took her glass and placed it on a convenient window ledge. He tucked her hand into the crook of his arm, pulling her hard against his body so that he could support her wilting form as he ushered her towards the door. She had never been held so close to any man before, except her father. It made her heart race to feel the heat of his body seeping through his uniform jacket. She could feel the flex of his muscled frame with every step he took, and a slight change of pressure every time he breathed in or out. And if she could feel him, then he must be aware she was trembling. Oh, pray God he would put it down to physical weakness, and would never guess that he had devastated her with his careless remark.

Her mother was sitting on a bench with several other chaperons, ladies whose task it was to ensure their charges maintained that delicate balancing act between doing their utmost to entrap an eligible bachelor into matrimony whilst simultaneously behaving with sufficient decorum to avert scandal.

'Mrs Gillies,' said Captain Fawley, executing a polite bow, 'I fear your daughter is feeling unwell.'

'Oh, dear!' Her mother's eyes shot past her, to where Susannah was twirling merrily around the floor with Baron Dunning. 'We have only just arrived, and Susannah is having such success… she will not wish to leave. Do you really need to go home?' She shifted to one side, so that Deborah could sit next to her. Taking her hand in hers, she gave it a squeeze. 'Deborah was so ill over

Christmas, I almost decided to put off coming to London at all. But Susannah was so keen…' she explained to Captain Fawley.

'I shall be fine, Mother. If I may but sit quietly for a while….'

'Perhaps a turn about the garden, to get some fresh air?' Lady Honoria Vesey-Fitch, an old friend of her mother's suggested with an arch smile. 'I am sure the Captain would oblige.'

Oh, no. It was bad enough that he did not wish to dance with her, never mind dragging the poor man round the garden on what would be a fool's errand. For no amount of fresh air was going to make her feel any better. On the contrary, knowing that Captain Fawley would wish himself anywhere rather than with her would only serve to make her feel ten times worse.

'Oh, no!' To Deborah's immense relief, her mother instantly vetoed the suggestion. 'The cold night air would be most injurious to her health, after the heat of this stuffy room. I do not want her to catch a chill on top of everything else!'

Everything else? Had her mother guessed that her only daughter had been smitten by a severe case of hero-worship? Though how could she, when Deborah had only just worked it out for herself? It could be the only reason why her heart twisted at the look in Captain Fawley's eyes every time Susannah turned him down, the little leap it performed when he turned, albeit with resignation, to her.

'Is there nobody who could escort Miss Gillies home?' Captain Fawley said, then, looking pensive, he ventured, 'Or perhaps you could take your daughter home, if you would entrust Miss Hullworthy to my care. I assure you, I…'

That did it. He would gladly think of an excuse to shovel her out of the way, so that he could have Susannah all to himself. Pulling herself upright in her chair, she said, 'There will be no need for anyone to leave, or any alteration made to our arrangements. I will be fine, if I may but sit quietly, for a while.'

'Oh, but thank you for your concern, Captain,' her mother put in quickly. 'Please do call on us tomorrow if you are still anxious over my daughter's health.'

An arrested expression came over his face. 'I shall certainly do so,' he said, a gleam coming to his eye.

Deborah glared down at her hands as she clasped them in her lap. He did not care a fig for her health! He had just worked out that, if he called, he would be able to ascertain which social events Susannah might be attending the next evening. For all his manly attributes, he was clearly inexperienced at wooing society women. He often arrived at a ball quite late, looking flustered, as though he had searched several venues before hitting upon the right one. But now he had cottoned on to the mysterious means by which his rivals had stolen a march over him. They called during the day, and by means of cajolery, flattery or downright bribery, wrought promises from their darling before even setting foot in the ballroom.

Tomorrow, he would join the ranks of admirers who called to deliver posies and drink tea whilst vying for Susannah's favours.

She rather thought she might have a relapse tomorrow. She did not think she wished to witness his humiliation.

There was a smattering of applause as the music ended, and the dancers began to leave the floor. Baron Dunning returned Susannah, very correctly, to Mrs Gillies. Flicking her fan open, she waved it briskly before her face, pointedly ignoring Captain Fawley.

'It is so hot in here,' she complained.

'Indeed,' he put in, in an effort, Deborah was sure,

to draw her sparkling gaze in his direction. 'Miss Gillies has been quite overcome with the heat.'

'Really?' Instantly Susannah dropped what Deborah thought of as her ballroom manner, and looked at her with concern. 'Oh, don't say you are going to be ill again, Debs.'

'I am not going to be ill,' she grated, flustered at becoming the centre of attention. 'I will be fine, if everyone was to just leave me alone.' To her mortification, the tears that had long been threatening welled up; despite blinking furiously, one spilled down her cheek. Hastily, she wiped it away with her gloved hand.

'Oh, Debs,' said Susannah, her own eyes welling in sympathy. 'You really are unwell. We must go home at once.'

'No, no, I do not want to spoil your evening.'

'And you have so many distinguished names on your dance card,' put in Mrs Gillies. 'You don't want to disappoint so many eligible gentlemen....'

'Oh, pooh to that!' said Susannah, bending forward and taking Deborah's hand. 'I can dance with them all tomorrow. Or the next night. But I would never forgive myself if Deborah sacrificed her health for my pleasure.'

Deborah was swamped by a wave of guilt. No

wonder the men all preferred Susannah to her. Not only was she far prettier, but she was a much nicer person too.

Captain Fawley certainly thought so. His eyes were glowing with admiration as he organised a footman to bring their carriage round. He was falling deeper and deeper under Susannah's spell with every encounter. Just as she, Deborah realised, stifling a sob, was growing more hopelessly infatuated with him. She had experienced an almost overwhelming urge to *cling* to him when he finally handed her over to her mother. To fling her arms around him and beg him to forget Susannah. In a ballroom!

She allowed Susannah and her mother to hustle her to the ladies' retiring room while *they* waited for their carriage and *she* grappled with the revelation that she had carelessly lost her heart to a man who scarcely noticed she existed.

'I am so sorry,' she said when they got into the carriage. 'I have ruined your evening, Suzy, and it is not as though I feel that unwell.'

Susannah grasped her hand. 'I shall not mind having an early night myself, truly, I promise you. Just lately, things seem to have become a bit of a whirl. It was easier, in some ways, when we first came to London, and hardly knew anybody.'

That was before Susannah had become such a hit. Her success had astounded Mrs Gillies, who had warned her not to expect too much from society. For though Susannah was so pretty, and so charming, and had so much wealth, that wealth came from trade.

'I can introduce you to a certain level of society,' she had explained. It was the reason that Deborah's mother was acting as chaperon, after all. Her own lineage was impeccable. Her only problem was lack of money. Since Susannah's family had plenty, they had come to a mutually beneficial arrangement. Mrs Gillies would introduce Susannah alongside her own daughter, and Susannah's parents would foot the bill for both girls. 'But there is no guarantee you will be accepted.'

Indeed, for the first few weeks of the Season, they had stayed in more often than they had gone out. Now, they had so many invitations, they had either to reject some, or attend several functions each evening.

And naturally, since Susannah's parents were meeting their costs, Mrs Gillies felt obligated to ensure that she had the opportunity to mingle with the sort of men she considered marriage-worthy.

They were not at all what Deborah wanted. She

had hoped that she might meet a young man who did not mind that she was not very wealthy. He would be looking for a helpmeet. A girl who would not demand he keep her in splendid indolence, but be prepared to run his household on a tight budget, and raise his children with a cheerful demeanour. There must be many younger sons of good families who wanted a dependable, resourceful wife. When they had first come to London, she had held out hopes of meeting such a man. But not now they were beginning to mingle in somewhat higher social circles, to satisfy Susannah's ambitions.

Deborah sighed heavily more than once as the carriage took them the few streets to their rented house. In the small market town where she had grown up, she would have scorned to ride such a short distance, when she was perfectly capable of walking. But in London, she was subject to all manner of ridiculous restrictions. A footman grasped her arm as she stumbled in the act of clambering out of the coach. Hired for the Season, naturally, just like the town house they had rented in Half Moon Street. She missed being able to hold a conversation without wondering if the servants, who were strangers she could not trust, were listening. She missed being able to go for a walk without one of them trailing behind, for the sake of propriety. And really, how silly was it to stipulate that a footman was necessary to knock on the door of whatever house they were paying a call at? As though a young lady's knuckles were far too delicate for the task?

She barely restrained herself from shaking him off, but when, upon climbing the steps to their front door, she experienced a moment of dizziness, she was glad she had not. A little later, she blinked, to find herself sitting in the armchair in her pretty bedroom, a maid kneeling at her feet removing her slippers, and Susannah hovering over her, fanning her face. Her mother was behind her chair, hastily loosening her stays.

'Did I faint?' she asked, feeling thoroughly confused.

'Not quite,' her mother replied, 'but your face was as white as paper. You must get straight into bed. Jones,' she addressed the maid, 'go to the kitchens and fetch Deborah a drink.' When the woman looked a little put out, she continued ruthlessly, 'Miss Hullworthy and I are quite capable of getting my daughter undressed and into bed. What she needs from you is a drink of hot chocolate, and some bread and butter. You have lost weight this last couple of weeks,' she said, clucking her tongue at the sight of Deborah's bony shoulder blades as she removed the stays and gown. 'You have been racketing about, growing more and more tired, and only picking at your food....'

'I am so sorry,' Susannah put in at this point. 'I should have noticed. Please say you forgive me for being so selfish. I have been so full of myself. My success has quite gone to my head....'

'I think,' said Mrs Gillies, raising her daughter to her feet, and supporting her towards the bed, 'that it will do both you girls good to spend a few days at home quietly. We may put it about that it is on account of Deborah's indisposition, but really, Susannah, I have been growing quite concerned about you too.'

'Me?' Susannah plumped down on to a bedside chair as Mrs Gillies rolled up Deborah's nightdress and pushed it over her head, just as she had done when Deborah had been a little girl, back home in the vicarage. It was almost worth being a little unwell, Deborah decided, to be rid of that maid, and have her mother and Susannah to put her to bed as though she was herself, and not this prim débutante she had to pretend to be in order to trick some poor man into matrimony.

'Yes, you. You know, Susannah, that I would never countenance any of those fellows making up to my Deborah.'

At this statement, both girls blinked at Mrs Gillies in surprise.

'You may think you are doing well to attract the attention of several men with titles, but I have made it my business to find out about them, and the sad truth is that they are fortune hunters.'

'Well…' Susannah pouted '…I have a fortune. And I want to marry someone with a title.'

'Yes, but I think you could show a little more discernment. Over the next day or so, I think it would be wise to consider the gentlemen who have been paying you attention, very carefully. Baron Dunning, for example, is only obeying his mama in paying you court. She wants him to marry, so that she will not have to make the drastic economies that his late father's reckless gambling have necessitated. He will not be any kind of a husband to you once he has got you to the altar. Why, he is hardly more than a schoolboy!'

'Don't you think he likes me?' said Susannah in a very small voice.

'Oh, I think he likes you well enough. If he has to marry a fortune, of course he would rather it came so prettily gift-wrapped. But don't you think,' she said in a more gentle tone, 'you deserve better than that?'

Susannah bowed her head, her fingers running along the struts of her fan.

'And as for the Earl of Caxton...'

But Deborah was never to find out what her mother thought of the Earl of Caxton. The maid had returned, bearing a tray laden with a pot of chocolate, a plate of bread and butter, and a small glass of what smelled like some form of spirituous liquor.

'Ah, just the thing for a faint!' Mrs Gillies remarked cheerfully, startling Deborah even further. Her father, the late Reverend Gillies, had lectured his flock frequently, and at length, upon the evils of drink. And there was never anything stronger than ale served at his table. 'That was very thoughtful of you, Jones, thank you. And now, Susannah, I think it is high time you went to bed, as well.'

She bent to kiss her daughter's forehead, pausing to smooth back a straggling lock of hair before turning her full attention to her other charge. Susannah paused in the doorway to pull a face at her friend, knowing she was about to endure one of her mother's patient, but excruciatingly moving lectures.

Under Jones's watchful eye, Deborah consumed the plate of bread and butter, then, holding her nose, she downed what she had been told was brandy in one go, like the vile medicine she considered it to be, then snuggled down against the pillows to enjoy her chocolate.

A pleasing warmth stole through her limbs as she sipped the hot drink, and she could feel herself relaxing. She must have been quite wrung out, what with one thing and another, she reflected, yawning sleepily. Perhaps, after a day or two spent recouping her strength, she would be able to put the unsettling feelings she had towards Captain Fawley into proper perspective.

And the next time she saw him, she would be able to smile upon him with perfect equanimity. Her heart would not skip a beat, her breathing would remain orderly and she would not blush and grow tongue-tied. And if he took her arm, she would not succumb to the temptation to lean into him and revel in the feel of all that masculine strength and vitality concealed beneath the fabric of his dress uniform.

She was far too sensible to give in to the first infatuation she had begun to harbour for a man. Only a ninny would let her head be completely turned by a scarlet coat and a roguish smile, she told herself sternly. She must nip such feelings in the bud. She was the sensible, practical Miss Deborah Gillies, who could be relied upon to behave completely correctly, no matter what blows fate dealt her. Had she not stood firm when her mother had collapsed after the sudden death of the Reverend Gillies? Though she, too, had been grief-stricken and shocked to discover her loving father had left them with scarce two farthings to rub together, she had dealt with the legal men, assessed their budget, found a modest house and hired the few servants they could now afford. She had shaken hands with the new incumbent, who had wanted them to move out of the vicarage within a month of her father's death, and even managed to hand over the keys of the only home she had ever known to his pretty young wife with dry eyes.

In comparison with that, this inconvenient yearning she felt for a man who was unattainable was nothing.

Yawning again, she pulled the covers up to her ears, reminding herself that she did not have the energy to waste on weaving dreams around the dashing Captain Fawley anyway. What she ought to be worrying about was what she and her mother would do once Susannah had bagged her eligible, and they no longer had any reason to let the Hullworthys foot their bills.

If tonight had taught her anything, it was that she might as well stop hoping to meet someone who would want to marry her and miraculously make everything right. And she had long since known that she could not simply return to Lower Wakering at the end of the Season, and continue to be a drain on her mother's scant resources.

It was about time, she decided as her eyes drifted shut, to come up with some plan to settle her future for herself.

By herself.

Chapter Two

Deborah yawned, opened her eyes and stretched languorously. And sat up abruptly. She could see sunlight burning through the curtains, so the day must be far advanced. Why had Jones not come to wake her?

Then the events of the previous night filtered back to her consciousness. After the dizzy spell, the near faint, and, of course, the scene she had almost caused in the ballroom, her mother had probably decreed she should be left to sleep for as long as she needed. She swung her legs out of the bed and went to the washstand. The face that gazed back at her from the ornate gilt mirror was drawn, her eyes looking incredibly large against the pallor of her skin. Yes, she decided wryly, she had been trying to do too much, too soon after her illness. The fact that she had been unable to control her emotions in public was an indicator of how pulled she must be.

Once she had recovered her strength, she decided, splashing her face with cold water, she would be much better able to control those ridiculous feelings she had been experiencing around Captain Fawley. And the uncharitable ones she had been harbouring towards Susannah.

She rang the bell for the maid, deciding that she would have her breakfast in bed for once, just like a lady of fashion. While the Hullworthys were paying the bills, she might as well make the best of it. This would very likely be the last time she would have the opportunity to experience such luxury.

After a hearty breakfast of ham and eggs, washed down with liberal amounts of coffee, she fell asleep again, not waking until the day was far spent.

This time, when she rang for her maid, she decided she must get up and get dressed.

'I'll put out the long-sleeved morning gown, the one with the green sash, shall I, miss?' said Jones. 'There are several gentlemen callers downstairs, and you will be wanting to look your best.'

'Will I?' she said bitterly, causing Jones to frown at her. It would hardly matter what she looked like, she reflected, raising her arms for Jones to drop the delicate muslin over her head. They would all be there for Susannah.

'Perhaps I am not well enough to leave my room, after all,' she muttered darkly, settling on her dressing table stool so that Jones could arrange her hair. She had thought she had recovered her equanimity, yet the minute she was out of bed, she was beginning to feel jealous of Susannah again.

'Oh, no, miss, I think it would do you good to go and drink a cup of tea and eat a little something.'

There was that, she agreed, as her stomach rumbled loudly. After brushing her hair briskly, Jones took a length of green ribbon in her hand.

'No sense in heating the curling tongs, if you are only going to be out of bed for an hour or so,' Jones said, deftly securing her hair off her face with the ribbon. Deborah wondered if she had infected the woman with her own pessimism, or whether Jones had come to the conclusion that, since her charge would never match up to the pretty Miss Susannah, there was no point in making much effort.

Funnily enough, Deborah approved of the new style Jones had created out of sheer laziness. She had not tried to torture her hair into the fussy mass of curls that had only ever made her face look even more pinched. It simply cascaded down her back. She looked far more like herself than she had felt since she had come to town.

'Let's not bother with the tongs again, Jones,' she said, making for the door. If the London bucks did not find her attractive enough to propose, she was no longer prepared to exhaust herself trying to get them to notice her.

As she descended the stairs to the first floor, she felt more cheerful than she had for some time. The result of all that extra sleep, or her decision to stop hankering after the unobtainable? She did not know. She only knew that she wanted a cup of tea. And some sandwiches. And maybe a few of the delicious little macaroons the cook always put out for afternoon callers.

She was not going to bother attempting to engage any of Susannah's suitors in conversation. She was tired of trying to discover some speck of intelligence in the fops and fribbles who were crowding her drawing room lately. No wonder she had begun to think so highly of Captain Fawley. He stood out from the herd whose minds were full of the cut of their coat, or the latest way of tying a cravat. Nor was his conversation peppered with tales of his exploits on the hunting field.

Oh, Lord, she thought, setting her hand to the doorknob with a self-deprecating smile, *here I go again*!

Susannah saw her the moment she entered the drawing room, and leapt to her feet, squealing 'Deborah!' in a most unladylike display of pleasure. 'I had begun to think you were going to sleep the clock round. Are you feeling better? Do come and sit by me.' She gestured towards the sofa seat next to her, causing the swain sitting there to scowl. 'Mr Jay will not mind making room for you.' She turned her sweetly smiling face to his, and the scowl miraculously disappeared. 'You can fetch Miss Gillies a plate of sandwiches from the sideboard, while I pour her a cup of tea.'

Deborah bit her lip to prevent herself from giggling. The last thing Mr Jay wanted to do was fetch and carry for a pasty-faced girl he would not have passed the time of day with, given the choice. But to win favour with Susannah, his pained look seemed to convey, he would walk across hot coals.

As she followed his progress across the room, her eyes snagged on the figure of Captain Fawley, lounging against the mantelpiece. He had been looking distinctly surly, but, on seeing her, the expression on his face softened somewhat.

In spite of her resolution not to allow herself to be affected by him again, her unruly heart began to thump as he picked his way through the throng to reach her side.

'I am glad to have had the opportunity to see you before I take my leave, Miss Gillies,' he said. 'Miss Hullworthy gave me to understand that it was unlikely.'

Out of the corner of her eye, Deborah saw Susannah blush and look a little uncomfortable. She wondered if her friend had tried, at long last, to make her dislike of this particular one of her suitors somewhat clearer.

'Are you feeling better?'

'Yes, much, thank you,' she replied.

'I did peep in once or twice,' said Susannah, handing her a cup of tea, 'in case you were just resting and in want of company...'

'Never tell me you stayed in all morning! I thought you meant to go to Hatchard's, for some new books!'

'Oh, well, I could not go out and leave you until I was sure you were not really ill. If your mother had needed to send for the doctor—' Susannah broke off, chewing at her lower lip.

Deborah could not help noticing how the Captain's eyes fixed intently on that little gesture, his own lips parting slightly.

'Your concern for Miss Gillies's well-being is most commendable,' he said. 'Not many young ladies would forgo their pleasure, to sit at home and tend an invalid.'

'Nonsense!' Susannah replied robustly. 'I do not think of Deborah as an invalid. She is my dearest friend,' she said, taking Deborah's hand and squeezing it. 'She has been kindness itself to me, when I needed her, and if she was not here with me in London now, I should consider myself most unfortunate.'

Deborah returned the squeeze, remembering some of the grim times the Hullworthys had endured when they had first moved into Lower Wakering. The local gentry had closed ranks against the common upstarts, excluding them from their select gatherings. It was presumptuous, they all agreed, of the Hullworthys to buy the bankrupt Lord Wakering's estate, shocking of them to demolish the ramshackle mansion that had been his ancestral home and downright vulgar to replace it with a purpose-built colossus equipped with every luxury and new-fangled convenience.

For some time, the only locals who had not been hostile had been the vicar and his family. And it was entirely due to their influence that the Hullworthys had gradually found a measure of acceptance.

Once more, Captain Fawley's eyes glowed with admiration. He appeared to think that Susannah was just being gracious, thought Deborah with a spurt of annoyance, when she had only spoken the literal truth. If her mother had not agreed to sponsor Susannah, she would not have the entrée to the circles in which she was now moving. Especially not if either of her parents had come with her. They would have ruined Susannah's chances, as Mrs Gillies had wasted no time in pointing out to them. Dearly though she loved them, there was no getting round the fact that Mr and Mrs Hullworthy were not at all genteel.

'I hope…' He checked himself, then went on, 'That is, I shall be asking the dowager Lady Lensborough to call on you soon, to extend an invitation to Lord Lensborough's engagement ball. I hope you will be able to attend. And that you will save me at least one dance.'

Susannah gasped, her grip on Deborah's hand growing uncomfortably tight.

'L…Lensborough? The Marquis of Lensborough?'

For a moment, Deborah thought she saw a flicker of amusement in Captain Fawley's eyes. Did he know that an invitation to such an event was the one sure way to capture Susannah's interest? She looked at him keenly. Perhaps it was not only débutantes who cast out lures to catch their prey. He had certainly baited his hook with the one worm that could make Susannah bite. She was almost obsessed with gaining an entrée to the *haut ton*.

'The same,' he said, his fleeting trace of amusement replaced with an air of gravity.

'Oh, well, that would be wonderful!' Susannah sighed rapturously. 'If you can indeed promise me an invitation, you may be sure I shall save at least one dance for you!'

'That was just what I thought you would say,' he replied, bowing over the hand she had extended, for the first time to Deborah's knowledge, willingly.

'Now I will take my leave,' he said, nodding curtly to Deborah. 'I am glad to hear you are recovering from your indisposition. And I hope you will accept the small token of my good wishes in the spirit in which it was given.'

'Token?' Deborah felt totally mystified.

'Oh, Captain Fawley brought you a posy. It is over there.' Deborah looked where Susannah had pointed, to see the usual mound of floral tributes piled upon the little table by the door. Her heart leaped to think that, at long last, one of them was for her!

'Miss Hullworthy informed me that you would not be able to accept it from me personally, so I left it with the other tributes to the beauties of Half Moon Street,' he said drily.

'Which one is it?' she asked, her pulse fluttering wildly.

'The orangey-coloured one,' he replied vaguely. 'I know not the names of the flowers. I just thought they were something like the colour of the ribbons you were wearing in your hair last night.'

All the breath left her lungs in a great whoosh. He had brought her a posy. And he had noticed what colour ribbons she had been wearing in her hair! She wanted to rush across the room, gather the flowers to her bosom and breathe in their fragrance. How silly of her. He had not brought it because he harboured any tender feelings for her. It had been expedient to arm himself with it, that was all, and feign concern over her health to gain entry to the home of the woman who really interested him. Rather stiffly, she said, 'I am sure

Susannah would have brought it up to me, had I not got out of bed today.'

'Yes, of course I would!'

'Of course you would,' he agreed wryly. 'But now there is no need. Miss Gillies is much recovered, and I am sure in a day or so, will be well able to withstand the rigours of the ballroom at Challinor House.'

'Where is Challinor House?' Susannah asked, the minute he had left. 'And what has it to do with an invitation to Lord Lensborough's engagement? And what is his connection with the family?'

'Hush, Suzy,' Deborah murmured. 'Wait till your callers have gone. Then we may ask my mama.'

Her mother was very well informed about the noble families of England. It never ceased to amaze her how a woman who had spent the majority of her life in a rural backwater had managed to keep her finger on the pulse of London gossip.

'Challinor is the family name, dear,' Mrs Gillies explained, when Susannah eventually got the opportunity to question her about the Marquis of Lensborough. 'And you say Captain Fawley is to use his influence with the dowager Lady Lensborough to get you an invitation to her son's ball? Hmm…' She sank on to her favourite chair, her finger tapping her chin as a frown came to her brow. 'Of course!' Her face lit up. 'Her younger son served in the same regiment as Captain Fawley. Dead now, of course, like so many of them after that dreadful affair of Waterloo…' She sighed, shaking her head. 'But I believe shared grief has created something of a bond between your Captain Fawley and the Marquis. I know for a fact that he trained a horse especially to cope with his…umm…disadvantages. He is bound to be on the guest list already….'

'But I heard that the engagement ball is one of the most exclusive events of the Season so far!' Susannah protested. 'Why should they include a penniless nobody like Captain Fawley?'

'Now, Susannah, my dear, I have told you before about judging a man too hastily. There is nothing wrong with his background. He is half-brother to the Earl of Walton, after all.'

Deborah's heart sank as Susannah's eyes lit up. She suddenly felt incredibly weary.

'If you do not mind,' she said, 'I would like to go and lie down again before dinner.'

'Of course, my dear,' said her mother. 'And do not be thinking you will be left alone this evening.

If you do not feel up to coming down and keeping company with us, one of us will come and read to you. Won't we, Susannah?'

To her credit, Susannah betrayed not the slightest sign of petulance, though Deborah knew she had been looking forward to the theatre trip planned for that evening. Instead, she leapt to her feet, saying brightly, 'Shall I come up with you now? We could have a good gossip while you have a lie down. For you surely don't need to sleep any more today, do you?'

Deborah mentally braced herself. She knew that the gossip would consist of hearing Susannah dissect every single one of her suitors—their dress, their manners, their connections and fortune—and she was not sure she was sufficiently in control of the frayed edges of her temper to hold it together.

'Fancy Captain Fawley being the brother of an earl!' Susannah sighed the moment they had shut the chamber door behind them.

'Yes, only fancy,' Deborah muttered glumly, sitting on a low stool to ease off her pumps.

'Why did you not tell me?'

'Would you mind helping me with the hooks?' Deborah prevaricated, turning her back to her friend. While Susannah was thrilled to find one of her suitors so well connected, so far as Deborah was concerned, it only seemed to put him further from her reach than ever.

While Susannah dealt with the fastenings of her dress, she confessed, 'I had no idea his father was an earl.'

'Which changes everything, of course. Do you think he is a viscount, as well as being a captain?'

'Don't you dare toy with him, Susannah!' Deborah whirled round, her eyes blazing with fury. 'He has suffered enough!'

'I wouldn't…' Susannah gasped.

'You may not mean to hurt him, but I have seen the way his eyes follow you round the dance floor, while you are making up to your latest conquest!'

'Well, I…'

'Oh, you do not need to tell me—you cannot bear to look at him!'

'With that face?' Susannah shuddered. 'Can you blame me?'

Deborah struggled to control her temper. 'I admit he has been knocked about a bit. But only consider how he received his wounds. Fighting for his country. He is worth ten of that fribble Baron Dunning, whom you hang upon because he has a title. He worked his way up through the ranks, earning promotion through merit….'

Drawing herself up to her full height, Susannah said quietly, 'Your mother has already made me revise my opinion of Baron Dunning. I see what this is, Deborah—you have designs upon Captain Fawley yourself.'

Deborah's mouth opened, then closed, as she sought to refute Susannah's argument, but realised she could not in all conscience do so.

'I do not have designs upon him,' she eventually managed to say. 'But that does not mean I am prepared to stand by and watch you break his heart. I think you are a better person than that, Suzy.'

Susannah's eyes narrowed. '*If* you do not have your sights set on him, and *if* you are only thinking of what is best for him, then I would have thought you would be glad that I have finally relented towards him. He is intelligent enough to know what my ambitions are. He knows I intend to make a brilliant match. Agreeing to go to one ball as his guest, letting him have one dance with me, is all he aspires to, I assure you. I won't encourage him to dangle after me.'

'I…I hope you will not.'

'Of course I won't! What do you take me for?'

She laid one hand upon Deborah's arm. 'Goose. I think you must really need to lie down if you are as snappish as this.'

'Yes,' Deborah mumbled, hanging her head guiltily. 'Yes, I think I must.'

Though she felt wrung out after that episode, sleep remained far from her as she lay rigidly on top of the counterpane, her fists clenched at her sides. She did not know what was the matter with her. Why had she got so angry with Susannah? Oh, if only this Season was over, and she could leave London and all its painful associations behind.

As soon as Susannah's future was settled, she would begin to scour the papers and apply for every post suitable for a lady of gentle birth.

She was never going to get married.

She did not want to get married!

Not if it meant playing the sort of games Susannah was indulging in.

A week later, as she entered the portals of Challinor House, Deborah was glad she had allowed Susannah to talk her into buying a new gown.

'Papa will pay for it!' she had airily promised. 'And don't think of it as charity. He has hired your mother to bring me to the notice of the best families, and I am sure he will think the cost of one gown well worth it to have us both looking our best when we walk into the house of a marquis!'

That had been all it had taken to sway Deborah. They both had to look the part, not just Susannah. If Deborah merely refurbished one of the few ball-gowns she had, or remade one of Susannah's cast-offs, as she had first intended, every woman there would know she was purse-pinched. And then they would look at Susannah, decked out in her finery, and see the true state of affairs. A girl who had to hire someone to launch her into society would not be looked upon with the same indulgence as one who was being sponsored, out of friendship, by a family with as good a pedigree as the Gillies.

Still, seeing the diamonds that glittered at the throats and ears of so many of the other guests as they slowly made their way up the stairs, made her feel as though it was she, and not Susannah, who was the impostor here. Though her ballgown was quite the finest thing she had ever owned, a superbly cut satin slip, with an overdress of gauze embroidered with hundreds of the tiniest beads whirling in intricate patterns, little puffed sleeves and a demi-train of spangled lace, her only jewellery was a single strand of pearls that had been her mother's.

'I don't need such gewgaws at my age, dear.' She had smiled as she clasped it about her daughter's neck just before they came out. 'In fact, I prefer to conceal as much of my neck as I can!' She had recently taken to wearing an assortment of floaty scarves draped about her throat. The one she had on tonight was a delicate wisp of powder blue, which, Deborah had to admit, somehow managed to put the finishing touch to an outfit that was as elegant as anything that the other older ladies were wearing.

At length, they came to the head of the receiving line, and she finally came face to face with her host and hostess. The Marquis of Lensborough bowed his head in greeting to her mother, expressed the appropriate sentiments to her, but then merely looked at Susannah as though...she gasped—as though she had no right to be there. As his features settled into a decided sneer, Deborah took a strong aversion to him. Why on earth did Susannah want to ingratiate herself with people of his class, who would only ever look down their aristocratic noses at her? And his fiancée, a tall, rake-thin redhead, was no better. She had the most haughty, closed expression of any woman Deborah had ever met. It was a relief to get past them and make for the ballroom.

'Ah, there is Gussy!' said her mother, spotting the dowager Lady Lensborough holding court from a sofa in an alcove just off the ballroom proper. Deborah felt her lips rise in a wry smile. It had come as a shock when, not two days after Captain Fawley had made his promise to get them an invitation, the dowager Marchioness of Lensborough had swept into their drawing room, and proceeded to treat her mother as though she was a close friend. She soon learned that this was not so very far from the truth. They had known each other as girls, and though their paths in life had taken very different directions, they had kept up a sporadic correspondence.

She had made both girls stand, and turn and walk before her, before she deigned to hand over the coveted invitations.

'I will not have any chit in my ballroom who will not do it credit,' she had said outrageously. 'You are both pretty enough, in your own ways.' She had raised her lorgnette and frowned at each in turn. 'It is a great pity that your daughter has not her friend's looks and fortune, Sally. But then again, *she* has not the advantage of breeding. But there…' she sighed '…that is always the way of things. And there is no real reason why either of them should not marry well. My own son has gone for character, over beauty, in the choice of his bride, as I am sure you will discover when you meet her.' She clicked her tongue in exasperation. 'Men are such odd creatures. No telling what will take their fancy.'

Susannah and Deborah followed closely in her mother's wake, like chicks seeking the warmth of a mother hen. The dowager's evident pleasure in seeing the girls served as a welcome antidote to their frosty reception, and reassured the other guests that these two girls were persons worthy of notice. Soon, Susannah's hand was being solicited for the dancing that was about to ensue. She very correctly saved the first dance for Captain Fawley, but when he came to claim her hand, Deborah was somewhat startled to find he had brought a tall, fair-haired man with him.

'Permit me to introduce my half-brother, Miss Gillies,' he said to her. 'Lord Charles Algernon Fawley, ninth Earl of Walton.'

He looked nothing like Captain Fawley. Not only was he fair-haired and blue-eyed, but there was nothing about their facial features to suggest they could be related at all.

Deborah curtsied. He bowed, then shocked her by saying, 'Would you do me the honour of allowing me to partner you for the first dance?'

It was with mixed feelings that she allowed Lord Walton to lead her on to the dance floor. It had been so kind of Captain Fawley to ensure she was not left on the sidelines, while Susannah formed part of the set that opened such a glittering ball. She had never danced with an earl, never mind such a handsome one. She should have been giddy with rapture. But as they trod the measure of the stately quadrille, she could not help being agonisingly aware that, though she formed part of the set that contained Captain Fawley, she was not his partner. Nor could she help but be aware of the satisfaction that gleamed from his eyes every time he linked hands with Susannah.

On the whole, she was glad when the exercise was over, and Lord Walton led her back to the bench where her mother was sitting, chatting happily with a bevy of dowagers.

As Susannah's next partner came to claim his dance, Captain Fawley bowed stiffly to Deborah. His face looked a little strained as he said, somewhat defensively, 'I am not going to ask you to dance,

Miss Gillies. But may I have the pleasure of your company during the next set, if your card is free?'

In spite of all the stern lectures she had given herself, her heart began to beat a tattoo against her ribs in response to his request. In truth, she would much rather spend time talking to him, than treading prescribed steps in time with the music. Especially since she could tell that performing the quadrille had cost him quite dearly. Lines of tension bracketed his mouth, and his eyes were dulled with pain.

'Yes, thank you. I should like that.' She smiled, laying her hand upon his arm as he held it out. 'In fact,' she suggested, sensitive to his evident discomfort, 'I should quite enjoy sitting and watching the dancers.'

He quirked one eye at her. 'You sound just like Heloise—that is, my sister-in-law, Lady Walton. As an artist, she likes to observe the *ton* at play. Do you sketch?'

'Oh, no, not really. No more than any young lady is supposed to.'

He suddenly frowned. 'Of course, you are not in the best of health, are you? Here, let us sit on this sofa, so that you may rest.'

'I do not need to rest. Not tonight. I am not generally invalidish,' she retorted. Then could have kicked herself for being so insensitive. He had probably homed in on her precisely because he thought she was frail, so that he could have the opportunity to sit without making it look as though it was what he needed to do.

He settled her on a cushioned window seat, far enough from the swirling crowds so that they could engage in conversation, yet still within sight of the chaperon's bench.

'Are you enjoying your Season?' he enquired politely, ignoring her last tactless remark.

'In some ways.' She sighed. She did not want to waste her few precious moments with him in polite nothings. Yet he did not look as though he was really interested in her answer. 'I am certainly glad to see my mother enjoying herself so much.' She looked across the room to where Mrs Gillies was dividing her time between chatting with her acquaintances and watching Susannah's progress with obvious satisfaction. 'From the moment we heard that a Season in London was going to be possible after all, it was as though she came back to life.'

'Your father died not long ago, I seem to recall?'

'Yes, and it hit her very badly. For several months she seemed to lose interest in everything.

I had to…' She paused. She did not want to sound as though she was complaining. 'Well, we were not left in very comfortable circumstances. But look at her now.' She smiled fondly at her mother across the room. Her cheeks were pink and her eyes were bright. 'It has done her so much good to launch Susannah. And finding so many of her old friends in London has successfully distracted her from her problems.'

'But what of you?' he persisted. 'I can see your friend is enjoying her triumph. And that your mother is in her element. But how does the delicate Miss Gillies fare in the hurly burly of London society?'

'I have told you before, I am not in the least delicate! It was only because…' She tailed off, blushing as she realised she was on the point of divulging just how desperate their straits had been before the Hullworthys had come to their rescue.

The little cottage, which had seemed perfectly charming when they had moved in during the summer, had revealed all its inadequacies during the first autumnal storm. The roof leaked, the windows rattled in their casements, and the chimneys smoked. Her mother had shrunk into herself as though finally realising that she was going to eke out the rest of her days in penury. Feeling as though she had contributed to her mother's state of mind, by not having managed to find somewhere better, Deborah's health had broken down.

That, at least, had roused Mrs Gillies from her apathy. Fearing that she might lose her daughter, as well as her husband, within the space of a few months, she had put pride to one side and finally accepted the Hullworthys' offer of rooms up at the Hall so she could nurse Deborah back to health in warmth and comfort.

Even though it meant they had become charity cases.

Deborah was only having this Season at all because she felt she owed the Hullworthys her very life. She had not wanted to come, especially not at their expense, but Susannah wanted her mother to launch her into society, and Deborah was necessary to make the whole thing look right.

'If you must know, this whole thing seems… unreal. Wasting entire days shopping so that we may fritter away the evenings dancing, or doing something equally frivolous…it is a bit like living a dream, from which I am waiting to awake, so that I can get back to my real life again.'

'Do you dislike it so much?' he frowned.

'Oh, no. It is quite a pleasant sort of dream…' she sighed '…for the most part.' She frowned down at the dainty satin slippers that peeped from beneath the hem of her gown, wondering what on earth had possessed her to speak so frankly. Yet having begun, she felt a compelling urge to unburden herself to the one person she thought might understand her sentiments.

'It is just that I cannot ever permit myself to enter into it all in quite the same way as Miss Hullworthy does. She is here to catch a husband, whereas I…' Her breath hitched in her throat.

'You do not wish to marry?' Captain Fawley looked puzzled.

'Of course, marriage would be my preferred option. But being of a practical nature, I have to consider what I will do when my time in London is over, should I not have received any offers.'

'And what decision have you come to?' he asked, with a smile.

'That I shall have to find some kind of paid position, of course. Either as a governess, or teacher. I would prefer to secure a post as a housekeeper, for I know that is a job I could do really well. However, I do not think anyone would employ a girl as young as me for such a responsible post.'

'Would anyone employ a girl of your background for a teaching post, either?' She shot him a look of chagrin. But there was nothing in his face to suggest he was mocking her. On the contrary, he only looked as though he was curious.

'I think they might, yes,' she retorted, lifting her chin. 'All I shall need to do is teach other young ladies the very same things I have had to learn. I can do household accounts, and bake, and sew. And, what is more, Papa taught me Greek and Latin,' she finished proudly.

'Do many schools for little girls have Greek and Latin on the curriculum?' He laughed.

'They might have,' she replied, fixing him with a challenging look. 'There might be some schools that work on the ethos that girls have a right to learn all the things that boys do, and not restrict them to sewing, and deportment, and drawing.'

'Are you equipped to teach them to fence and box, by any chance?'

Part of her wanted to take offence at his words, but the smile in his eyes as he teased her was so appealing, she found herself laughing instead.

'Oh, very well, not perhaps everything, but you know what I mean.'

'Yes, I rather think I do.' He smiled, getting to his

feet. 'Pray forgive me, Miss Gillies, but I must take my leave of you. Now that I have had my dance with Miss Hullworthy, and spent this delightful interlude with you, it is time I was elsewhere.'

Delightful interlude. He had said this had been a delightful interlude.

She stared up at him, her heart sinking as she noted the blankness of his face as he bowed his farewell. It was just the sort of nonsense men spouted all the time. Something to say. He hadn't really meant it.

'Goodnight, then, Captain Fawley,' she managed to say, though she could not muster the smile she should have raised to go with the polite utterance. Nor could she tear her eyes away from him, as he limped away. As he bade farewell to his host, Lord Lensborough's face darkened. And after he had gone, the Marquis turned and glared at Susannah, as she made her way down the current set, his fists clenching as though he was restraining the urge to seize her and throw her bodily through the nearest window.

At first, his demeanour shocked her. But then she reminded herself that she did not like the way Susannah treated Captain Fawley, either. Lord Lensborough might not be a very pleasant man, but he was clearly capable of loyalty towards those he considered friends.

And it *was* hard to sit and watch Susannah enjoying herself, when Captain Fawley, who had been responsible for bringing her here, had just slunk out, alone, into the night.

Oh, why could not Susannah appreciate what it was costing Captain Fawley to court her? He found it physically painful to dance, and yet he had persistently begged for the privilege of doing so with her, so ardent was his admiration. He could not even bear to remain in this ballroom, when he knew his own case was hopeless. He had laid himself open to rejection, time and time again, and yet it all meant nothing to her! Why couldn't she see that the esteem of a man like him was worth far more than landing a title? What did it matter if his body was no longer completely whole? It was the heart of a man that mattered.

And Captain Fawley's heart was Susannah's for the taking.

Susannah's.

She must not forget that. Not for an instant.

Snapping her fan open, Deborah rose to her feet, and made her way rather unsteadily to the bench on which her mother was sitting.

Chapter Three

It was a glorious afternoon. Though there was hardly a cloud in the sky, a deliciously cool breeze skittered playfully through the chestnut trees, making the air beneath their boughs sweet enough to drink. Sadly, Deborah's pleasure in being out of doors was dimmed somewhat by the company she was in.

Although Susannah no longer viewed Baron Dunning with much enthusiasm, she had not turned down his invitation to promenade through Hyde Park during the fashionable hour. Particularly since he had been thoughtful enough to bring along his friend, Mr Jay, to escort Deborah. The girls had both hoped that having male escorts would make the walk rather more like the brisk outings they were used to taking in Lower Wakering. But the men were no more willing to stride out than the hired London servants were. They strolled along at a snail's pace, pausing frequently to acknowledge acquaintances or point out persons of interest who were bowling along the carriage drive in smart barouches or landaulets.

Deborah's heart sank as yet another friend of Mr Jay's called out a greeting, then, upon catching sight of Susannah, pulled his rather showy chestnut mare alongside them.

'What brings you to the park at this hour, Lampton?' Mr Jay asked him as he swung down from the saddle. 'Wouldn't have thought it was quite your thing.'

'Oh, you know,' Mr Lampton said vaguely, his attention riveted upon Susannah. 'Won't you introduce me to your charming companions?'

Deborah's first impression was that he must be one of the most handsome men she had ever seen. He was tall and well built. A lock of fair hair strayed from under his curly-brimmed beaver hat, but she would have guessed at the colouring anyway, from the fairness of lashes and brows that framed forget-me-not blue eyes.

'Oh, this is Miss Gillies,' Mr Jay said briefly. 'Miss Gillies, the Honourable Percy Lampton.'

'Charmed to make your acquaintance,' said Mr Lampton, turning on a smile so patently false, it immediately put Deborah's back up. Men as handsome as this were not charmed to make her acquaintance. They usually ran their eyes over her swiftly, assessing her scrawny figure, the cheapness of her dress, and then the expression in their eyes became dismissive, or sometimes even downright scornful.

'Mr Lampton,' she repeated, making the proper curtsy, though she found it hard to muster up a reciprocal smile.

'And who, pray, is the dasher upon young Baron Dunning's arm?' he enquired, turning to make an exaggerated bow to Susannah.

While the introductions were made, the horse became quite skittish.

'You were correct about this brute,' Mr Lampton said to Mr Jay, tugging ineffectually on the horse's reins while its hindquarters surged across the path. 'Too high spirited by half.'

'Yes. I say, don't you think you ought to…?' Looking somewhat alarmed, Mr Jay let go of Deborah's arm and darted under the horse's tossing head. Shooting a look over his shoulder, he said to Baron Dunning, 'Perhaps you should move the ladies a little further away.'

While he set about calming the horse, with a competence Deborah had to admire, Baron Dunning linked arms with her and moved her out of range of those potentially dangerous hooves.

And somehow, once the incident was over, Mr Jay had the horse, Baron Dunning had Deborah on his arm, leaving Mr Lampton in sole possession of Susannah.

That was how it remained, all the way home. And Baron Dunning, far from exerting himself to be pleasant to Deborah, could not disguise his annoyance at being so neatly cut out by the newcomer. Deborah felt amused, rather than offended, only wondering how on earth Susannah would decide between all her suitors in the end. Although, if she could not make up her mind, there was nothing to stop her from returning to London again the next year. She was wealthy enough to be choosy. Her parents would not mind in the least if she went home without a husband in tow. So long as she enjoyed herself, and did not throw herself away on a nobody.

She sighed, remembering their conversation the morning after the Marquis of Lensborough's ball.

'I am not to throw myself away on a nobody,' she had said defiantly, when Deborah had challenged her for asking her mother to make further enquiries about Captain Fawley. 'Even if he is not what I thought him at first, I must not encourage him if he does not have any prospects.'

Sadly for Captain Fawley, it had not taken her mother long to discover that his prospects were non-existent.

'The eighth Earl of Walton married twice,' she had explained. 'The first marriage was arranged by his family, while he was scarce out of his teens, to ensure the succession, for he was the only son. They matched him with one of the Lampton girls, who, eventually, presented him with a healthy boy. He chose his own wife the second time he married, for reasons of sentiment, rather than duty. There was some sort of scandal about the time he died, which I have not been able to get to the bottom of, but the upshot was that the boys were parted and reared separately. The current Earl,' she said, leaning forward in her chair to dispense her nugget of gossip in a thrilled tone, 'scoured the battlefields of Spain to find Captain Fawley when he got news of how severely injured he was. He brought him home, and spent a fortune having him nursed back to health, thus effecting their reconciliation.'

'So,' said Susannah, getting to the nub of the

matter, 'does that mean he is eligible, or not? If he is truly the younger son of an Earl, he must have a title, as well as his rank of captain from the army, must he not? And…' She bit at her lower lip as she hesitated over broaching the indelicate topic of money.

But Mrs Gillies knew what interested her charge, without having to have it spelt out for her.

'No, he was never officially recognised as the eighth Earl's son. Nor did the old man leave him anything in his will. It all went to the current Earl. All Captain Fawley has is his army pension.'

'That's shocking!' cried Deborah, her fists clenching in indignation. 'Why was he cut out of the inheritance? It is not as if the present Earl cannot afford to spare a little. He must be one of the wealthiest men in England!'

Susannah laughed. 'Don't be such a goose, Debs. Isn't it obvious? Haven't you wondered why the two so-called brothers bear not the slightest resemblance to one another? No wonder the Lamptons threw the second wife out.' Picking up her cup of tea, and taking a dainty sip, she added, 'Well, that rules him out, for certain. Papa would never countenance me marrying a man who was born on the wrong side of the blanket.'

'Now, Susannah, dear, I hope you won't go around suggesting that I even hinted that Captain Fawley might not be legitimate. The Earl of Walton gets most upset with anyone who repeats that old scandal. He guards his brother's reputation zealously. And if you offend a man of his standing...'

Susannah had shrugged, calmly putting Captain Fawley out of her mind now that she had no further use for him.

It was a relief to get home from their walk in Hyde Park and slough off the disappointed suitors who would, if etiquette had not forbidden such tactics, have cheerfully shoved Mr Lampton off the pavement in order to pry Susannah from his side. Deborah was not surprised when, upon entering her mother's room, her friend's first words were of her latest conquest.

'What do you know about the Honourable Percy Lampton?' she said, perching on a chair beside the bed, where Mrs Gillies had been taking her afternoon nap. 'Is he one of the Lamptons who are related to the Earl of Walton? He looks as if he might be!'

Mrs Gillies struggled into a sitting position, while Deborah plumped up her pillows.

'From the way you have bounced into the room, I assume he has taken your fancy?' said Mrs

Gillies, with a yawn. 'Of course, he will probably be a handsome devil, if he is anything like his father.' Her eyes took on a dreamy look as she delved back into reminiscences of her youth. 'And, yes, he is cousin to the present Earl. Very good *ton*, the Lamptons.' Suddenly, her eyes snapped back into focus. 'Eminently respectable family. Pride themselves on it, in fact. I do not know exactly how young Percy is situated financially, but if you like, I shall find out.'

Susannah leant forward, giving Mrs Gillies an impetuous hug. 'Thank you!'

Deborah and her mother watched her practically dance out of the room, with similarly thoughtful expressions.

'I think Susannah may have met her match,' said Mrs Gillies, at length.

Remembering the ruthlessly charming way he had outmanoeuvred his two rivals in the park, Deborah was forced to agree with her.

'What the devil is Lampton playing at, that is what I want to know.' Captain Fawley scowled at his brother, across the dining table, some ten days later. 'The way he is monopolising Miss Hullworthy is becoming the talk of the clubs. And don't tell me he is thinking of marrying her, for I won't believe it. Apart from the fact he enjoys his bachelor status far too much to hazard it for any woman, no Lampton would stoop to marrying a cit's daughter.'

The Earl of Walton frowned thoughtfully into his glass of port. 'He lacks only four months to his thirtieth birthday,' he said at length, enigmatically.

'What has that to say to anything?'

The Earl sighed, then looked his younger brother full in the face. 'What is Miss Hullworthy to you, Robert? Do you care for her?'

'I certainly don't want to see her ruined. Good God, you know what a menace Lampton is around women. Only remember the trouble he caused Heloise when she first came to London!'

Percy Lampton had joined forces with the Earl's discarded mistress in an attempt to soil his young bride's reputation. The marriage had very nearly foundered before the Earl had got wise to what was going on.

'I don't forget it,' said the Earl crisply. 'Although, in this particular case, I think I can see what motivates him.'

'Well, I cannot! Much as I dislike the man,' he said with a pensive frown, 'he strikes me as too fastidious to get embroiled in the kind of scandal that would erupt if he really did seduce her….'

'He won't need to go so far. All he means to do, I think, is to keep her away from you until he attains the age of thirty.'

'What has his age to do with anything?'

The Earl sighed. 'Upon his thirtieth birthday, Percy Lampton will come into a substantial inheritance.'

'But what has that to do with me? Or Miss Hullworthy, come to that?'

'You brought her to his notice, Robert, by pursuing her so hotly. Inviting her to Lensborough's engagement ball caused the devil of a stir.'

'That was my intent,' Captain Fawley replied brusquely. 'But why should Lampton think my affairs are any of his business?'

'Because of my Aunt Euphemia's will, I should think,' he said wryly. 'Which rather ambiguously named either you, or Percy Lampton as her heir.'

Captain Fawley went very still. 'I have been named in the will of some woman that I have never heard of? Why has nobody informed me of the fact until today?'

The Earl shifted uncomfortably in his seat. 'Aunt Euphemia died not long after I brought you home from Spain. My mother's family always regarded her as something of an eccentric, but when her will was finally read out, they declared she must have been unhinged. I do not think so. And nor did her lawyers or her doctors. Naming you as her beneficiary was not an irrational act, but rather her attempt to redress the injustice she felt her brothers had done to you over the matter of your upbringing.'

'*Felt* they had done?'

The Earl acknowledged his brother's objection. 'Did do. We both know your mother should have been moved to the dower house and granted an annuity, and that you should have been brought up at Wycke, along with me.' He clenched his fist on the tabletop. 'They would have contested Aunt Euphemia's will, too, if I had not convinced them I had the resources to fight them tooth and nail until there would have been nothing left for anyone to inherit. Eventually, we reached a compromise with the trustees of her estate, which ensured that at least her fortune would remain intact until such time as one of you met with certain conditions.' He swirled his port round in his glass, staring into it meditatively. 'I rather think they ceded to my terms, instead of embarking on what would have been a protracted legal case because, at that time, nobody really expected you to survive.' He smiled mirthlessly.

'All right,' Captain Fawley grated, 'I accept that at the time this will was read, you acted on my behalf, since everyone thought I was about to stick my spoon in the wall. But I have been living under your roof for nigh on two years. Why is this the first I have heard about the will?'

'Would you believe me if I told you I did not think it would do you any good?'

'Not do me any good? I have a substantial sum of money owed me—at least I must assume it is, or the Lamptons would not have considered contesting the will to get it—and you say it would not do me any good?' Captain Fawley got to his feet, blood surging hotly through his veins. This was not the first time he had felt such hatred for his brother. No, he checked himself, only his half-brother. Though they shared the same father, his mother had never quite made the grade with the Earl's starchy relations. They had evicted her from his father's home before he was cold in his grave, threatening her with all sorts of dire consequences should she try to claim anything from her late husband's estate. Bereft, pregnant and without powerful friends to advise her, she had quietly returned to her middle-class family and dwindled away.

'What are you about, Walton? You pretend to act in my interests, but how can I forget that your mother was a Lampton too?'

Walton barely reacted to his brother's thinly veiled accusation.

'You forget, perhaps, that I mentioned there were conditions attached to you inheriting anything,' he said with icy calm. 'Until a few weeks ago, nobody, least of all myself, could have guessed you might want to meet them.'

'If I had known what they are, I would have been able to make the decision for myself!'

'Then do so now,' the Earl stated coldly. 'If you truly wish to escape the ignominy of living on my charity, all you have to do is make a respectable marriage. For one thing my aunt made resoundingly clear. She had no wish to have a bachelor living in her house. But do not tarry, Robert. If you are not married by the time Percy attains the age of thirty, then the trustees have decreed everything will go to him. He is, after all, a blood relative, which you are not.'

Robert felt as though the wind had been knocked out of him. No woman in her right mind would marry him. He knew it. Charles knew it. *That* was why he had not told him about the legacy. Knowing that a fortune lurked for ever just beyond his reach would only have added a further layer of torture to his existence.

He slumped back into his chair. Once again, he had lashed out at his brother, who had only ever had his welfare at heart. And sadly, though they both knew he hated having to subsist on his brother's charity, they also knew there was no viable alternative. Charles had offered on numerous occasions to make over to him the estates and trusts that should have been his, as the younger son of the Earl of Walton. Had he inherited them from his father, he would have been glad to live the life of a gentleman farmer, pottering about his acres. But the old man had not named him in his will…how could he, when he had not even been aware his wife was pregnant when he had died so suddenly? To accept them now, from his brother, out of some kind of misguided charity… He grimaced with distaste. No, he had been brought low enough, without stooping to accepting handouts, like some beggar on the streets.

If only he could be independent! His mind revolved over what Walton had just told him about this will. All he had to do, apparently, was to persuade a respectable female to marry him. Yes, that was all, he reflected bitterly. Persuade some poor woman to wake up to the nightmare of his face upon her pillow every morning.

Yet, Lampton must have thought he might have been able to persuade Miss Hullworthy to marry him. Or why would he have gone to such lengths to detach her from him?

'Damn him!' He lurched to his feet. 'Damn all the Lamptons. And damn you too.' He rounded on his half-brother. 'Oh, yes, you claim you acted for the best, but because you decided to keep me in the dark, Percy Lampton is dangling that girl on a string. If only I had known, I would—' He stopped, bitter rage roiling in his gut. 'You have a lot to answer for, Walton,' he grated, turning on his heel and striding from the dining room.

He crossed the hall and slammed into the suite of rooms Lord Walton had set aside for him in his London residence. Linney, his manservant, who had been with him since his days in the army, was sitting at a table covered with newspaper, a tankard at his elbow and a pair of boots across his knees.

When Captain Fawley slumped into the chair opposite him, Linney reached under the table for a stone bottle, wiped round the rim of a rather smeared glass tumbler with the sleeve of his shirt and poured his master a full measure.

Captain Fawley drank the bumper off in one go, and pushed it across the table for a refill. He could not let Lampton get away with this! Apart from the fact he hated all the Lamptons on principle, the way he was falsely raising Susannah's expectations was downright dishonourable. Was there nothing that family would not stoop to, to increase their already substantial personal wealth?

It was not even as though Percy Lampton needed the money as much as he did. Lampton lived a comfortable, independent bachelor lifestyle, whereas he was completely dependent on his brother. His half-brother, he corrected himself.

He leaned his forehead on his hand, struggling against the sense of resentment that thoughts of his half-brother still roused, even after all the man had done for him.

Too much! That was half the trouble. Walton always claimed he was acting in his best interests, but he was effectively robbing him of any choice. Smothering him!

If only there was some way out. Or, at least,

some way he could prevent the blackguard getting his hands on his Aunt Euphemia's fortune.

He damned the Lamptons volubly, and comprehensively, before addressing his second glass of brandy.

He had hated the name of Lampton for as long as he could remember. They had destroyed his mother, blighted his childhood with their insinuations of his illegitimacy and made no secret of the fact they had hoped he would die in some foreign country while he was on active service. The French had done their damnedest, but he was not an easy man to kill. He had survived an explosion, two amputations, a fever and gruelling months of rehabilitation.

Even in his darkest hour, when he had felt he had nothing left to live for, he had refused to let them beat him.

And he was not going to let them beat him now.

If Percy Lampton thought he was going to sit back while he waltzed off with his inheritance, then he was very much mistaken.

He would find a way to best all the Lamptons.

His face twisted into a mask of hatred.

And he didn't much care how low he might have to stoop to do so.

* * *

Deborah started at the sound of someone knocking at the front door. Susannah had gone out for a drive in the park with Mr Lampton, and she had been looking forward to spending a peaceful afternoon reading. She had already become engrossed in her book, and was a little annoyed that she would be obliged to put it aside, and entertain some dull man who would be crushingly disappointed to find his quarry flown. Her mother, who was sitting on a chair by the window to get the best light for her embroidery, let out a sigh.

'Oh, dear,' she said, having evidently caught sight of the visitor as he waited on the front steps. 'He will be so disappointed to have missed Susannah.' Turning to Deborah, she said, 'Ring for some tea. We must make the poor boy especially welcome, must we not?'

It was only when Captain Fawley walked through the door that Deborah understood what had prompted her mother's sympathy. She had not approved of many of Susannah's suitors, before Mr Lampton had come on the scene, but she had a soft spot for the Captain. It was the way he looked at Susannah, she had confided to Deborah one evening not long after they had first made Mr

Lampton's acquaintance. So wounded, so bitter, so tragically certain he had no chance against a man who was everything he was not. For not only was Mr Lampton staggeringly handsome, he had expectations. It was common knowledge that he stood to inherit a substantial fortune upon reaching the age of thirty. So he could not be pursuing Susannah for her money. He would make a better match for Susannah, Mrs Gillies had decided, than an ageing earl, or a spotty young baron. Nor would her parents look askance at him, even though he had no title, since Susannah herself seemed to have her heart set on him. And he was being so particular in his attentions, it was surely only a matter of time before he proposed.

Deborah laid her book to one side, as her mother said, 'Oh, Captain Fawley, how good it is of you to call on us this afternoon. We are all alone, as you see, and so dull! Please, do sit down. We have ordered some tea. I am sure you will stay and drink a cup with us, even though Miss Hullworthy is not here...' She faltered, looking a little self-conscious as she alluded to the Captain's disappointment.

'Thank you, Mrs Gillies,' he replied, though he remained standing stiffly by the door, rather than advancing towards the seat she had indicated he should take. 'I was aware that Miss Hullworthy was out. In point of fact, I waited until I was certain she would be. It is your daughter I have come to see. Miss Gillies,' he said, his cheeks flushing as he turned towards her, 'I know this is a little unorthodox, but might I have a few words with you in private?'

Deborah did not know how to answer him, nor to even begin to guess what on earth he might wish to say to her that would require privacy. Besides, it was completely improper! She was sure her mother would not allow any such thing.

'Why don't you two take a turn about the garden?' her mother stunned her by saying. 'But stay in sight of the windows. I am sure if Captain Fawley feels he needs to speak to you privately, he has a very good reason,' she said, in answer to Deborah's puzzled look. 'I will take a seat in the back parlour, from where I will have a good view of the lawn. Will that be acceptable, Captain?'

'Most acceptable. Thank you for your generosity, madam,' he said, opening the door and indicating that Deborah should accompany him.

One of the reasons for hiring this particular house was that it had a good-sized garden, by

London standards. There was a narrow strip of lawn, bordered by low, shrubby sage plants, interspersed with clumps of sweet-william. Against one of the walls that separated their garden from the neighbouring property, some chairs had been set out around a wrought-iron table in a position to catch the early-morning sun. The area could still be used for sitting out later, too, since a pergola had been placed to provide some shade at the height of the day. And the roses and honeysuckle clambering over the structure in a marvellously scented tangle made it a pleasant place to sit well into the evening.

Captain Fawley headed unerringly towards the flowered arbour, making sure Deborah was sitting down before glancing back towards the house. When Mrs Gillies waved to him from the window, he bowed in her direction, before turning to address Deborah.

'Before I broach the matter I have come here to discuss, may I have your assurance that you will hold everything that passes between us in the strictest confidence?'

He returned her mystified gaze with a scowl so ferocious, Deborah began to feel a little nervous.

'If it means so much to you,' she answered,

touched by his intention to confide in her, 'of course I will. Though I should not like to keep anything from my mother….'

'There will be no need to keep her in the dark for long,' he assured her. 'But I must insist that you do not reveal anything, not even to her, until I give you leave.'

'That sounds a little high-handed.'

'If I cannot trust you, then say so now, and that will be an end to it!'

Deborah scarcely paused to think. It would be quite impossible to let him leave without discovering why he had thought it imperative to breach etiquette by seeking an interview with her alone and then swearing her to secrecy. She would die of curiosity.

'You can trust me,' she vowed.

For a minute or two, he frowned down at her, searching her face as though he needed to be absolutely sure before committing himself any further. Finally, he squared his shoulders, as though coming to a decision about her, and muttered, 'If I did not think I could trust you, I would never even have considered coming to you. One thing I have noticed about you—you seem to possess more integrity than most girls of your age.

I know that you have endured much during this past year, and borne it all with fortitude.'

Deborah filled up with pleasure at his praise, though gruffly delivered.

'You have also confided in me that when your Season comes to an end, you will have little to look forward to. I hope you will not take it amiss if I speak bluntly?'

He was about to trust her with some burden that he carried. How could she object if, in his extremity, he phrased it bluntly?

'You may speak freely to me,' she assured him.

'Well, then,' he said, taking the seat beside her and staring earnestly into her face, 'not to wrap the matter up in clean linen, the facts are these. You have neither the wealth, nor the looks, nor the wiles required to snare a wealthy husband.'

Deborah gasped, wounded to the core by his harsh assessment of her complete want of feminine allure. But he did not even pause in his catalogue of her failings.

'You might, perhaps, have secured the interest of a more ordinary man if you were not so frail. But I have no need to tell you that a man who must earn his own living, as, say, a soldier, or a diplomat, will want a wife in robust health, with the stamina to raise his family, and order his household in possibly less-than-comfortable circumstances.'

She was about to point out, in no uncertain terms, that she was not some frail creature that could not withstand a little hardship. And argue that, while such a man as he had spoken of was exactly the sort of husband she had come to London to find, Susannah's ambitions had catapulted her into spheres where such men did not venture. She was quite sure, that if she ever met such men, *they* might see she had some redeeming features. But he gave her no opportunity to say a word.

'You have admitted to me that you do not expect to receive any proposals of marriage,' he ploughed on with brutal candour, 'and that at the end of the Season, because of your straitened circumstances, you will have to seek paid employment. If you do not become a governess, you must serve as a teacher, for ever confined to some stuffy class-room. You will be quite miserable, for you would much rather marry, and be mistress of your own establishment than be for ever at the mercy of some other family's spoiled brats.'

Deborah's heart was pounding hard. She could not remember any man ever insulting her so comprehensively. Even though all he had said was true, it was cruel of him to fling it in her face. How dare he taunt her with her wish to marry, having told her she stood no chance of snaring a man!

'I do not think I wish to continue with this conversation,' she said, rising to her feet and turning her back on him.

'Miss Gillies, do not turn me down before you hear the whole.'

Turn him down? She froze. What was he trying to say?

'The…the whole?' Reluctantly, she looked at him over her shoulder.

'Yes. Miss Gillies, I have recently discovered that if I can but persuade some respectable female into marriage, I will inherit a substantial property.' He got to his feet, reached for her upper arm and spun her to face him. 'I thought you, of all women, might overcome your revulsion for such a man as I am in return for lifelong security.'

'You are asking me to marry you?' Deborah's heart was pounding with quite another emotion than she had been experiencing a moment earlier. She might have known his intention had not been to deliberately hurt her. He just obviously thought of himself as such a bad bargain for any woman, he had to highlight what he thought her alternative to accepting his proposal would be. 'The devil or the deep blue sea,' she whispered, her eyes filling with tears. Oh, how could he think no woman could love him!

'Don't dismiss the idea out of hand,' he implored her. 'Please, hear me out.'

Deborah's heart soared, even as she lowered her head to fumble in her reticule for a handkerchief. She did not know why she was crying, really. It was so silly when it felt as if a huge dark mass, which had been crushing her hopes and dreams, had finally rolled away, leaving her giddy and dazed. The man she loved had asked her to marry him!

She dropped back down on to her chair. The only reason, she now admitted to herself, that she had decided to forswear marriage and seek work was that she could not see herself marrying anyone except Captain Fawley. If she had received a proposal from any other man, she would have been gratified, but she did not think she could really have accepted it. But of course she would marry him. In a heartbeat! As soon as she had got this ridiculous urge to weep tears of relief under control, she would tell him so….

'Miss Gillies, I know I have little to offer you myself. But consider the property that comes with the marriage.' He sat down next to her, leaning forward as he put his case. 'I believe it would make an ideal family home. There will be room for your mother. I am sure you wish to be able to provide for her in her old age. I know her pension to be so meagre you thought it would be better to work than be a burden on her. And would you not rather raise children of your own than be paid to teach other people's? I would even permit you to hire a fencing master for our daughters, if that is what you wish,' he added, the touch of humour reminding her of the conversation they had shared at the Marquis of Lensborough's ball.

Though his reference to children was made in a jocular fashion, she knew he was spelling out to her that he was offering her a real marriage, not just a convenient arrangement. She had a brief vision of a boy and a girl capering about a broad, sunlit lawn, waving wooden swords at each other, while Captain Fawley, lounging beneath the shade of a gnarled oak tree, shouted instructions to them. Another little boy, with a grubby face, grinned down from the branches of the tree, while her mother, seated on a rustic bench nearby, smiled contentedly at her grandchildren. She watched them all from the windows of a rambling stone house, a tiny baby nuzzling at her breast. And then the Captain Fawley on that sun-drenched lawn turned to look at her. And he smiled at her. And his expression was not that of the bitter, careworn cripple who was putting this proposition to her, his eyes full of hopeless entreaty. He had become a contented family man.

She scanned the harsh features, scarce six inches from her own face. The warmth of his breath fanned her cheek. She could smell the faint aroma of bergamot, a scent she had associated with him since the night when he had supported her, half-fainting, from the heat of that crowded ballroom. Her hands remembered the texture of his sleeve, and, through it, the strength of the arm that it clothed.

How she longed to be the one to wipe away those lines of suffering that a lifetime of disappointments had etched so deeply on his face! To make those eyes, that burned with suspicion, glow with contentment or light with laughter.

Oh, she knew he was only asking her to marry him out of disappointment in losing Susannah to a rival. But she could empathise with the streak of practicality in his nature that had him reasoning that if he could not have the woman he had set his heart on, there was no reason that he should forgo the property, as well. Had she not planned her own future along similar lines? Having given up hope of marrying the man she loved, she had decided she would at least stand on her own two feet and not be beholden to anyone.

Though it was depressing that he thought so poorly of her. He saw her as a girl with so little going for her that she would be grateful for the chance to live in comfort, even if it meant allying herself to a man he assumed no woman could look upon with anything but revulsion.

'If any other man had asked me in such terms,' she declared, determined to justify her intention to accept him, in spite of his insults, 'I would have turned him down flat. Don't you know that the way you just addressed me was hurtful, almost beyond bearing?'

'If that is what you think,' he said, rearing back and making as though he was about to stand up, 'then I will trouble you with my unwelcome attentions no more.'

She regretted her impulse to put him straight, as soon as she saw the pain in his eyes. She had never intended to hurt him. Oh, blow her stupid pride. It was not worth defending if doing so wounded him.

'Your attentions are not unwelcome,' she hastily

reassured him. 'And of course I will marry you. It was just the way you put it…'

He got to his feet, looking down at her with an expression so fierce she felt almost afraid of him.

'You must not expect honeyed words, or any insincere flattery from me, Miss Gillies. I may not have put my proposal with any great eloquence, but at least you know exactly what it is I am offering. I am offering you financial security, a chance at a good, comfortable future. You are about to marry a man who has been a soldier all his adult life. A man who has fought hard and lived rough. I am not going to spout some silly romantic nonsense to try to deceive you into expecting what I cannot give.'

She blinked in astonishment. Hurt tears sprung to her eyes. Had any woman ever received such an insulting proposal or had her acceptance met with such a stinging rebuke? If she had a grain of sense, she would tell him what he could do with his proposal, and walk away.

But then she would never see him again.

She would become a teacher, just as she had planned, but with the knowledge that, had she had more courage, she could have been Captain Fawley's wife.

She could have endured that lonely life of drudgery, had he never proposed to her. But now, such a future would be unbearable.

A cold hand seemed to reach into her bowels, and twist them into a knot as another horrible thought occurred to her. Seeing the ruthless way he had tried to bludgeon her into a marriage he was convinced she could not want, was he not bound to bully some other hapless female into taking him on, so that he could get at his inheritance? She could not deceive herself into thinking she was anything more to him than the first on a list of prospective wives, drawn from the pool of available females in desperate straits.

'I do not expect anything from you,' she said despondently. How could she have forgotten, even for a second, that he was in love with Susannah? She might have fanciful visions of creating a happy family with the man she loved, but as far as he was concerned, she could be any female.

A means to an end.

Chapter Four

A sense of elation swept over him, so strong that it made him almost dizzy. Vengeance, for all of it, was almost within his grasp! He could not believe it had been so easy. He had all those fools to thank—the fools who had made this lovely girl believe no man could want her.

He sank down on to the chair next to her, and would have seized her hand in gratitude, had he not been aware that she saw acceptance of his proposal as the lesser of two evils. Poverty and drudgery on the one hand, or marriage to a man no other woman could stomach on the other. What was it she had murmured, tears in her eyes? The devil or the deep blue sea!

So what if she felt she had made a bargain with the devil? She would soon learn that though he might not be the kind of husband most girls dreamed of, she would most definitely enjoy the comfortable lifestyle marrying him would bring her. From what he had been able to glean from his brief visit to the lawyers, to verify exactly what he needed to do to inherit, the old woman had left a tidy sum of money, as well as the property that would become their home.

'Thank you, Miss Gillies. I cannot begin to tell you what this means to me.' He almost winced at his own choice of words. He had been deliberately economical with the facts. For he never wanted her to discover that he had taken advantage of her vulnerability in order to exact revenge on a Lampton. Such knowledge was bound to chafe at her tender conscience.

He had suspected, before he came to put his proposal to her, that she would refuse him outright if she knew that marrying him would be tantamount to ruining another person's future. She seemed capable of putting everyone's happiness before her own. Look at how pleased she had been to observe Susannah's success. She had displayed no trace of envy, though Susannah had totally eclipsed her more understated beauty, denying her a chance to attract her own suitors. And she had been pleased that the London Season, which was clearly sapping her strength, was helping her mother to get over her grief.

No, he had no intention of burdening her with the knowledge that he was determined to deprive Lampton of a fortune the man had always regarded as his.

But he had to secure it swiftly. Lampton was bound to take steps to prevent him marrying if he got wind of it.

'We must marry at once.'

'Must we?' she replied, in bewilderment.

'Yes, for if I do not fulfil the terms of the will, within a specified time, I may lose out on the inheritance altogether.'

'Oh,' was all she said, but he could hear acceptance in her tone. Relieved to have surmounted yet another hurdle, he braced himself for her objections when he stipulated, 'And I must insist that we send no announcement to the papers until after the ceremony. Nor tell anyone who is not directly involved either when, or where, it is to take place.'

She looked at him with a troubled frown. 'You want me to marry you in secret?' She shook her head. 'No…that would be…quite repugnant to me.' To marry in secret, as though there was something to be ashamed of…it did not bear thinking about.

'It seems so underhanded,' she persisted.

'I know I am asking a great deal of you. But, please, look at it from my point of view.'

Sometimes, a battle had to be fought with subtlety, using whatever stratagems necessary to outwit the enemy. He was not exactly lying to Deborah. Only throwing a little dust in her eyes. It was no worse than lying in ambush for an enemy who had superior numbers, rather than meeting him on open ground, where defeat would have been inevitable.

'I do not want there to be any more witnesses to our wedding than are absolutely necessary.' That much was the literal truth. But then, relying on her sympathetic nature, he added, 'Do you think I enjoy having people stare at me? Wondering what on earth I had to do to induce a beauty like you into taking on a wreck like me?'

'Beauty?' she gasped indignantly. 'You just said that you were not going to spout silly romantic nonsense! So don't resort to insincere flattery just to get your own way. I would much rather you kept to the plain speaking you say you pride yourself on.'

'Miss Gillies, I am being perfectly sincere. You posses an inner beauty that any man with an ounce of sense—'

'Oh, inner beauty,' she snorted in derision. That was how a man always tried to cajole a plain girl into doing his bidding. Well, he would soon find out that she was not as biddable as all that. She must tell him she simply could not act in a way she felt was morally reprehensible.

She took a deep breath.

'I refuse to keep this news from my mother, or marry without her to attend me….'

'Well, naturally,' he said, taking the wind out of her sails. 'Miss Gillies, I am not asking you to enter into a secret marriage. Only a very private one. There will be nothing havey-cavey about it. I shall be asking my brother to stand up with me. And once the ceremony is over and we are on our way to our new home, I will be only too pleased to advertise the fact.'

That did not sound too unreasonable, she supposed.

'However, I would rather you did not tell your mother that we are to marry, until you are in the coach and on the way to the ceremony.'

Deborah blinked.

'It is the only way to be sure she does not let slip what is about to take place. She is clearly very fond of Miss Hullworthy. Would she be able, do you suppose, to keep the news of your marriage from her? Would she be able to keep it from anyone? Most mothers are so pleased to know their daughters are to wed, they cannot keep a still tongue in their head.'

Deborah chewed on her lower lip as she pondered this aspect of the case. Her mother would indeed be thrilled to hear she was getting married, doubly so that it was to Captain Fawley. And if she knew that he planned to take her into the marital home, and care for her in her old age, nothing would keep her from flinging herself on his neck and weeping all over him, before she proudly announced to all her cronies what a splendid son-in-law she had managed to net.

And as for keeping the news from Susannah… She sighed. Captain Fawley would not want her to be present at the ceremony that represented a final farewell to the woman he loved. In fact, if she was honest with herself, having Susannah there would ruin the event for her, as well. It was bad enough knowing she was a poor second-best, without having her husband's first choice there in person to remind her what a second-rate marriage he was embarking upon.

She hated subterfuge, or anything that smacked

of dishonesty in any form, yet refraining from telling her friend her news would certainly save both Captain Fawley, and herself, some pain.

'How long would you expect me to keep our engagement from my mother?'

She could not miss the flare of triumph that lit his eyes as he recognised her capitulation to his terms.

'Now that I have your promise, I can obtain the special licence required to marry without the need for banns. We will have to meet with the lawyers who are acting as executors of the will of which I am a beneficiary too. It is no use marrying without their prior knowledge and agreement. Providing all goes well, the ceremony itself can take place the day after tomorrow. We shall leave town immediately after the ceremony. Walton can send the notice to the *Morning Post* once we are safely out of the way.'

'Just a minute—what will happen if the lawyers do not give their agreement?'

'I am sure they will. You have no need to worry. I did not mean to imply they might not approve you. I just need to make sure I fulfil all the terms to the letter, so that nobody may contest my claim.'

'Contest your claim? Is that likely?'

What would happen to her, if she did not fulfil

the requirements of this will? Or if someone contested his claim? He had only proposed because he wanted to inherit this property. He would have no use for her at all if the lawyers decided she was not fit for some reason. She went cold inside. What would he do in such an event? Take her home and wash his hands of her? Could he be so ungallant?

Was that why he had sworn her to secrecy? So that she would not be able to complain that he had proposed and then jilted her? For she had too much pride to admit to another living soul that she had done something so improper as entering into a secret engagement. Suddenly, she felt very alone, and very afraid.

But then, to her surprise, Captain Fawley reached out and placed his hand over hers as she twisted them together in her lap.

'I know it will not be easy for you to creep out of the house, without your mother's knowledge.'

She had not even considered the practical aspects of attending an appointment at the lawyers' office without her mother's knowledge until that moment. Now she had another worry to add to those already tormenting her!

'But only think how happy she will be when she finds out it was all in a good cause,' he cajoled her.

'And you will not have to keep her from our plans for more than a day, if all goes well.'

If all went well. But would it? It would be the longest day of her life. Lying to her mother, dreading that something might occur to prevent the wedding taking place....

'Trust me,' he said, giving her hands a little squeeze. 'I will arrange everything.'

Trust him? Oh, how she wished she could!

'It is only one day, Miss Gillies. I am sure you have the courage to endure just one day. You have gone through far worse since your father died, and emerged unscathed.'

She blinked up at him. He had said he would never resort to honeyed words, and yet here he was uttering another compliment. Did he mean it? He must do, for he had declared he could only speak the plain truth. He must think she had fortitude.

Yes, this was an aspect of that dratted inner beauty he had claimed to admire.

'Just one day.' She sighed. It would not seem all that much to him, for he did not know that she loved him. He assumed her torment would end, after that one day, whatever the outcome.

She looked up into his face, wondering whether

this was the moment to tell him the truth. Surely he would not abandon her, even if she did not pass the examination of his lawyers, if she told him she loved him. He could not be so cruel....

But if she pressured him into keeping to his vow to marry her, how would they live? They would not have a feather to fly with. Every time a bill landed on their doorstep, he would resent her for preventing him from marrying a woman who would have enabled him to inherit that property.

Better for her to become a lonely, desiccated teacher, and know that at least she had not robbed him of his happiness, than to endure his hatred.

She would have to keep her feelings for him to herself then, until after they were married.

'It will only be for a day,' she said again, returning the pressure of his hand. Even if it meant a lifetime of misery for her, she would not let him down. Was that not what love meant? Putting the beloved's happiness before one's own?

'You will not regret it,' he declared fervently.

But she was regretting it even before she got back to the house. Her mother was bound to want to know what had passed between them in the garden. What was she to tell her?

In the event, she told her mother as much of the

truth as she felt she could, without betraying Captain Fawley's confidence.

'He spoke to me on a…on a financial matter, Mother,' she said, fiddling with one of the tiebacks of the drawing-room curtains. 'And he asked me to keep the matter in confidence.'

'A financial matter…' Mrs Gillies frowned. 'Not a personal matter?'

'Mother, I promised not to speak about it until…until he gave me leave.'

Seeing how red her daughter's face was turning, Mrs Gillies let the matter drop.

Deborah was glad, for once, when Susannah returned and filled the room with an endless stream of chatter, which required very little input from anyone else. Her mother had not questioned her further, but kept darting her troubled looks, and taking a breath, as though she was about to speak. Then she would shake her head, and purse her lips, as Deborah felt her cheeks grow red at the prospect of returning another evasive answer. Susannah was a welcome buffer from the tension that steadily mounted all afternoon.

Both mother and daughter concentrated on conversing with her, rather than each other, during their outing to the theatre that night. But as the evening dragged interminably on, Deborah began to resent the situation Captain Fawley had placed her in. It was all very well for him to say she would not have to deceive her mother for more than one day, but while his day would be filled with activity, dashing about getting the licence and arranging appointments with lawyers and vicars, she would have nothing to do but count the minutes, while her mother kept looking at her with those mildly disapproving eyes until she would feel she was guilty of some heinous crime.

It was a relief to get into bed, where she did not have to encounter her mother's reproachful looks any more. But by then she was too wound up to sleep. She thumped her pillows, and threw off the covers, furious at his cruelty in placing her in this untenable position. But it was not much later that she sat up, shivering in the chill night air, and dragged the covers back over her shoulders. The conviction that it would all come to nothing filled her with a cold sense of dread. Then she sank back into her pillows, her eyes searching the shadowy alcoves of her room. How on earth was it possible to love him, yet resent his behaviour with such ferocity, all at the same time?

* * *

By the time morning came, she felt almost wretched enough to declare she intended to stay in bed. She did not think she could cope with either her mother's suspicious looks or Susannah's self-centred oblivion to her distress.

But her mother took her hand when she tried to evade the social obligations of the day, saying in a firm voice, 'It will be much better if you got up, and kept busy, my dear. Distract your mind from…whatever it is that ails it. How long, by the way, did you promise to keep Captain Fawley's confidence?'

'Just for today, Mother,' Deborah replied, a little uneasy that her mother had so perceptively linked her distress to the conversation she'd had with Captain Fawley. 'By tomorrow, I should be able to…'

'Give him an answer.' Mrs Gillies nodded. 'He has a deal of pride, that young man.' She leaned down and kissed her daughter on the forehead. 'But my advice to you is to carry on as best you can, as though you did not have…a decision to make. If he has asked you to keep the matter confidential, you must act as though you were not considering…umm…whatever it was you discussed so intently in the garden yesterday.'

Deborah could not believe her mother had so nearly guessed at the truth. From her knowing smile and meaningful nods, she made it obvious she thought Captain Fawley had proposed to her, and was giving her time to consider her answer. She sat up straight, in alarm.

'Mother, you won't speak of this to anyone else, will you?'

'Of course not! Especially if you decide not to…umm…that is, I am sure you would not wish it to be known that you… And naturally, he will not want anyone knowing that you would not… No, no! Far better to keep the whole thing under wraps, until you have decided you will… I mean, when we may speak freely, without risk of hurting anyone's pride.'

Deborah felt much better, knowing that her mother had an inkling of what was in the air. It would be much easier to tell her the whole once they were on the way to her wedding than if she had to spring it on her out of the blue.

It would be easier to make some excuse to go out to the lawyer's too. She would assume she would be meeting Captain Fawley secretly, in order to give him an answer.

* * *

She rose early in the morning, after another restless night, wondering how he would manage to communicate with her. He could hardly come to fetch her himself. They could not just go out, without a chaperon of any sort. But she could not imagine how she was expected to find the lawyer's office unless he sent her a message. Her stomach roiled at the thought he would send her a letter, which she would have to somehow keep from the curiosity of both her mother and Susannah. They normally read all the post over the breakfast plates, discussing the various invitations they received, or comparing news from home. She shook her head, a nagging pain building across her forehead, which, she realised, had been ridged with worry almost since the moment he had made his proposal.

But in the event, Captain Fawley had, as he had promised, arranged things so she did not have to tell any lies at all. They had scarcely risen from the breakfast table, when the butler strode into the room, looking full of self-importance.

'The Countess of Walton is here, Miss Gillies,' he said, handing her a card. 'I have shown her into the front parlour.'

All three ladies gasped at the unexpected honour of having such a grand person visit them, especially at such an unsocial hour.

'Go on, go on,' her mother urged her, making shooing motions with her hands. 'Do not keep her ladyship waiting. We will join you as soon as we have…' She trailed off, straightening her cap as Susannah scurried to the mirror, where she patted her curls and tugged at the neckline of her gown.

'Oh, no, is that a smear of butter on my dress?' Deborah heard her saying, as she followed the butler from the room. 'I had better go and change!'

'Ah! Miss Deborah!' the Countess greeted her incorrectly, in a decidedly French accent, as soon as she entered the room.

Deborah had been introduced to the Countess at Lord Lensborough's ball, and had spent a few minutes trying in vain to think of some topic of conversation that might interest the diminutive and rather vague-looking woman. She had learned later, from her mother, that the Countess was generally considered something of a failure, socially speaking, although the universally poor opinion of the Earl's choice of bride had mellowed somewhat when she had eventually fallen pregnant.

'Alone too!' she beamed, leaping to her feet,

and taking Deborah's hands to pull her down on to the sofa next to her. 'This is good! For I come from Robert, to bear you to him who is waiting at the office of his lawyers. He has told me how I must keep this a secret, and how I am to say to your mother that we are to go shopping, that I admired the gown I saw you wearing at Lensborough's ball, or some such piece of nonsense. As though anyone would believe I would wish to spend the day shopping when I am this size!' She indicated her clearly visible pregnancy with a rueful moue. 'But there, that is Robert for you!'

The countess was dressed in layers of pink muslin, which draped over, and emphasised, the roundness of her tummy. Together with her chirruping voice and her fluttery hand movements, she put Deborah in mind of a chaffinch hopping about her drawing room. This impression was reinforced when her mother entered the room, and Lady Walton briskly folded those hands in her lap, regarding the newcomer with her head tilted to one side.

'Mrs Gillies?' she enquired without preamble. 'You do not mind that I borrow your daughter for the morning to go shopping? It is a fancy of mine.' She checked, an expression of inspiration coming to her face. 'Yes! For we women who are *enceinte*, we get these fancies, you know. Nothing will do, but to have the delightful Miss Gillies to come shopping with me this morning. We met at Lord Lensborough's ball. I have very few friends in London,' she finished, with an abstracted air. 'Except for Robert, of course, who is quite like a brother to me. I mean to say, Captain Fawley,' she explained, at the mystified look Mrs Gillies gave her.

Deborah decided she would have to get the woman out of the house before she blurted out something that would give the game away. How could Captain Fawley have entrusted such a delicate mission to such a scatterbrained creature as this? She dashed upstairs, gathered her coat and bonnet, almost tripping on the hall carpet in her haste to get back to the drawing room.

Both women heaved a sigh of relief when the door of the Walton carriage shut behind them, and they set out on their mission.

'Oh, this is so exciting!' Lady Walton trilled, settling herself into a corner and regarding Deborah out of a pair of black, beady eyes. 'To think that I should be able to help Robert to outwit that vile Lampton, at last!' She checked herself, going a little pink in the cheeks when Deborah looked at her in astonishment.

'Lampton? What has Lampton got to do with this?'

'Oh, dear, now I have ruined everything. Robert will be so cross with me. I promised I would not spill any beans and now I have done it before we even get to see the men who control his fortune. Miss Gillies...' she leaned forward, her face creased with distress '...please tell me that you will not turn him down, now that you know he has done what you must think reprehensible.'

Deborah felt a strange sensation in her chest, as though someone was squeezing her there, making it hard to breathe. 'Reprehensible?' she echoed. 'I do not know what you mean. What has Captain Fawley done?'

'He has done nothing! It is that vile worm of a pig, Percy Lampton, who has tried to steal everything from him. Please, if you care anything for him at all, do not side with his enemies today. From much he has recovered in the past, but not this, I think. It has been so hard for him to summon the courage to ask a woman even to dance with him, thinking himself so ugly, but to beg for your hand… You cannot think what courage he had to summon to approach you.'

She took Deborah's hands between her own. 'You see beyond the scars, to his heart, do you not? You have not just agreed to marry him because you wish to have a big house in the country and not to have to become a governess? I would not have agreed to take part in this deception if I did not believe you were worthy of him. But I saw how you looked at him at Lensborough's ball. You love him, don't you? Please tell me I have not this all wrong?'

'Y-yes, I love him,' Deborah breathed, tugging her hands out of the Countess's grip. 'But I don't understand….'

'You don't need to understand! Only love him. Trust him! Men…they do the foolish things sometimes, because they think to protect us. Wrong things, perhaps. But Robert will be so good a husband to you. I know it! He is so grateful that you give him this chance….'

'I don't want his gratitude!' Deborah snapped. The funny feeling in her chest was developing into a burning pain. She had felt from the outset that there was something not right about all the secrecy Captain Fawley had insisted on. Now the

Countess had confirmed that it was not just his sensitivity to the way he looked that had made him insist the wedding should be held in secret.

But the worst thing of all was knowing that he had taken this ninny completely into his confidence, even to telling her all about her plans to become a governess, when he had kept her in the dark. It had been bad enough when she had thought she came in a poor second to Susannah. Now she had to accept she did not even come in second. This woman, his sister-in-law, stood closer to him than she did.

She blanked out the Countess's persistent chirruping as the coach bore them into the City, as she tried to make some sense out of what she had let slip the moment they had got into the coach. She remembered the look of contempt Captain Fawley had directed at Percy Lampton the first time he had seen him with Susannah. And the malicious smile Lampton had returned. At the time, she had thought it was odd, but now she saw it was the look of two long-standing adversaries. She recalled the way Lampton had ridden up to them in Hyde Park, requesting an introduction, as though the meeting was purely accidental. She remembered her instant distrust of his charm. And felt certain that he was not merely another in Susannah's long line of conquests. Could his pursuit of her been deliberately calculated for the sole purpose of preventing Captain Fawley from marrying her, and thus gaining his inheritance?

She alighted from the carriage in a daze. Captain Fawley was waiting for her on the steps of a functional building in a narrow, though cleanly swept, side street. He looked tense.

As well he might. He was using her as a weapon in his ongoing struggle with the Lamptons in general, and Percy Lampton in particular.

And it hurt.

'Thank you for coming,' he said, limping forward to offer her his arm. 'I was beginning to think my ruse would not work. Heloise is such a pea goose. A dear little pea goose, but sadly featherbrained.'

'I heard that, you ungrateful beast!' Lady Walton put her head out of the carriage window to inform him, her eyes full of laughter. 'Now you will have to wonder if I will return, in Walton's carriage, to take your Miss Gillies home, or if I will take offence and wash my hands of you once and for all!'

'You wouldn't do anything so hard-hearted,' he returned, with a fond smile. 'Besides, you will be burning with curiosity to discover how this interview turned out.'

'Pig!' she answered, slamming the window and thumping with her parasol on the roof to indicate the driver should set off.

Could she really believe the Countess would connive at doing something that was really reprehensible? Though her words had set alarm bells ringing, the insouciant way she had driven off, after laughing and joking with Robert, made it sound as though she were participating in some kind of prank, at the very worst.

She shook her head, too hurt and bewildered to do more than follow meekly where Robert led her, which was into a narrow hallway and up a wooden staircase to the cramped office of the lawyers, Kenridge and Hopedale.

As they entered the room, two men looked up from behind a desk almost obliterated by the mounds of papers and files stacked upon it. One, a kindly-faced, stout gentleman, got to his feet, indicating that she should take the ladder-backed chair set out for the convenience of his clients. As Captain Fawley took his place directly behind her, the other lawyer scowled at them over the top of a pair of half-moon spectacles.

'Now, then, Miss…Gillies, is it not?' the cherubic lawyer muttered, shuffling a sheaf of papers in front of him. 'We just need to ask you a few questions.'

She felt Captain Fawley place his hand upon her shoulder, as though offering her reassurance. She felt an almost overwhelming urge to shake it off. Why had he not been open with her about his real motive for wishing to get married? Could he imagine for one second that she would side with the family who had wronged him even before he was born? She could not believe a man as starchy as the Earl of Walton would acknowledge a man as his brother, if there was even a hint he might be illegitimate. The Lamptons must have deliberately robbed Captain Fawley's mother, and him, of what should have been theirs. Now Percy Lampton seemed to be trying to do the same thing, all over again!

'We only need to know that she is of age, and entering into marriage with Captain Fawley freely,' the acid-faced lawyer interrupted. 'Are you?' he shot at her.

But before she could answer in the affirmative, the kindly lawyer shook his head. 'No, no, we must establish not only the legality, but also the suitability of this union. The marriage must be watertight.

We do not want the Lamptons thinking they might have any possible grounds for contesting our decision to wind up the trust. If she does not come from an impeccable background, they might—'

'Codswallop!' the thin lawyer snapped. 'It is quite clear that Euphemia Lampton intended all her estate to go to this young man. Her nephew never even got a mention in the original will. Not even to a keepsake. You and I both know that she only added the codicil under duress.'

Something like a cold dart shot through Deborah at the use of the word *nephew*. Nephew to a Lampton? Could this other legatee mentioned in a codicil be…Percy Lampton? Was this the inheritance he had been fully expecting to come into? If so, what Captain Fawley was doing was worse than she had imagined. Not only was he using her to get his hands on this legacy, but it was a property that morally belonged to somebody else. Or at least…she chewed at her lower lip…Lampton had always assumed it belonged to him. So he would feel as though he was being robbed. Now she felt like an accessory to a crime.

The plump lawyer's cheeks went a little pink. 'Now, now, we do not need to mention specifics in front of this young lady….'

'Why not? You are practically demanding she provide references!'

The plump lawyer lost his cherubic look, his brows drawing down in an angry V as he swivelled to face his partner. 'Only in order to satisfy a legal point. Normally it *is* preferable for a property to go to a blood relation than somebody who has no connection with the testator.'

'The connection is there. You heard what Miss Lampton told us when we drew up the original will—'

'Excuse me,' Deborah said, rising to her feet, her pulse tumultuous with agitation. 'But I am quite able to vouch for my suitability to marry any man I choose,' she said, addressing the plump lawyer. 'My mother is granddaughter to the Earl of Plymstock, through the female line. You may check her lineage in *Collin's Peerage*. My father was a Gillies of Hertfordshire. Again, check away as meticulously as you please. Third son of Reginald and Lucinda Gillies, of Upshott. Not perhaps a noble family, but old.'

She drew in an indignant breath. Not only had Captain Fawley been dishonest in the manner of his proposal, but he had exposed her to this piece of impertinence!

'You may also investigate as long as you please, and you will discover I have *never* done anything that would give *anyone* any justification for claiming I was not completely respectable. My father was a man of the cloth. As his child, he taught me how important it was not to let him down by so much as an unseemly gesture. Go and inquire in the town of Lower Wakering, where I grew up. You will not find anybody who could cast an aspersion on my moral rectitude. And as for the other matter, yes, I am of age! At my last prayers, in fact,' she said, her face twisting with bitterness as she recalled that it was precisely this fact Captain Fawley had used to lure her into what he thought was her last chance of ever marrying. 'And do I marry Captain Fawley of my own free will?'

She whirled round to glare at him. She felt humiliated, used, deceived. He held her regard without the slightest sign of guilt or remorse. There was only what might have been interpreted as a slightly mocking challenge in his eyes.

Trust him, the Countess had urged her. Do not side with his enemies.

She swallowed. Furious as she was with him, right at this moment, could she really back out of this horrible tangle, having come this far? Would he not see it as a betrayal, far worse than anything that had been done to him to date? He would regard her as an enemy. He would hate her.

Shaking with impotent fury, she turned back to the lawyers, who were awaiting her answer with quills poised.

'Yes,' she croaked, her voice clogged with emotion. She cleared her throat. 'If I do not marry him, I shall not marry anyone,' she declared firmly.

Then, her eyes full of humiliated tears, she whirled from the room and stumbled down the stairs into the dusty street. Leaning against the wall, her forehead grinding into the brickwork, she fought to regain her composure.

What was she doing, allying herself to a man who could deceive her, use her without regard for her feelings? Condemning herself to a lifetime of hurt, that was what!

'Miss Gillies!' She blinked as the Walton coach drew up at the kerb, and the countess leaned out, her face puckered with concern.

'Miss Gillies!' She heard another voice, a masculine voice, calling her from within the lawyer's offices. Captain Fawley must be making his way down the stairs, of necessity slowly and carefully.

A footman jumped down from the box and

opened the carriage door for her. She strode across the pavement and got in.

'Where is Robert?' the Countess asked, peering behind her.

'I don't think we ought to be seen together, do you?' Deborah said, on a flash of inspiration. 'Wouldn't want to give the game away!' she finished bitterly.

The Countess's face lit up. Clapping her hands, she gave the order for the coach to set off.

Just as Robert emerged from the doorway, his face as dark as a thundercloud.

Chapter Five

'Oh, isn't the Countess coming in?' Susannah wailed in disappointment as the Walton carriage pulled away the moment Deborah had entered her front door. 'I was so hoping to meet her. What is she like? Where did you go? You have been an age, and I am dying with curiosity!'

'She is rather like a small, determined whirlwind,' Deborah answered, thinking it typical of Susannah to display that unfamiliar emotion on a day she was least willing to satisfy it. 'She whisked me off in her coach without waiting for a proper introduction to you both. I am so sorry,' she said, joining her mother and Susannah in the front parlour, where they were partaking of a light nuncheon. 'But I did not like to keep her ladyship waiting….'

'That is quite all right, my dear,' Mrs Gillies replied, pouring her a cup of tea. 'Since she is

French, we cannot expect the same standards in her manners as if she had been brought up properly, can we?'

'I have been consumed with jealousy all morning!' said Susannah, heaping ham on to the plate in Deborah's place setting.

'Jealous? You?' she gasped, taking her seat at table.

'Yes! It is one thing having men dangling after one. But what really gets one into society is to make a friend of some influential or aristocratic female.' She placed a slice of bread and butter to Deborah's plate, adding, 'I don't blame you for dropping everything and dashing off after her. If she takes you up, you will be made.'

'Oh, I don't know,' Mrs Gillies interposed. 'She is not exactly a leader of fashion. And she will not be much use to Deborah after another month or so anyway, since she is increasing.'

Deborah paused in the act of lifting a slice of ham to her lips, a troubled frown knotting her brow.

'One does not just make friends that can be of use, surely!' she protested. She had never liked this side of Susannah's nature, and was appalled to hear her mother speaking of connections in similar terms.

'But it is always a point to take into consideration,' said Susannah, popping a slice of tomato into her mouth. 'You are too unworldly for your own good, sometimes.'

'Unless…she may be looking for a companion to go with her, when she has to return to her country estate for the lying in,' Mrs Gillies pondered. 'Her husband is bound to insist his heir is born at Wycke, and I have heard that she detests the place. She grew up in Paris, you see, in such exciting times, and finds the countryside tedious.'

'Oh!' cried Susannah. 'Perhaps, if she does take a fancy to you, she will take you with her, to keep her amused.'

'Like a pet monkey,' Deborah remarked sourly.

Susannah began to giggle.

'I can just see you in a little knitted c-cap, with a Spanish j-jacket, like the one we saw dancing in the park that day….'

Her mother's mouth, too, twitched with amusement and from then on, by applying a little ingenuity, Deborah was able to ensure that the conversation never returned to exactly how she had spent her morning. By the time they rose from the table, her mother was ready to take her afternoon nap, and Susannah declared she simply had to write to her parents, since she had not done so for two days.

Deborah escaped to her room with a feeling of profound relief.

It did not last long.

Once she was on her own, there was nothing to prevent her from dwelling on what a dreadful situation she had got herself into. She had known it would be quite wrong to turn Captain Fawley down in the lawyer's office, while she was so angry with him. She needed to consider the situation rather more dispassionately, and make the decision which would affect her whole future, with a clear head. Concentrating her mind on fielding Susannah's curiosity had certainly helped her to calm down somewhat, but now she was alone, and free to think as she would, all her doubts and anxieties came flooding back with a vengeance.

Could she really marry a man who showed so little regard for her, who was embroiling her in some scheme about which she had the deepest suspicions?

She sank on her bedside chair, her head in her hands.

No, the real question was, could she live with herself if she spurned him? It hardly mattered what had motivated him to ask for her hand, even though she now had some evidence to suggest he was using her as an unwitting accomplice in snatching a legacy from some person. Some person that she refused to assume was Percy Lampton. That would be too dreadful a coincidence.

Oh, how she wished she had not promised to keep the whole matter from her mother! She would have known all about the family connections, and been able to give a name to the poor wretch who was expecting to inherit the property she and Captain Fawley were about to…steal from him. It amounted to that!

Though…the cross-looking lawyer had said that the lady who had died had wanted everything to go to Captain Fawley to begin with. So she was not stealing anything from anybody. She was only helping to fulfil the dying wishes of a poor elderly lady with no children of her own….

She sat up, pushing a stray wisp of hair from her forehead. She had only a few hours to make her mind up about what she should do. During the carriage ride home, Lady Walton had informed her that the marriage was going to take place that very evening, at six of the clock, in the library of Walton House.

While everyone who aspired to be fashionable was promenading round Hyde Park, she would be sneaking into a private room, to take part in a clan-destine marriage, which would rob some other poor fellow of a substantial inheritance.

It was morally repugnant!

She got to her feet and paced to the window.

Yet how could she back out? If she refused to go along with Captain Fawley's plan, *he* would be the poor fellow who had his inheritance snatched from his grasp. She paced back to the chair.

Perhaps the issue was not so bad as she was imagining. Lady Walton had said she should trust Robert.

Robert. Hot jealousy had her pacing back to the window, her fists clenched at her side. Lady Walton called him Robert. She had not even known it was his given name, until she had prattled on about all the confidences he had shared with her! It would serve him right if she did jilt him!

No, no, it wouldn't, she gasped, searing pain almost doubling her over as she thought of the effect such an act would have upon him. Jilting him would wound him irreparably. How hard it had been, Lady Walton had said, for him to beg a woman for a dance, let alone for her hand in marriage! He would not understand why she had refused him. He would think it was because he was too deformed, even for a woman as desperate as her, to marry!

She could not do it to him.

She did not want to hurt anyone.

She paced back to the chair, sat down and wrapped her arms round her waist. Since somebody was clearly going to lose out because of the actions she took today, she would rather it was this faceless, nameless nephew, than Captain Fawley.

And even if the other legatee of the will turned out to be Percy Lampton, as she suspected...well, she had never liked him. In fact, she wouldn't put it past him to have sought Susannah out on purpose to prevent things from progressing to the point where Captain Fawley might have proposed to her. He had already lived with the unnecessary stigma of illegitimacy all his life because of the Lamptons' lies! And now, they were trying to prevent him from inheriting his own fortune.

She was not going to side with them. She was on Captain Fawley's side, no matter what!

Getting to her feet, she stomped to the wardrobe and yanked open its doors. Now, what kind of dress did she have that would be suitable for taking part in a clandestine wedding?

No sooner had Susannah set out for her ride round Hyde Park in Percy Lampton's high-perch phaeton, than Deborah urged her mother to get her bonnet and pelisse on.

'The Countess is returning for us both,' she explained. 'She is going to take us to Walton House….'

'And she did not want to include Susannah in the invitation?' Mrs Gillies frowned. 'Is her husband so high in the instep that he will not admit someone from her background into his home? I do not think I wish to encourage you in this friendship, if that is the case.'

'No, no, Mother, that is not it at all. Only please hurry to get ready, and I shall explain it all on the way.' She cast a significant look in the direction of the butler who came with the house, and Mrs Gillies subsided at once.

They waited for the Countess to arrive in tense silence. When the Walton town coach finally drew up outside their door, Deborah was surprised by a sharp pain that shot across the back of her hand as she leapt to her feet. Looking down, she saw she had been twisting the strings of her reticule so tightly they were cutting through her gloves into her flesh.

Lady Walton beamed at them as they scrambled into the coach before her footman even had time to climb their front steps and knock on the door.

'Oh, I am so glad you have decided after all to

come! Robert has been in the state most terrible since this morning after that he came home from the lawyers. He said you were so cross, you would not go through with it. But I knew you would come! For you love him enough to forgive him anything, is that not so?'

She turned to Mrs Gillies, who was regarding her with frank amazement.

'Ah, you have not told your mother yet? But, no, since that silly girl who could not see how wonderful Robert is has only just left the house, I suppose you have not had a chance.'

'Er…Mother…' Deborah began.

Mrs Gillies made a dismissive sound as she dived into her reticule for a handkerchief. 'You have decided to marry Captain Fawley, after all. I am happy for you,' she said, blowing her nose, 'if you are happy?'

'Thank you, Mother,' Deborah fudged, unwilling to admit that right at that moment, she was not at all sure she was going to be happy marrying a man who had so clearly demonstrated how little he valued anything about her, except as a name on a piece of paper.

'I take it we are going to meet with the family and discuss settlements?' Mrs Gillies got out, stuffing her crumpled handkerchief back into her reticule. 'Though, really, this sort of thing should be done through a man of business. I am sure Mr Hullworthy would be only too happy to act for you, if you applied to him.'

Deborah laid her hand firmly on her mother's sleeve. 'There will be no need for that. We went to see some lawyers this morning. We are getting married today. Now. In the library at Walton House.'

'But…without a man of business to see to the settlements? Really, Deborah, dear…'

'Mother, I have no dowry, so what good would a lawyer do me?'

'But you cannot have considered what a fragile thing life is. What if he dies and leaves you widowed? He has hardly a penny to his name. Your portion might be so slender that—'

'Mother, you have no need to worry. I told you that we discussed the financial side of things on Tuesday afternoon, did I not? Once I marry Captain Fawley, he will qualify for a substantial property. We will be able to live very comfortably. Indeed, he has even agreed that, should you wish it, you may come and live with us….'

'Oh, the dear boy!' Mrs Gillies cried, digging her handkerchief out of her reticule once again.

'So long as it is not entailed, this property?' she said sharply, crushing the damp piece of lace between her arthritic fingers.

Deborah saw that she had taken a great deal on trust. Far too much. She had no idea what kind of allowance Captain Fawley was likely to settle on her, nor how she would fare should she indeed be widowed. Not bringing in some man of business to negotiate all these points had been extremely foolish of her. But she was not about to burden her mother with her doubts.

'I am sure there is no need to worry about anything, Mother. We can trust Captain Fawley to do the right thing.' She only wished she could have felt the conviction she tried to put into her words. She was almost positive he was not doing the right thing, in marrying her secretly this afternoon.

Lady Walton, who had been watching them both, her beady eyes flicking from one to the other as she followed the conversation, clapped her hands, beaming at Deborah.

'Of course you may trust Robert! He may not have the polished manners of so many of the men who think themselves so attractive, but he has what they have not. The integrity. Yes, and the courage to fight for what is rightfully his!'

To fight for what was rightfully his. Yes, Deborah mused, settling back into the luxuriously soft leather squabs, that was what he was doing this afternoon. Lady Walton clearly knew all the details in regard to this inheritance, and regarded it as a just fight.

Perhaps it was understandable that he had not taken her fully into his confidence. He did not know her all that well. Besides, what was it Lady Walton had blurted out, earlier, on the way to visit the lawyers? That men sometimes did not explain why they were acting in a way that might be interpreted as a bit questionable, in an attempt to protect their women. She certainly had moral qualms about what she was doing. Had he been trying to protect her from going into a questionable situation, to spare her conscience?

A warm glow began to melt the knot of ice that her insides had become over the past few days. His woman. She was Captain Fawley's woman. Of course he was attempting to shield her from anxiety. Of course he would provide generously for her. For today, by marrying him, she was going to stand shoulder to shoulder with him in his fight, though he had deliberately kept her ignorant of the details.

* * *

By the time they reached Walton House, Deborah was glowing with the kind of happiness any bride might display on her wedding day. Her mother was still dabbing at her eyes as they mounted the front steps, just as the mother of a bride should do. When they went into the hall, one footman produced a fresh handkerchief for her mother, while a second presented her with a posy of roses and honeysuckle. Her heart almost stopped. They had been sitting in an arbour perfumed with roses and honeysuckle when he had proposed to her. He had remembered! Just as he had remembered the colour of the ribbons in her hair the other time he had bought her flowers.

This time, she did bury her face in the blooms, inhaling their scent with a mounting sense of elation. She drifted through the magnificent hallway in a haze of romantic hopes. It seemed like an omen that the bonnet and gloves she had picked out were the exact shade of pink as the centre of the honeysuckle blooms. How could she fail to love Captain Fawley? Even though he did not return her regard, he was perceptive and considerate. She was sure he would do his utmost to be a good husband to her.

Two massive double doors swung open, and she wafted into a library. But she scarcely registered anything about the room, save for the fact that it housed a lot of books. For Captain Fawley was standing in one of the window embrasures, watching her approaching him, and all she wanted to do was fill her eyes with the sight of him, as she had filled her lungs with the fragrance of her wedding bouquet.

He looked drained. But some of the tension that rode his shoulders slackened when he saw her enter the library. With a pang, she realised the way she had flounced out of the lawyers' offices must have contributed to his worries. Hadn't Lady Walton told her he had not been at all sure she would turn up today?

For a second or two they just stood there, looking at each other. Deborah felt so guilty for thinking only of herself, and adding to the lines of care upon his face that only days before she had dreamed of erasing. She could not interpret the expression on his face as he examined her in his turn. If she did not know better, she would think that the initial relief that her arrival had prompted was turning into a look so cynical it was almost akin to disappointment.

The Earl of Walton cleared his throat, breaking the tense silence that had bound them immobile.

The ceremony got under way.

Deborah marvelled that the words in the prayer book described so aptly, yet so poetically, exactly what marriage meant to her. She already loved Captain Fawley, and from that emotion sprang the will to honour and obey him. And, oh, how she longed to offer him comfort and become a companion in whom he would confide. They had already spoken of their plans to raise children. He had vowed she could have an input into their education beyond what most husbands would allow. She knew he did not love her yet. But she would be such a good wife to him—he was bound to grow fond of her eventually, wasn't he?

Though as he began to make his vows, she found herself clutching at the posy increasingly tightly. Captain Fawley sounded so angry, so bitter.

Her foolish romantic dreams evaporated like the morning dew in the first blast of the sun's rays. How could she have forgotten that he was in love with another woman? If it had been Susannah standing here, he would have gazed into her eyes with adoration as he spoke of worshipping her with his body. Instead, he shoved the ring on to

Deborah's finger, his jaw working as he paused before declaring he endowed her with all his worldly goods, emphasising to her, at least, that this was all that could have induced him to marry such a poor specimen of womanhood as he considered her to be.

And suddenly she wanted to weep.

They were man and wife. But when Captain Fawley was given the opportunity to kiss the bride, there was an awkward little pause.

Then Lady Walton rushed up to her, gave her an impulsive hug, and said, 'Now you are like a sister to me! Of all the women Robert could have brought into the family, I am so glad it was you!'

'Yes, welcome to the family, Mrs Fawley,' said the Earl, shaking her solemnly by the hand.

Her mother, just as Deborah had predicted, flung her arms about her new son-in-law's neck, almost overbalancing him in her enthusiasm, crying 'Oh, you dear boy! You dear, dear boy!'

It seemed that the only two people who did not wish to embrace one another were the bride and groom.

A butler, who must have been standing in the background somewhere during the ceremony, began to pour champagne, while Lady Walton tugged Deborah over to a table on which lay a selection of delicacies.

'We cannot linger,' Captain Fawley announced to the room in general. 'We have a long journey, and I wish to use what hours of daylight we have left to get as far from London as I can today.'

The Earl nodded, looking serious as he replied, 'I took the liberty of having a message sent down to the mews as soon as your bride arrived. The carriage should be ready for you by now.' Then in a voice so low only his brother could hear, he added, 'You don't need me to tell you how I shall relish dealing with the aftermath of this day's work.'

'Then, if you have no objection,' Captain Fawley said to Deborah, plucking her untouched glass of champagne from her fingers, 'we will leave at once.'

Deborah could think of plenty of objections. The first rose to her lips before she could prevent herself.

'I did not realise we were to leave town tonight. I have not packed a bag—'

'Oh, but I have!' Lady Walton put in cheerfully. 'Everything you will need for tonight, and a day or two, is already in the coach. Your mother and I can pack the rest of your things and have them sent on to you.'

Once again, he had taken Lady Walton into his plans, leaving her firmly out in the cold. 'I don't even know where we are going!' she protested, as Captain Fawley took her by the arm and propelled her towards the door.

'Our new home,' he grated. 'That is all you need to know.'

'Oh, how romantic!' she heard her mother cry, as he hustled her across the hall and down the front steps.

But she did not feel it was in the least romantic to be dragged away from her wedding breakfast, to who knew where, without even being permitted a proper leave-taking from her mother. 'How do you know what I need to know?' she complained, as he tugged her across the pavement to where a smart post-chaise and four awaited them.

'Do not be difficult,' he replied curtly, as a burly individual with a face like a potato leapt out of the carriage, let down the steps and held the door open for them to get in.

To her surprise, as soon as they were settled inside, the potato-faced man got in with them.

'This is Linney, my man,' said Captain Fawley when she looked the question at him.

She supposed she ought to feel grateful he had

bothered to introduce her at all. Not that he bothered to tell Linney who she was.

No, she thought resentfully. For he already knew all about her. So—here was yet another person her husband took into confidences he denied his own wife!

Alone in a carriage with two silent, grim-faced men, she had never felt so isolated in all her life. It was bad enough to whisk her away from the wedding breakfast without letting her take even one sip of the celebratory champagne, but now here he was, positively glowering at her as though she was an unexpected, and very expensive, bill he had to pay.

She was angry, and humiliated and, yes, a little afraid too.

Fortunately, the tremor of fear went from her mind entirely when it occurred to her that he had no right to stare at her with such marked hostility when she had just done him such a tremendous favour. If she had not agreed to marry him, he would still be a pauper. Instead of which, he was setting out to claim a property that would keep him in comfort for the rest of his life!

Narrowing her eyes, she shot him one look that she hoped told him exactly what she thought of his treatment of her, before lifting her chin and staring out of the window, determined to ignore him, and his manservant, for the rest of the journey.

Captain Fawley did not know which he wanted to do more—throttle her or kiss her. Naturally he could do neither with Linney present. Though the cheering thought struck him that, should he decide to murder his wife, he could rely on his man to help him dispose of the body, no questions asked.

He had no idea how far he could trust his wife.

He looked at her determinedly averted profile, wondering how long she could maintain this pose of affronted dignity. Not long, he would guess. Women were just not capable of keeping a still tongue in their head. They were the natural enemies of silence. Whenever they encountered it, they felt they had to fill it with chatter. It did not matter if they had nothing of import to say.

Linney folded his arms, closed his eyes and shoved his bulky body sideways so that he was wedged into the corner. There! A practical solution to dealing with the tedium of a journey. Use it to get some rest. Women always complained that they were tired after undertaking a long journey.

They wouldn't if they just stopped talking and made a profitable use of the time!

But there she was, sitting ramrod straight, forced to clutch at the strap to keep her balance when they went over a pothole instead of letting the cushions absorb the impact.

But then, she was a foolish creature. She would not be sitting in this coach with him at all if she had an ounce of sense. She would have traded on her looks, on her family connections…good God, when she had parroted off her antecedents to his lawyers he was amazed she had entertained his proposal for a second!

Mutton-headed, that's what she was, to have accepted the first proposal she had received, out of some kind of panic that she might never get another.

But that was women for you. So determined to escape the stigma of spinsterhood they would sell themselves to a hunchbacked dwarf—isn't that what he had told Lensborough, when he had complained women only saw his title, and wealth, but never the man he really was?

He slouched a little deeper into his seat. Those very words had come back to haunt him already today. Namely when she had sashayed into the library, looking like the cat that had got at the cream, and it had hit him like a blow to the midriff that she was as avaricious as they came.

Why had he not seen the warnings earlier? She had not shown a flicker of interest in his proposal of marriage until he had described the extent of the property she could become mistress of. After that, she had been willing to roll over and give birth to his children.

A shaft of heat darted from his stomach to his loins.

He had to shift in his seat to accommodate his body's inconvenient reaction.

This was not the first time he had experienced such stirrings of lust in regard to Miss Deborah Gillies. That memorable occasion had been the afternoon when he had gone to her house, to offer Miss Hullworthy the one sure piece of bait that would have her clamouring to dance with him, and Deborah had tripped into the room, dreamy-eyed from sleep, with her hair flowing about her shoulders and down her back. She had looked so natural, so…yes, innocent. So out of place amongst the plotters and schemers who filled the room.

His reaction then had surprised him, to say the least. It had been a very long time since he had felt even the faintest stirrings of desire towards a woman. So long, that he had begun to wonder if his injuries had completely unmanned him.

That was why, when he had decided to lay claim to his inheritance, he had known Miss Gillies must be the woman he took to wife.

He had always liked the unaffected way she had spoken to him, as though she did not care what he looked like.

But then, he reflected sourly, she was always pleasant to everyone.

Whereas what he had discovered he really wanted, he grimaced, was the reality of that image she had created when she had breathed her vows. That was when he had begun to get really angry with her—when she had promised to love and obey him in a voice quivering with emotion. Who had she thought she was fooling, with that sickening show of pretence? He knew she did not care a rap for him. She couldn't. Not to have stormed out of the lawyers' offices, at such a crucial moment, without so much as a backward glance. She had sent no word as to her intentions. He had spent the entire day almost paralysed by dread she had gone for good. He'd had to tell everyone to carry on with preparations for the ceremony as though it was all settled, when for all he knew he was about to face the ultimate humiliation of being jilted.

And worse than that, had been the slowly dawning realisation that, if she did not show up, it would destroy him. He would never have the stomach to browbeat another female into an engagement. He would remain eternally dependent on his brother's charity.

A beggar, that is what he would become.

So when she had strolled in, mingled with relief that she had shown up at all, was a good deal of resentment that he had somehow allowed this slip of a girl to gain such a hold over his life.

While all she seemed to have on her mind was playing the part of blushing bride to the hilt.

Which brought him back to the question—why did she feel she had to pretend anything? Why did she have to wound him by giving him a glimpse of what it might have been like to find a woman who…?

Breathing hard, he turned to glare at her stubbornly averted profile.

Oh, yes, she had dropped the act the minute there was nobody to see it!

But what made him angriest of all was the fact that though he knew she cared nothing for him, somehow, by some strange process of alchemy, she had the power to stoke him to this seething pitch of arousal merely by sitting there with her shoulder turned to him and her nose in the air.

Did she expect him to attempt to cajole her out of this mood?

If he started down that road, he would soon be reduced to the state of supplicant, begging for her favours.

Well, she was about to learn he would never beg her for anything!

'There is no sense in maintaining this ridiculous stand off,' he growled.

'I have no idea what you mean,' she replied stiffly, darting a glance in Linney's direction.

'Do you object to having Linney with us?' He scowled. 'You had better not. Linney is my right-hand man, I go nowhere without him—' he began, then checked himself, looking down at his empty jacket sleeve. 'Perhaps it would be more accurate to say, he is my left arm. I cannot do without him. I need him to help me into and out of the coach. And when we stop for the night, he will cut up my food, undress me, wash me and put me to bed. He is an integral part of my day-to-day routine. And will become an integral part of yours. Get used to it!'

'I beg your pardon,' Deborah said, abashed. She had not considered her husband's disability. He seemed so much more of a man than any other she had ever encountered, that she had completely forgotten how awkward certain aspects of his life must be.

'In fact, while we are discussing my daily routine, I had best inform you that under no circumstances will I permit you to have your own bedchamber.'

He'd had to accept that she had only married him for his money. Now she must accept the conditions under which she would earn it. The time for play-acting was over. There were a few grim realities it was about time Deborah faced.

'We will sleep together, in the same bed, right from the start. Once Linney unstraps my false leg, and I lay my crutch aside on the nightstand, I will have difficulty leaving it, unaided. You must surely see how impractical it would be, should I feel the urge, and you were sleeping in some distant chamber? Would you not feel humiliated if I were to ring a bell and summon you, then send you packing when I had done with you, as though you were a whore? Or perhaps you imagine Linney will help me into your bed, wait until the deed is done, then assist me back to my own?'

From the dull flush that was creeping across Linney's cheeks, Deborah could tell he had heard every word.

'May we not speak of this in private?' she begged, shocked that he could discuss such an indelicate matter in front of his servant. Why was he in such a foul mood? She could understand he was hurt that he'd had to settle for marrying a woman it was becoming more and more obvious he felt little for, but he was embarrassing his serving man into the bargain. Linney did not deserve that, even if Captain Fawley thought she did.

'You are embarrassing your man.'

Captain Fawley turned to look at Linney, who was keeping his eyes resolutely shut, maintaining the pretence of being asleep.

He shrugged.

'So long as you understand that we *will* have this conversation. And that there will be no point in you ever trying to defy me.' He was not going to suffer any more days like today, spent aching and uncertain, dependent on her whim for his peace of mind. He leaned forward, murmuring in her ear, 'If you refuse to accede to my wishes, I will have no compunction about sending Linney to fetch you from your virginal chamber, when I have need of a woman, and carrying you to me, if needs be, kicking and screaming. And don't think he will not obey such a command. For he will.'

Deborah flinched from the harshness of his words. She had no idea why he would think she would object to sharing a bed. That was what married people did. Her mother and father had always done so.

No, what shocked her was the idea that he would compel his servant to manhandle her if she did not submit to his every dictate. That did not sound at all like the image of what she thought a husband should be to his wife.

Perplexed, and repulsed by the vision of marriage his words were beginning to conjure up, she shrank as deeply into the cushions as she could, averting her eyes so that he should not see the hurt tears that were gathering there.

Chapter Six

Deborah felt quite perplexed when the landlady of the coaching inn where they were to break their journey led her into a chamber quite separate from her husband's.

'I think there has been some mistake,' she said, recalling his insistence she must share a room with him.

'No mistake,' she heard his harsh voice ring out from a shadowy alcove, which turned out to be a connecting door to another room. 'Walton sent a man ahead to book us a suite. That will be all, thank you,' he informed the landlady, who bobbed him a deferential curtsy and left.

She must have looked as perplexed as she felt, for he explained, 'Unless you expect Linney to help you get undressed and into bed, as well?'

She gasped, appalled at the very idea.

'No, I thought not,' said her husband. 'A girl who works in this establishment will come to see to your needs. I will ring for you when I am ready for you, then you will come to me.'

Having delivered his edict, he turned and stomped from the room.

Deborah had always thought of herself as an even-tempered person, but right at that moment, she experienced an almost overwhelming urge to smash something. Or stamp her feet and scream.

Being far too much a lady to yield to either temptation, she settled for flinging herself into a chair and scowling at the door her irascible husband had just gone through.

If the Earl had not booked a suite for them and arranged for a maid to help her come and undress, would he really have been beastly enough to humiliate her by making his man undo her hooks and eyes?

She was his wife, she sniffed, untying the ribbons of her bonnet and lowering it to her lap. Just this afternoon, he had promised to cherish her.

She heaved a shuddering sigh, fighting back a wave of self-pitying tears. So far there had been precious little cherishing going on. On the contrary, it felt as if he had gone out of his way to demean her. She was tired and hungry and totally disoriented. She had no idea what town she was in, nor which direction from London they were heading. Even the news that the Earl had taken a hand in these wedding-night arrangements made her feel of less value to her husband. Everyone seemed to have had more input into the arrangements for her wedding than she had. Her wishes, her preferences, seemed to count for nothing!

A tap on the door heralded the arrival of a buxom young chambermaid, who said, 'Would you be wanting a wash before I bring your supper up to your private parlour, madam? I can fetch a can of hot water in a trice.'

'Oh, I…I am not sure…' A private parlour? Supper? And if the maid did bring hot water, was there any soap? Had Lady Walton packed a towel in the little bag of essentials that sat on the ottoman at the foot of her bed?

Something of her confusion must have shown on her face, for the maid said, 'Your wedding night, isn't it? If you don't mind me saying so, you will feel much more the thing once you've had a bit of a wash. And you'll take a glass or two of wine with your supper, if you take my advice. Help you calm down, it will. Make it much easier for you.'

'What!' Her spine stiffened. She might be

feeling bewildered and isolated, but surely she was not such a poor specimen that even a serving girl felt she needed to give her advice.

'Was only saying, that's all,' the girl pouted.

'Yes, well, thank you. I would like a wash, I think.'

She did not know if she did or not, but at least sending the girl for the promised hot water got her out of the room. And while she was gone, she could hunt through the overnight case and find out exactly what it contained.

Though she was most definitely not going to face her wedding night in a state of inebriation. Lord knew Captain Fawley was hard enough to deal with when she had all her wits about her!

At least once she had washed and got the maid to help comb out the travel tangles from her hair, she felt a little less nervous about facing her husband across the supper table.

Her husband did not rise when she entered their private parlour, but merely motioned to Linney to help her into a chair facing him. She was just racking her brains to think of some suitably haughty remark, which would indicate her refusal to feel intimidated by the set-up, when her stomach rumbled loudly.

Linney shot her a startled look, then, his mouth working as though he was trying not to laugh, remarked, 'Hungry, miss? I mean, madam?'

'Yes. Ravenous, actually.' She shot her husband what she hoped was a darkling look. 'I have not had a chance to eat anything since noon.' She felt satisfied that the dart had gone home when he looked a little chagrined.

A tavern servant brought in a tureen of soup and set it on the corner of the table. Linney dismissed the man, serving her first, and then his master.

It was a delicious, wholesome broth containing a lot of pearl barley and a small amount of mutton. She slathered butter on to a deliciously fresh bread roll, and once she had finished, leaned back in her chair with a contented sigh. She had been trembling when she had come to the table, but her hands were quite steady now. She did not even feel anywhere near so cross with her husband now she had taken the edge off her appetite.

Linney rang for the next course, which turned out to be a whole roast chicken, and a game pie, along with several side dishes of vegetables.

It was not until Linney began to cut up the food he had placed on Captain Fawley's plate into tiny pieces, that Deborah had any inkling of just how awkward her husband found it to feed himself. She lowered her eyes to her own plate as he scooped up a mixed portion of meat and vegetables with a spoon.

Now she knew why he never stayed to supper at any of the gatherings where she had met him in London. He must feel so clumsy, so…so exposed to the pitying stares or snide comments of others.

She raised her eyes to his, briefly, and met a challenging, almost hostile look. It was as though he was daring her to make any comment. Startled, she realised that, in having her to sit down and eat with him, he was permitting her to witness a vulnerability that he normally never revealed to anyone. True, he was uncomfortable with her being here, but it was a start. She dropped her eyes at once, flustered by a strange feeling of intense intimacy.

'That was delicious.' She sighed once she had demolished the contents of her plate. Raising her eyes to his, she attempted a smile. 'No wonder Lord Walton hired rooms for us here, if he has sampled the cooking.'

'I see that it was certainly to your taste. I only wonder, having witnessed that demonstration of just how much you manage to put away at one sitting, that you manage to stay so thin,' he replied, cuttingly.

Deborah eyed him with sadness. It was as if he was determined to rebuff her attempts to lighten the atmosphere or establish any sort of rapport with him. He confirmed that suspicion by then saying, 'If you are finished, you may return to your room until I send for you.'

He did not even wish to while away the last few moments of the day in conversing with her. Where had the man who used to be so kind to her, at the balls where she had been a wallflower, gone?

Puzzled and hurt, she pushed back her chair, and left him in solitary possession of the dining parlour.

Why bother to send for her at all? Or insist he wished her to share his bed? It was not as if he wanted to cuddle her, or talk over the problems of the day, which was what her parents had always told her was the main purpose of having their own big bed. He did not seem to want her as a companion at all.

And when he saw her in the nightdress Lady Walton had packed for her, he would probably laugh out loud. She was far taller than the Countess, and much thinner. She had known that the confection of silk and lace was entirely insufficient to keep her warm in a draughty inn, from the first moment she had set eyes on it. But once she had put it on, and seen how little of her it managed to cover, she felt positively annoyed. Why had Captain Fawley not warned her he intended to leave town at once? She could have packed her own, warm nightgown, and the thick flannel wrapper that would have covered her from neck to toe. Even the Countess's wrapper exposed more than it covered, she grimaced. Once she had dismissed the maid, she went to the bed, seized the coverlet, and wrapped it round herself like a cloak. Then she padded barefoot to one of the armchairs that flanked the empty fireplace—for, naturally, the Countess had not thought to pack her a pair of slippers—and curled up in it. Before she knew it, she had pulled her plait over her shoulder, and begun chewing on the end of it.

Disgusted with herself for reverting to a childish habit she had firmly believed she had grown out of, angry with her husband for pushing her until her nerves had reached such a pitch, she spat it out, got to her feet and padded over to the window.

Night had fallen while they had been eating supper, but the yard below her window was still a hive of activity. With a determination born of desperation, Deborah concentrated on the little figures bustling about, refusing to allow her mind to drift back to her own sense of ill usage. She did not wish to arrive in her husband's chamber in an angry frame of mind. Their first night together would set the tone for the whole of the rest of their married life.

She forced herself to remember that she had married him because she thought she loved him. It was not easy to dredge up any fond thoughts of him, after the abominable way he had treated her today, but she could refuse to allow her mood to teeter over into downright hostility. She frowned down into the bustling yard, wondering what demons had driven him to act as he had done.

At the supper table, she had glimpsed how uneasy he felt to have her sharing something as simple as a meal. Unwittingly, she slipped the end of her plait into her mouth again, chewing at it absently as she struggled to make sense of his attitude towards her. She already knew that he was convinced he was ugly, and clumsy and that no woman could possibly like him, never mind love him. How could she make him see that she did?

She sighed. She had thought she could tell him she loved him, once they were married, but right now, she was so upset with him, she knew such a declaration would ring hollow. And she was afraid that if she tried to show her affection in a physical way, he would rebuff her. Her mind went back to the day when she had caught a party of village boys scrumping apples from her orchard. In their haste to escape, one of them had fallen out of a tree and broken his arm. When she had gone to his aid, he had pushed her away, the belligerent expression on his face almost exactly like the one she had seen in her husband's eyes today when she had been watching Linney cut up his food.

'An injured male is a dangerous creature,' she remembered her mother explaining to her when she had asked why the boy had been so rude, when all she had been trying to do was help him. 'Rather than accept sympathy, they are inclined to lash out. Just like a wild animal, which would bite your hand should you try to help it escape from a trap.'

Suddenly everything he had done and said today made sense. Far from being grateful to her for helping him to achieve financial independence, he resented the necessity of having her involved at all. He equated admitting to any kind of need as a slur on his masculinity. That was why he had behaved with such uncharacteristic unkindness, she decided, letting her plait fall from her mouth. Though how she could convince him to cease hostilities, she could not imagine. The little village boy's hostility had been obdurate. In the end, she had been obliged to leave him in a crumpled heap at the foot of the tree and go and fetch a doctor.

She rather thought her husband's hurts were of the sort no doctor could treat. While she was still pondering how she could express her regard, without wounding his male sensibilities any further, there was a knock on the door, followed by the gentle cough, announcing Linney had come to fetch her.

He said not a word, merely opening the connecting doorway, and ushering her through. If anything, he seemed even more embarrassed than she felt as she marched past him, the coverlet clutched to her chin.

'What the deuce have you got on?' were her husband's first words when she entered his chamber.

'A blanket,' she replied, as Linney softly closed the door on his retreat. She noticed that a fire was smouldering gently in the grate, and though she had vowed not to give in to her sense of ill usage, she could not help saying, 'My room is really cold. And you should have seen the ridiculous get-up Lady Walton packed for me to wear!'

'I should like to see it,' he agreed. 'Knowing Heloise, it was probably intended to show off rather more than it covered.'

'How did you know that?'

He shrugged one shoulder, with a knowing smile.

'How any woman could consider wearing such an impractical outfit to bed mystifies me completely. Never mind lending it to a friend. What was she thinking?'

'Impractical,' he said, an arrested expression on his face. 'How do you mean, impractical, exactly?'

She advanced on the bed, in which he reclined against a bank of pillows. His right hand lay on top of the coverlet. His left arm, the one which she knew ended just below his elbow, was concealed beneath the blankets. A single candle burned in a holder on a nightstand, to the right of the bed, illuminating his uninjured side, and casting his left into deeper shadow. Her heart went out to him. Just having her invade his room was a monumental concession for him. In fact, she frowned, she did not really know why he was forcing himself to go through this torment.

'Well, it is certainly not designed to keep a body warm. There is hardly anything to it. And what there is, you can see right through! What is the point of donning a covering that does not cover anything?'

'I expect she thought I would keep you warm tonight.'

'Oh!' She looked dubiously at his chest, which was completely bare. Her father had always worn a nightshirt to bed. And usually a cap too. And had drawn thick velvet hangings round the battered old four-poster, to keep out the draughts. 'You don't exactly look as though you will be very warm tonight, either,' she said with concern. 'Were you in too much of a hurry to remember to pack a nightshirt?'

It was slowly dawning on Captain Fawley that his wife was a complete innocent.

'Did your mother never explain what went on in the marriage bed?'

'Not exactly, no.'

He bit down on a savage oath. He had been so intent on rushing the ceremony through in complete secrecy that he had forgotten she might need to learn a thing or two from her mother before sharing a bed with a man. Only now did her mystified looks when he had spoken of dragging her to his bed make sense.

To his surprise, while he was wrestling with the

concept of having to explain to a naïve virgin what a man generally did with his wife, whilst repressing the overwhelming desire to just get on with it, she smiled, and shrugged off the blanket.

'I suppose we will just have to keep each other warm, then, won't we? At least there is a fire in here.'

His mouth went dry at the sight of her in her borrowed nightwear. The bodice consisted of a few slivers of peach-coloured silk holding together panels of lace, which were strategically positioned to entice a man's gaze.

He gazed. And saw the skirt was split to her thigh, revealing tantalising glimpses of her pale slender legs with every tentative step she took towards him.

She hesitated in the act of climbing up into the bed, her face turning bright pink as he growled when the silk slithered from her bent leg in sinful invitation.

'What is the matter?' she whispered. 'Do I look dreadful in this gown?'

He saw the uncertainty in her face, the need for reassurance.

And something dark and bitter welled up within him. *She* was seeking reassurance from him, for the way *she* looked! Didn't she know she was perfect? Perfect face, perfect body, perfect skin. No man looking at her, in that seductive outfit, could fail to react as he was reacting at the sight of that bared thigh. He was rock hard. Sweating.

'Take it off,' he growled.

She flinched back, an expression of shock on her face.

'I said, take it off,' he repeated, as a fine tremor began to ripple through the blighted arm he had hoped to conceal from her sight by placing a pillow over the mangled stump where his hand ought to be.

'You don't like it,' she said, shaking her head ruefully. Then, lifting her chin, added, 'Nor do I.'

She kept her gaze fixed on his bare chest, as she reached for the ties that bound the wrapper over her breasts. He probably felt naked, and vulnerable, without the artificial limbs his servant had removed to make him comfortable for the night. In his mind, it probably seemed fair that she, too, should be stripped of some of her dignity.

She wondered if he was completely naked under the covers. A strange shiver went right through her at the thought of lying next to all that hair-roughened flesh. Her knees had gone weak, her heartbeat had fluttered when she had leaned up against him the night she had almost fainted. Being in such close proximity had affected her profoundly, even through her clothing and his. What would it be like with no barriers at all?

Her legs began to tremble as her heartbeat accelerated. Her fingers shook so much that she was convinced she would tear the delicate garment in her clumsy haste to divest herself of it.

Finally, as she stood completely naked before her husband, she drew the courage to look into his face. His expression was stark, unyielding—not at all welcoming as he flicked back the covers, indicating that it was time to get into the bed and join him.

'Wait!' he said, just as she began to climb up on to the bed for the second time.

She paused, one knee already bent on the mattress, her hands splayed out to balance her. Had she misinterpreted his wishes? He certainly did not look at all pleased to see her attempting to scramble in beside him. Slowly, she retreated and stood up, catching her lower lip between her teeth at the dreadful prospect that he was going to send her back to her room after all. He had tried, but when it came to the crunch, he just could not bear to have her near him. Just as he did not like anyone to see him eating, he probably hated anyone except his trusted manservant getting a good look at the full extent of his injuries.

She wanted to reach out and put her arms round him. But, remembering the reaction she had got from that village boy, she sensed it would only make him resent her all the more.

She shifted her weight from one foot to the other, wondering what on earth she ought to do.

'Undo your plait,' he growled, settling back into the pillows.

'My plait?' she echoed, at a loss to understand what could possibly lay behind that request.

'You promised to obey me this afternoon, woman,' he growled. 'Undo your plait. I want to see your hair down.'

Giving a mental shrug, she reached over her shoulder and undid the ribbon that held the ends of her hair in place. His eyes roamed her body as she worked the strands loose, the expression on his face growing fiercer by the second. By the time she had freed her hair, she was trembling from head to foot. He did not appear to like what he saw at all. She knew she must compare unfavourably with Susannah, the woman he wished was here with him tonight. She felt a strong urge to cover the breasts that were so much smaller than her friend's. She felt gangly, and awkward and ashamed of the ribs and hipbones that were so clearly visible through her skin, instead of being covered by the feminine lushness of a woman in the peak of health. She was not sure how much more of this testing she could take before she ran back to her room and gave way to the tears of humiliation that were only an eyeblink away.

If she did not love him…if he did not need to reduce her to the level of exposure he was suffering, by having her invade his personal space…

'You are shivering,' he finally observed. A wave of goose pimples had swept across her body, tightening her nipples into the hard peaks that also betokened arousal. He knew she was not aroused. She was just plain scared. Her eyes were huge in her pale face, fixed on him as though he were a wolf, and she Little Red Riding Hood.

He felt wolfish. He wanted to devour her. Claw at her and bite her, and hear her cry out as he sank into her soft warm flesh.

Yet he also wanted to wipe away that look of uncertainty, and replace it with yearning, and wonder and rapture.

She knew nothing of what went on between a

man and a woman. How could she? She was standing there, completely naked, completely bemused by his request to take down her hair. She shifted her weight from the foot she had been favouring, stroking the sole over the arch of the other, chewing at her lower lip, like a little girl, completely unaware of what the sight of her naked body was doing to him.

Any man with a shred of decency would let her grow accustomed to intimacy by gradual stages, he sighed. Not plunge her straight into the sort of torrid encounter he had planned to subject her to tonight.

'Get into bed now,' he said, ashamed of himself for toying with her like this, 'and I will warm you.'

'Th…thank you,' she breathed, scrambling in beside him with alacrity, and pulling the covers up to her chin as she lay down. 'I am all over goose bumps.'

'I saw.' He put his arm about her waist, pulling her closer. 'Is that better?'

'Mmm…' She nodded, the top of her head bumping the underside of his chin. She kept her arms demurely by her sides, knowing he would not wish her to hug him, dearly though she wished to. But the entire length of her leg rested against his. He was warm, and hard and his skin was covered all over, it seemed, with coarse hair that made her want to rub herself against him—twine herself about him like a cat. Each breath he took, expanding his chest, brought him temporarily, tantalisingly closer to her upper body and made her yearn to roll on to her side, and press herself up against him, till there was not a single inch of air between their naked bodies. She wanted her breasts pressed against his chest, her legs entangled with his. She wanted the right to put her arms about him, and kiss the scars on his face, and, yes, the ones she had briefly glimpsed bubbling down the left side of his chest. She wanted to plunge her fingers into his overlong hair, while she kissed him with all the love she felt welling in her heart.

But she was so afraid he would repulse her.

He gritted his teeth, lying rigidly upon his back, while he felt his naked young bride shivering with cold, and probably a large dose of trepidation, against his side. He did not know where to start. Not so long ago he had feared he would never want to lay with a woman again. Yet now he was experiencing a hunger so fierce he scarce knew how to hold it back. The things he wanted to do to this innocent young woman were so brutal they even shocked him. He gritted his teeth, knowing she needed a gentle introduction to a pastime she scarce knew existed. Not a clumsy, blundering cripple, who, even at his peak, had never known an innocent. His encounters, as a soldier, had been of the mercenary kind. Pleasurable enough for him, but not exactly good training for the polite coupling that he guessed ought to go on in a marriage bed.

She deserved far better than to marry a wreck like him. She had made it possible for him to have everything he had ever wanted. A home of his own, financial independence and revenge on the perfidious Lampton family.

And all she was getting in return was a bad-tempered cripple, who had scant idea how to initiate a virgin. Perhaps he ought to tell her to put her nightgown back on. If she was not naked…but then he imagined her getting out of bed, and bending over to retrieve that seductive confection of textures from the floor, raising her arms to slide it over her head…he would just want to rip it straight off her again.

He stifled a groan.

'Is aught amiss?' she asked, peering up at the rigid lines of his throat.

'No, nothing that need trouble you.' He sighed,

shifting so that no part of him quite touched any part of her any more. There was no way he could talk to her about what her marital duties would entail, not tonight. It was bad enough just thinking about it. If he tried to verbalise exactly what was going through his mind, he would end up wanting to give her a demonstration. And end up traumatising her, no doubt. For he was pretty sure he was not going to be able to take it slowly enough not to hurt her.

'Go to sleep.'

There was a short pause. Then she said, in a very small voice, 'May I kiss you goodnight?'

She must have felt him tense, because she added hastily, 'My mother and father always used to kiss each other goodnight. And we are married now, so, should I not kiss you?'

'Only if you really want to.' He was sure no woman could really want to kiss him. 'You do not need to,' he said, suddenly angry with Deborah's need to do her duty, as she saw it. 'It is not required.'

'But I do want to,' she stunned him by saying. Raising herself on to one elbow, she looked down into his face, right into his eyes, adding uncertainly, 'If you don't mind. It is what married people do, is it not?'

'Part of it,' he grated, his heart breaking into a gallop as her hair brushed across his chest, and he thought of what else married people did. And people who were not married, either, when the urge took them.

He had arranged it so that she was lying on his left side, his injured side. But she did not think he would like her to kiss the scarred side of his face. So she leaned across him, and placed a gentle kiss on his right cheek. As she did so, her breasts grazed across the hair-roughened surface of his chest. He sucked in a sharp breath.

'What did I do wrong?'

His eyes were squeezed shut. 'Nothing,' he grated. 'Lie down. Lie down at once.'

Chastened, she did so.

And shifted away, until she was right on the very edge of the mattress. But he could feel the warmth emanating from her skin. Could hear her breathing. Shaky, uneven breaths, as though…

'You are not crying, are you?'

'Of course not!' came her muffled response.

He rolled on to his side, raised himself up on his injured arm and looked down into her face with concern.

'Yes, you are…' he groaned '…and it is all my

fault. I have been a complete b-beast today, have I not?'

'N…no…'

'Yes, I have. I know it.' When he thought back over the way he had treated her, he was amazed she had not given way to tears much sooner. What kind of man forced a timid young virgin to strip naked on her wedding night? Repulsed her so curtly after she had drawn the courage to place a shy kiss on his ravaged face?

'Forgive me, Deborah?' He ran his thumb along the poor, bruised lower lip that she had been chewing more and more as the stresses of the day had piled up.

'Of course I forgive you.' She sighed, looking up at him solemnly with tear-drenched eyes.

God, but he wanted to kiss her. If he could manage to be gentle, could she manage to stomach it? He thought she, of all women, might really be brave enough. Look at what she had already endured at his hands. All day long she had borne the brunt of the emotions that churned inside him. And had stoically maintained a dignified mien.

He lowered his head and gently sucked her lower lip into his mouth, soothing it with his tongue.

He felt a tremor run through her, and broke the

kiss, with a feeling of intense regret. He should have known she would recoil.

'Are you afraid of me?' he asked ruefully, looking down into her face. Her hair had fanned out across the pillows, making her look…he gulped…incredibly alluring. He gritted his teeth as a fresh flood of desire surged through him. 'You do not need to be. Though I don't suppose after today's performance you will believe me….'

'No!' she replied, as he made to shift away from her. 'I am not afraid of you. Not at all. Only—' She broke off, and began chewing at her lower lip again.

'What are you afraid of?'

'That I might not please you,' she admitted, her eyes darting away from his.

'There has been no pleasing me today, has there?' he admitted, brushing his thumb over the lip she seemed so intent on abusing. As he recalled how soft her mouth had felt under his own, his breath hitched in his chest.

'I am sorry,' she said solemnly. 'I wish I knew…'

'You have nothing to be sorry for!' he insisted. She could not help the way she was. He did not even know now why seeing her in her true light should have hurt him so deeply. Women were none of them what they appeared. Even Lensborough's wife, a woman who had a reputation for being shy and demure, had turned out to have a sordid secret buried in her past. Before that marriage could proceed, they'd had to deal with a villain who had been blackmailing her for years.

'Truly?' she asked, with a hopeful expression. 'Even the kiss...' she persisted. 'Was that all right?' Her face fell. 'You did not seem to like it all that much.'

'The kiss was perfect.' He thought of the way her breasts had brushed across his chest, the way her hair had hung round both their faces like a curtain of living silk, cocooning them in a moment of dark intimacy. And how he had wanted to pull her fully on top of him, hold her in place and thrust up inside her. He swore under his breath.

'I wish to God I could trust myself to kiss you again.'

She frowned up at him. 'I don't understand. If you want to kiss me, then why don't you?'

'Because, my sweet little innocent, it will not stop at kisses. You would be shocked if I were to tell you...to show you...' The breath hitched in his chest again as his mind flooded with a series of images so erotic, he was amazed the sheets did not go up in flames.

'No, I won't,' she assured him in a breathy little voice. 'You said kisses were only part of what married people do. And…I don't want to stop at kisses. I want all of it.'

'You don't know what you are asking,' he growled.

She looked crestfallen. 'And you don't want to show me,' she said, turning over on to her side.

'What!' He pulled her over so that she lay on her back. 'What I want right now, is…what I want…' He groaned, finally abandoning his attempts to hold back. He plundered Deborah's mouth, plunging his fingers into her hair to anchor her against the force of his kiss. Need ripped through him, sweeping aside any thoughts of restraint. He looped one leg over hers, pinning her body beneath his, wanting to feel the softness of her skin against the full length of his own hardened need.

She arched up against him. For one terrible moment he thought she was trying to push him off. But instead, she looped her arms round his neck and kissed him back for all she was worth.

It was like striking a spark into dry kindling.

Just as he had known it would, any hope of initiating her gently went up in smoke. Amazingly, she seemed as greedy for sensation as he felt. She matched him, kiss for kiss, touch for touch, until the moment when he went to push her legs apart. Though she opened for him willingly, and he found her lusciously ready for his possession, it still hurt her. He felt no regret when she gave a yelp of pain, only a soaring triumph at the audible proof she was his now, utterly his in a way no other woman had ever been. And when she began to move against him again, winding her legs about his waist, her little hands clawing at his back, he felt a rush of power, that he had somehow, miraculously, against all the odds, brought her to this pitch of wild abandon.

He felt as though their rising pleasure was fusing them together. It was swifter, more intense, than anything he could ever have envisioned. For a blinding second or two, when he felt her convulse around him, crying out her rapture, he felt as though he had left the hell of his existence behind, and found a slice of heaven. When he came back to earth, he was shocked to find his face was wet with tears. He had to bury his face in her neck to stifle the shuddering sobs that shook his whole body.

How could a mere woman reduce him to this? He pulled away, rolling on to his back and flinging his arm over his face. He could not let her see what she did to him. If she said one word that mocked him, gave him so much as one look that showed she knew the power she could wield over him, he would make her rue the day she was born!

When he had regained control over himself, he lowered his arm and turned his head to confront her.

Her eyes were closed, her lips parted, her cheeks flushed with sleep.

Relief flooded through him, leaving him limp and shaken. There was no need to deal with her now. If he played his cards right, she would never know how deeply her response had moved him.

For she must never know. Once a woman got the upper hand, a man was doomed. Let her but guess how much he desired her, and she would start to trade on it.

Women were all the same. Deep down, they were scheming, manipulative creatures who would twist a man round their fingers, to get what they wanted.

Well, no woman was going to manipulate him. And if Deborah tried it, she would soon find she had picked the wrong target.

Chapter Seven

Bliss. There was no other word for it. Deborah stretched, and yawned, her whole being thrumming with lazy sensuality.

Her sleep had been deep, and completely restful, nestled against the strong body of the man she loved. Sighing, she snuggled closer, daringly placing one hand upon his waist and pressing a kiss against his back.

He rolled over, and looked down at her with a perplexed frown.

He had hoped that last night had been an aberration. He had reasoned that he must have been more worried about his ability to function normally than he had admitted to himself. That was why he had wept. It had been relief on finding he was whole, in that respect. It was not unprecedented. One of the company sergeants, one of the most hard-bitten men he had ever known, had wept with relief when the regimental surgeon had told him they could save his arm.

Last night's outpouring of emotion had nothing to do with the particular woman he was with.

And there was no reason why his heart should seem to be expanding and melting within his chest, just because she was touching him voluntarily this morning.

He was damned if he was going to melt into emotional mush every time his wife reached out to him!

He sat up abruptly, plucking her hand from his body, and flinging it from him.

'We have no time for that. We need to get up, and on the road. Go to your room, now, and get dressed.'

Shaken by the vehemence of his rejection, Deborah slid from the bed, fumbling her arms into the totally inadequate silken wrapper that had lain on the floor all night. He would not even look at her, but lay with his arm flung across his eyes as though the very sight of her made him angry.

Not that she could believe he held her personally in aversion, or he would not have asked her to marry him at all. But she could not forget the stunned look on his face when he had rolled over, and seen that it was her. Just before the shutters had come down, and he had repulsed her, he had looked positively confused.

Then it hit her with blinding clarity.

She was not Susannah.

Head bowed, she fled from the room, shutting the door firmly behind her.

For a few moments, she sat on the edge of her untouched bed, her arms wrapped about her middle, which seemed to be completely hollowed out.

She was glad that Linney would be sharing the carriage with them today. She did not know how she would have coped being shut up with her husband, not today. She felt he had reduced her to nothing, somehow, by throwing her out of his bed this morning.

And she was nothing, to him.

Last night, she had interpreted his groans of pleasure as a sign that he had felt something for her. But while she had been pulsing with love, all he had wanted was a convenient female body. She understood now, in the clear light of day, why he had spoken of urges, rather than love, when he had insisted they share a bed.

She found it hard work to climb into the carriage later, weighed down as she was by the conviction that not only did he not particularly care which woman he used to satisfy those urges, but that in order for him to be so proficient at it he must have done it with many other women. He had known exactly how to touch her, where to press his lips, to reduce her to a quivering mass of throbbing need.

He did not seem inclined to talk today, either, though she could feel his eyes upon her from time to time. Once, she returned his look, flinching at the ferocious blast of hostility that met her gaze.

Depression settled over her then, like a greasy pall. She felt unloved, and used and so lonely! Why had she ever imagined she could reach him and heal him? He did not want to be healed, least of all by her.

Had she made a terrible mistake, in marrying such a deeply wounded man? She certainly felt way out of her depth with him this morning, and half-convinced that she would not be able to keep her head above water for very much longer, unless he threw her some kind of lifeline.

'We are here,' he said, jolting her out of her silent misery.

They were slowing down to pass through a pair of wrought-iron gates, set between two stone pillars.

'Wh-where is this, exactly?' she plucked up the courage to ask. 'Am I permitted to know, now?'

'There is no harm in telling you now we are here, no,' he grunted. 'You cannot blab to anyone, and it would be too late to do anything about it, anyway. This is The Dovecote. In the county of Berkshire. Our new home.'

He craned his neck to look out of the window, as they swept round a curve in the drive, and a house came into view.

It was not as big as Deborah had imagined it would be from the way he had talked about it. The four-square, three-storey building was not even as big as the vicarage where she had grown up. She would guess it had no more than six or seven bedrooms, and the grounds that surrounded it were more of a large garden than an estate. Had he put her through so much unhappiness for this?

The carriage drew to a halt before a shallow flight of stone steps, leading to a covered entrance-way. A group of household staff came pouring out, as though they had been waiting in the hallway for their arrival. When Linney leaned out to open the coach door, they surged forward, gathering around in a semi-circle as he let down the steps. They were all smiling.

Linney helped Captain Fawley out first, then offered Deborah his burly arm. As she emerged from the coach, the entire group of staff burst into a spontaneous round of applause.

'Welcome, welcome to The Dovecote,' a large woman of middle age said, stepping forward, her face wreathed in smiles. 'I am Mrs Farrell, your housekeeper, and right glad we are to see you come home at last, Captain Fawley. And you, Mrs Fawley, of course!'

'Thank you,' said Deborah, when her husband remained mute. One glance in his direction was enough to tell her that he appeared to have been stunned into silence by the enthusiastic reception. 'I am sure we will be very happy here.'

Mrs Farrell's smile, if anything, grew even broader. 'We all hope you will be, and will do all we can to make sure of it. Terrible it would have been, if that Percy Lampton had pushed his way in here.' She shook her head in disapproval. 'My mistress would not have rested easy if he had got his hands on all she had worked so hard to build up.'

She felt her husband's tension flow from him in waves at the mention of Percy Lampton's name. From the swift look he gave her, the anxious frown that drew his brows down, she guessed he must think his housekeeper had betrayed a secret he still wished to keep from her.

'But you won't want to stand about talking after your journey. I'll just introduce all the staff, and then you will want to see your rooms, I don't doubt.'

'Thank you, yes,' Captain Fawley said, taking Deborah's arm as the housekeeper turned to do the honours.

'This is Cherry, the upper housemaid, and Nancy, the lower. We don't have a butler. I do all a butler would do, save order the wine cellar, which there was no call for in Miss Lampton's day. She never drank, nor would she have a male servant in the house.'

It finally hit Deborah what had seemed odd about the group of servants who had come out to greet them. Not a single one of them was male.

'And here is our cook, Susan,' Mrs Farrell continued happily, 'and May the kitchen maid. We have Bessie as the boots, and Betty the under-housemaid. Freda does the garden with her helpers...' a group of women and girls with weatherbeaten faces bobbed curtsies '...and Joan looks after the stables. We did once have a male groom, but he proved unsatisfactory.' She wrinkled her nose in distaste. 'Joan does much better. But then we only have a couple of carriage horses in the stables. Miss Lampton rarely went out, save in the gig to the village. Used to have a couple of hunters, when she was younger, but she had to get rid of them once her joints got too stiff for her to mount.'

'I see,' said Captain Fawley, looking thoroughly discomfited, though whether by the complement of female staff, or the housekeeper's volubility or the fact that Deborah now knew Percy Lampton was the other man in line for this property, she was unable to guess.

'Of course,' the housekeeper remarked, running her eyes assessingly over Linney's burly frame, 'we know things will not be run the same, not now you are here. You will want a man to see to your clothes, and so on.'

'And to stock the wine cellar,' Captain Fawley said firmly. 'And my own horse will be arriving in the next day or so, with the rest of our things.'

The housekeeper nodded again. 'Only natural, a married man would want to run things different from a single lady, but I assure you that had we not all been prepared to work for you, we would not have stopped on, is that not so?' She turned to the other female staff, who all nodded, or spoke their affirmation.

'Then perhaps you would show us to our rooms, Mrs Farrell?' he said, politely.

Mrs Farrell led them through the front doors, and into a room to the right. 'Sitting room,' she said. 'Miss Lampton would always receive callers here. Office,' she said, flinging open a door to the rear of the guest sitting room. An oak desk squatted with its back to the window, dominating the room. Around the walls stood glass-fronted bookcases, each containing ledgers of a different colour. 'Travers, her factor, will be coming by tomorrow, to discuss Miss Lampton's affairs with you. Only male she had any time for, and that only because he did exactly as he was told.' The housekeeper grinned.

'Kitchens and offices.' She pointed out the green baize door to the back of the hall, but seemed not to expect they would wish to pass through it. 'Your private rooms are over here,' she said, crossing the hall. 'Stairs got too much for her, in latter days, and knowing your particular requirements, we left things as she last had them.' They entered a small, cosy-looking sitting room, crossing through it to reach a bedroom. It contained a large double bed, of japanned pine, with floral chintz valance and curtains, topped by a snowy white quilt and pillows foaming with lace. Next to the door stood an old-fashioned clothes press, painted all over with flowers to match the bed hangings. It was all rather ornate and fussy and so feminine Deborah was sure her husband would want to change it all at the earliest opportunity. To the rear of the bedroom was a door that led to a dressing room, containing a hipbath and towel rail, as well as a traditional marble-topped washstand with a floral china basin and pitcher.

'Upstairs?' Mrs Farrell looked dubiously at Captain Fawley, but he elected to climb, albeit slowly, to the upper floors, where they found six guest bedrooms, two of which, the housekeeper cheerfully suggested, could be made into a nursery and schoolroom, when the time came.

Deborah's insides gave a peculiar lurch. What they had done last night was not unlike what the farm animals did during their mating seasons, which resulted in fresh batches of calves, and lambs and chicks. It was very lowering to think that such a sublimely pleasurable activity was no different, in the long run, from the very basic instinct of all God's creation to procreate.

'The servants' attics are above,' said Mrs Farrell, startling her out of her reverie. 'No need to examine those. I will show your man later, if he wishes?' she finished, darting a brief glance at Linney, who had been shadowing his master closely.

When the tour ended, the housekeeper said she would bring tea to the front parlour.

'How do you like our new quarters, then?' Captain Fawley asked Linney as soon as the housekeeper had left them. 'Think you could cope with promotion to the position of butler?'

Until that moment, Linney's face had stayed impassive, but he broke into a grin as he admitted, 'Dare say I could.'

'Good man. I don't want some stranger coming in, thinking he knows how to run my household. And you'd best cast your eye over the stables too,' Captain Fawley said, settling into a comfortable-looking wing-backed armchair before the fireplace.

Deborah slid into one that was angled so that whoever sat in it could look out of the front window, feeling utterly superfluous. He had not deigned to ask what she thought of the house, or its peculiar set-up, nor whether there were any changes she might wish to make.

When the maid brought the tea in, he dismissed Linney, and the maid, saying, 'My wife can pour for me.'

Perversely, now that she was alone with him, she

felt rather shy and very conscious of her limbs as she moved over to the table where the girl had deposited the tray. Her hands shook as she lifted the lid of the pot to see whether the beverage had brewed long enough to pour.

'Do you take milk, or lemon?' she asked, in a rather high-pitched voice. 'And sugar?'

He shrugged. 'Surprise me.'

When she shot him a bewildered look, he explained, 'I don't drink the stuff at all, to tell you the truth. Would much rather have a tankard of ale, but I daren't offend the sensibilities of Mrs Farrell within the first five minutes I am here. Linney knows my tastes. He will arrange it all how I like it, without me having to make a fuss. We'll need to get supplies in, but for the first day or so, we must both just make do with things as they are,' he ended quite sternly, as though daring her to make any complaints.

Linney knew his tastes. Linney would arrange things, she thought angrily, heaping an extra spoonful of sugar into her cup.

'You did not seem all that surprised to learn that, had we not married, Percy Lampton would have inherited The Dovecote,' he said, an irritable edge to his voice.

Though what had he to feel irritable about? He was the lord and master of this domain, while she was like some slave girl, brought in solely for the purpose of satisfying his animal urges. She felt so brittle, she feared one more unkind word would snap her in two like a twig.

She poured tea into both their cups, adding a splash of milk to hers, and leaving his black and unsweetened. She hoped he found it as un-palatable as she would have done.

'I wondered if he might be the other legatee the lawyers mentioned, yes,' she admitted. 'Having observed your aversion to each other,' she said, carefully placing his cup within reach of his right hand, 'I then wondered if you were attempting to deprive him of something he took for granted belonged to him.'

'And it did not bother you?' he sneered.

'It was only a vague suspicion,' she defended herself, suddenly loathe to admit how comforting it had been to hear Mrs Farrell confirming her hope that the former owner really had wanted her husband to inherit. 'And anyway, why should it bother me, if it did not bother you?'

'My motives were nothing like yours!' he flared. How like a woman to lay the blame for her mercenary actions upon another! She had not cared that she was pushing another claimant out of the way. She just wanted to get her hands on his inheritance. 'Lampton deliberately attempted to prevent me from inheriting when he thought I was about to make a match with Miss Hullworthy. If he had not acted so despicably, I would not have felt the need to retaliate!'

Deborah flinched, as though from a blow. It was bad enough that she knew he did not care for her, but to have him fling it in her face, the moment they had set foot in their marital home, was the act of a callous beast!

'You married me to get revenge on Mr Lampton…' Because he had stolen the woman Captain Fawley loved.

'And why not? He deserved some punishment. He will drop Miss Hullworthy, now she can be of no further use to him. Do you think he should get away with such cruelty to a woman—your friend, might I add?'

She swallowed down her hurt, clenching her fists in her lap as she reminded herself he did not know how cruel he was being. He did not know she loved him. He firmly believed she had agreed to the marriage for purely financial reasons.

She wondered what he would do if she bawled out, 'I love you, you idiot! That is why I married you!' before flailing out at him with those clenched fists.

She took a deep calming breath. Letting it out, she rose unsteadily to her feet. 'If you will excuse me, I should like to go and lie down for a while.'

He frowned at her. 'You do look pale. Are you ill? Should I ask Mrs Farrell to fetch a doctor?' He lurched to his feet, and tugged on the bell pull. 'Mrs Farrell!' he bellowed, going to the door, and flinging it open, 'My wife is unwell… Ah, you, girl, what is your name?' he snapped at the young maid who had come running in answer to his summons.

'Cherry, sir.' She bobbed a curtsy.

'Help my wife to our room, and get her whatever she needs. She is not well….'

'I am only tired, that is all,' said Deborah. 'If I might just lie down quietly for a space, I am sure I shall recover.'

'If you are sure?' He watched her with a troubled frown as she crossed the hall to their rooms.

'Quite sure,' she said, head lowered so that he would not see the effort it was costing her not to cry. She felt quite disgusted with herself for being so feeble as to want to weep, simply because he had shouted at her. She was pathetic. Quite pathetic.

The maid, however, took one look at her, before huffing, 'Men! Don't know why Miss Lampton thought that one would be any different just because he had a rough start in life.' She hustled Deborah to an upholstered chair by the window and bent to loosen her boots. 'Tyrants, the lot of 'em! Shouting at you like that, and you only just wed! That man of his is no better, either, looking us up and down while he tramps round the place in his noisy boots.'

'Captain Fawley is not a tyrant,' Deborah hastily intervened. 'He was not shouting at me.'

'If you say so, madam,' Cherry said, looking totally unconvinced.

'No, really, he shouted for help because he was concerned for me,' she explained. Though why she should be defending him, she did not know. 'I know he has a loud voice, but he was in the army, and used to giving orders to men. I am sure, after a period of adjustment, he will get used to ordering female staff, just as you will get used to having him about.'

'And was that great lummox of a serving man of his in the army too?' Cherry huffed, going round the back of her chair to loosen Deborah's laces.

It pained her that she did not know. So she said,

'I really would feel better for a lie down. I am not ill, but I was ill, and I seem to get tired very quickly.'

'Country air, that's what you need,' Cherry said firmly. 'Plenty of walks, and good plain cooking and lots of sleep. You'll be right as a trivet in no time. London…' she pulled a face '…that's what you need to recover from. Never went up to town, but what Miss Lampton came back with a white face and a need to sleep for a week,' she said.

'Miss Lampton visited London often?'

'At least three times a year, though we was never to let on.' Cherry went a bit red in the face. 'I don't suppose it will do any harm to tell you, though, especially not now she's gone. It was only her brother that would have put a stop to her doing her business, if he had known about it. But he never found out. Lor!' Her face lit up. 'You should have seen his face when the will was read out, and he found out how much money she had made. And that it weren't to go to his precious son! Madder than a wet hen, he was!'

Deborah was prevented from learning anything more about the previous owner of The Dovecote, when a knock on the door heralded the arrival of the housekeeper, with the tea tray.

'Your husband said as to be sure you drank your

tea, and had a morsel to eat.' She beamed. 'And I was to ask if there was anything else you needed. Does a body good,' she said, depositing the tray on a low table next to the chair, 'to see a man actually taking care of his wife. Out you go, Cherry,' she addressed the maid, who bobbed a curtsy and scuttled out. 'I had thought Cherry could serve as your personal maid, if you have no objection. Miss Lampton's woman left after she died, and went to live in Ramsgate on the nice little pension she got for her troubles. Cherry is not exactly trained, but the most suitable for now, since you have not brought your own maid.'

'Everything was rather rushed,' Deborah said weakly, as the woman handed her the same cup of tea she had poured herself earlier. She decided she could not fathom her husband out at all. He would shout at her one minute, then send a servant to see to her welfare the next.

'Well, no need for rush and hurry as though you was in London now. Nice and steady we take things here at The Dovecote. I'll just pull the curtains across, and you can take forty winks. I'll send Cherry to wake you in time to change for dinner.'

Rather overwhelmed by the woman's determined helpfulness, Deborah went to the bed, climbed up and lay down on top of the silky counterpane. She closed her eyes as the woman bustled round the room, needing, more than anything, to be left alone to think. She did not open her eyes after she heard the door close behind the housekeeper. She might as well try to doze. She had not slept properly for the two nights before that dreadful, hastily arranged wedding. That probably explained why she was finding it so hard to cope with her new station in life. In time, she would get used to her husband's abrupt manner, and learn to read his moods to the extent she would not provoke him to anger.

He *was* trying to be kind to her in spite of the fact that she annoyed him. He had sent both the housekeeper and a maid to look after her.

It wasn't his fault that she would rather be in the parlour, discussing the peculiar woman who had arranged the household in such an eccentric manner, or laughing together over Linney's face when he realised he was the only male servant in a house full of women.

That was not the sort of relationship he wanted with her. He had not offered her friendship. Only financial security and children.

Somehow she had to find the strength to bear the

limits he set on their relationship. Nor must she yield to the temptation to feel sorry for herself. It would only make him dislike her even more.

Wearily, she turned on to her side, laying her cheek upon her open palm. And before she knew it, she had fallen asleep.

She was not sure what woke her, but when she opened her eyes it was to see her husband leaning on the bedpost, gazing down at her with a pensive frown.

'How are you?' he asked, running one finger along the bevelled edge of the footboard. 'Better, I trust, after your rest?'

Her heart went out to him. It was not his fault he was not in love with her. Nor that he had not a glib tongue, to soothe over any awkward moments. He had warned her he would speak bluntly. In truth, it was one of the things she had liked so much about him, that slightly gruff manner, which made him stand out from the other men who had swarmed about Susannah. It had made him seem so much more manly than the others. She could easily imagine him barking out orders to a troop of battle-hardened soldiers, and them respectfully obeying him.

She smiled at him, sleepily. 'I am sure I will feel much better, when I am properly awake. Just at the moment, I still feel a little drowsy.' She yawned, and stretched, raising her arms above her head. He watched her sinuous movements with a dark, hungry look. She stilled, pierced by the force of desire she read in his stance. She couldn't help remembering how it had felt to be the recipient of all that pent-up longing the night before. Unwittingly, she shifted on the bed, revelling in the way his fingers clenched on the footboard as his eyes focused on her body. Her dress, which Cherry had loosened so she would be more comfortable, had partially slipped from her shoulders while she slept. She had kicked her shoes off, so her feet were bare, and she could feel that her skirts no longer covered her ankles, or calves. As he ran his eyes over her recumbent frame, she felt as though he was touching her all over.

'We need to wash and change for dinner,' he said abruptly, straightening up. 'I will use the facilities first, since you look as though you are still half-asleep.' Swinging away from her, he marched into their dressing room.

She watched him go, not sure whether to be glad or sorry. He did not want to want her so much, that was obvious, even to a woman of her inexperience. But want her, he did. There was no mistaking the hunger she had seen in his eyes as they had roamed over her recumbent form. She hugged the knowledge to herself as she sat up, and lowered her legs to the floor.

It was a start.

As she got to her feet, she felt a rush of feminine satisfaction surge through her. She caught her lower lip between her teeth. He wanted her, in spite of himself. And, oh, how she wanted him! Her body tingled in all the places he had paid the most attention to the night before. And her stomach gave a lurch at the prospect of receiving his attentions all over again.

In the dressing room, Captain Fawley grinned to himself as Linney helped him out of his jacket. He need not have worried that he was growing sentimental, after all. The jolt of lust he had felt, upon looking down at her, had been reassuringly carnal. All he had wanted was to lift her skirts and sink himself into the warm wet welcome, he could tell from the wanton wiggles she made, that he would find in his wife's sleepily pliant body.

There had been, apparently, no need to worry that she might find him repulsive, because of his scarring. As Linney helped him pull his shirt off over his head, he wondered if that had been because he had been so careful to shield her from the full horror of his injuries. He had kept the room dark, making sure what little light there was illuminated his good side.

Though, just now, she had looked up at him, in broad daylight, and given him clear signals that she felt aroused just by sensing the need in him. That was what she had been thinking of, as she had lain on the bed just now, watching him. Not how ugly his face was, but the way he had made her feel.

He frowned as he worked a soaped washcloth over his face and neck. It was surprising to think that a properly brought-up young lady like she should find such pleasure in the marriage bed. Although, he huffed, splashing away the soap with clean water from the basin, perhaps that was entirely due to the fact that her mother had not had time to warn her she ought not to enjoy it. She had, in effect, been surprised into her sexual awakening.

It felt good, he reflected, drying himself on the towel Linney handed him, to know that, in the dark of their bedroom, it had not mattered what he looked like. He had raised Deborah to heights of rapture, with his one good hand, his mouth and his own manhood. She was too innocent to have faked her response.

It felt good.

It evened things out, somewhat, to know that while she had made it possible for him to live in comfort, and independence, he had introduced her to pleasure she had never guessed at.

His chest swelled; he walked a little taller as he went to the upstairs salon to await the serving of the evening meal. In one department, at least, as a man, he had no lack.

Deborah sidled into the salon some time later, feeling completely exasperated. She had made the mistake of lying down in the only dress she had with her. It had not withstood the abuse well. She had agreed with Cherry that there was nothing for it but to borrow one of the late Miss Lampton's gowns until her own could be brushed and pressed into some semblance of respectability.

Miss Lampton had clearly been somewhat shorter, and a great deal more plump, than she was.

'What,' her husband said, his eyes lighting with amusement, 'are you wearing now?'

'Another borrowed garment,' she flashed,

'since you did not give me time to pack anything of my own.'

His amusement faded, to be replaced by a look that in another man she might have described as contrition.

'Now, Deborah, you surely understand by now the reason for my haste in getting you to the altar. I could not risk Lampton getting wind of my plans, or he would have done his utmost to overset them. He had tried such a trick before, don't forget.'

She nodded, her hands tugging ineffectually at the voluminous skirts that left her legs bare almost to the calves.

'No, do not try to pull your skirts lower. You have very pretty ankles. I like looking at them.'

'It is hardly proper to be talking about my ankles,' she snapped, although she knew it was not talking about her ankles that had annoyed her, so much as hearing once again of his reluctance to confide in her.

'Deborah,' he said, holding out his hand towards her, 'I know I must have taxed your patience to the limit. I whisked you away from your home without giving you time to prepare, and I have been so anxious that something would prevent our marriage I fear I have been less than polite to you at times.'

'Well, yes, I have to confess your manner has been a little… abrupt,' she conceded.

He smiled his lopsided smile, the one that always tugged at her heartstrings.

'I do regret the necessity for keeping you so much in the dark,' he said, removing her excuse for maintaining any anger with him. 'But given your close friendship with Miss Hullworthy, and her own infatuation with that boor, how else could I have acted?'

You could have trusted me… She sighed, settling on to a chair and taking the glass of lemonade someone had placed on the table beside it.

'If I had laid my cards on the table,' he continued, 'would it not have been a burden on you?'

She bit at her lower lip, watching a pip bobbing about near the bottom of the cloudy liquid. Yes, she admitted, she would have found it hard not to have gone to Susannah and warned her about Lampton's duplicity. She supposed it was just possible that he had been trying to shield her from anxiety, just as Lady Walton had suggested.

However, she reflected bitterly, taking a tentative sip of the drink and finding it surprisingly pleasant, it was more likely that her husband was so used to barking orders at inferiors, and never having to explain himself, that he had just not considered her feelings at all.

Although to be fair to him, she sighed, taking a large, unladylike gulp of the refreshing beverage, he was not a man given to trusting anyone. Why should he? He had been surrounded by treachery and betrayal since before he had been born.

Mrs Farrell came in to announce dinner was served, and they both rose and went to the door.

'Oh, how lovely!' Deborah exclaimed on passing through the double doors of the dining room. Crystal glasses sparkled in the rays of the setting sun that slanted in through the mullioned windows. Silverware glittered at the place settings laid out on a heavy damasked tablecloth, and the whole room was scented by masses of fresh roses prettily arranged in bowls along the table.

Her reaction brought a delighted smile to Mrs Farrell's face.

That look faded to one of affront, as Linney helped her into her chair, saying, 'Thank you, Mrs Farrell. I will take over from here.'

He had arranged things so that the food came from the kitchen to a sideboard just inside the door. He brought it to table, served his master and mistress, and removed the empty plates and dishes when they were finished with.

She would have to have a word with Mrs Farrell, and explain her husband's aversion to having strangers watching him eat, so that she did not take offence at Linney's peremptory dismissal. Thankfully the servants were used to serving an eccentric employer. They would grow used to her husband's foibles far more readily than some.

'Your things should be arriving in a day or so,' Captain Fawley remarked, as Linney brought out a dish of quince jelly.

'I shall be glad of it,' she admitted, shifting uncomfortably in the dress that, in spite of all she could do, would keep slipping off one shoulder.

'Yes, the sooner we can get you out of that dreadful gown, the better pleased I shall be.'

Deborah felt a flame of heat engulf her at the prospect of her husband taking off her gown. Guiltily she lowered her head, concentrating fiercely on her pudding. She was sure Robert would not have deliberately said something so indelicate in front of Linney. But when she eventually regained her composure, and lifted her head, he shot her a quite unrepentant grin.

She felt her cheeks heat to an unbecoming degree.

'You are looking a little flushed, my dear,' he said, leaning back and contemplating her thoughtfully. 'Are you feeling unwell again?'

'N-no, that is…'

He nodded, his face solemn, as he lay his napkin down beside his place setting. 'You probably just need another lie down. An early night would do us both good, I think. Linney!'

'Yes, Captain?'

'Get someone else to finish clearing away in here. My wife needs to get to her bed. I do not want to keep her waiting.'

Deborah wished she could sink through the floor. How obvious could he be making it that going to sleep was the last thing on his mind? She found herself exerting a vice-like grip on her dessert spoon, as he rose and limped past her to the door.

'As soon as I am ready, I shall send Linney to fetch you,' he shot at her over his shoulder, as he went out.

She looked at her dessert. She measured the distance to the door that had just closed on her insufferably insensitive husband. She picked up the bowl…and thought of Miss Lampton's staff. It would not be fair to indulge in a childish tantrum on her very first night here. Why should they have to clean up the mess she had made of her life?

She slammed the bowl down on the table, slinging the spoon in with a little cry of vexation. He had warned her how it would be, yet somehow, she had not believed he could be so…crude.

Well, she was not going to put up with being ordered to his bed, in front of a servant, as though she were a woman of easy virtue.

Getting to her feet so abruptly her chair overturned, she left the dining room and went down the stairs in pursuit of her husband.

She hesitated on the threshold of their bedroom, knowing he was probably in the process of having Linney remove his false limbs. Even though he had just humiliated her, she did not think it right to descend to the same level. She just needed to draw a line, across which she refused to let him go!

Raising her fist, she banged on the door.

When Linney opened it, she drew herself up to her full height. 'I do not care what your master asks of you. I will not have you marching into my dressing room, while I am in a state of undress! Send a message to my maid, when it is appropriate for me to come to bed, and she can relay the information to me.'

'Yes, miss—madam,' he corrected himself. 'Will that be all?'

Would that be all? As though she had requested he bring her a cup of tea, rather than touch upon a subject that was so delicate she wondered at herself in broaching it!

'Yes. That will be all,' she said, with as much dignity as she could muster, before turning with a twitch of her voluminous, borrowed skirts, and heading down the corridor to the other door that opened on to her dressing room.

Chapter Eight

She reminded him of a bristling alley cat when she finally stalked into his bedroom. Her eyes were snapping, her fists were clenched at her sides, and if she'd had a tail, it would have been twitching.

She had never looked more beautiful.

Wondering what it would take to goad his very correct young wife into losing her tenuous grip on her temper, he eyed her ill-fitting nightwear, and said, 'Take it off.'

She did not mistake his meaning, and, though her eyes narrowed, she just tugged the ties of her wrapper open, flung the garment to the floor and kicked it away from her feet.

And stood before him gloriously, furiously naked.

'Satisfied?' she demanded, planting her hands on her hips.

'Not yet,' he growled, though he knew satisfaction was not far off. It had not escaped his notice that tonight she had left her hair loose. Anticipating his demands. 'Get into bed now.'

The smouldering look that went with that peremptory command scythed right through her anger. Dropping her gaze to the folded-back edges of the bedcovers, she clambered in beside him.

Immediately, he hooked his arm round her waist and pulled her close. His weight pressed her back into the pillows as he kissed her forcefully.

'Ohh…' She shuddered when, eventually, he paused to draw breath. She wondered whether it was silly of her to feel flattered that he had not hesitated, as he had done the night before. She must have pleased him, though she was so inexperienced, for him to have set to work so swiftly.

'Oh, indeed,' he murmured thickly against her throat.

As his mouth worked hungrily against her neck, she felt as though she was melting. He raised himself slightly, just far enough so that he could run his tongue around the delicate whorls of her ear, and she found that she was running her hands up and down his flanks. He nipped the lobe gently with his teeth. She hooked her leg over his, so that she could run her foot over the calf muscles.

And they went up in flames, just as they had done the night before.

Deborah was amazed that he could want her with such ferocity, in the darkness of their bed, when by daylight, he did not seem to want her anywhere near him. But her awareness of how little she meant to him did not stop her from responding with her own fierce delight. And marvelling that this time, when he finally entered her, there was no pain, only an intensifying of her own pleasure.

Afterwards, they sank back into the soft feather mattress, side by side, not quite touching, though she was aware of every breath he took. She felt as though she was waiting for something for him. Some sign. And wondered why she should suddenly feel wary, when they had just been so closely engaged.

It was a bit like a truce after a bloody battle, she mused, when each side gave the other time to collect their wounded from the field of combat, each aware of the other, but in no fit state to engage in further action. They had even communicated their passion through their sighs and moans, neither of them quite daring to shatter their tenuous bubble of harmony by putting anything into words.

As Deborah slipped into an exhausted sleep, she

wondered if she would always feel as sad as this after they had been together.

The bedchamber was still shrouded in darkness, the heavy curtains firmly shutting out the feeble rays of early daylight, when she woke, to hear Linney moving about the room.

All the previous night's anger surged back. It was one thing having her husband see her naked, though that had been embarrassing enough. But she drew the line at having his servant wandering about the room while she had no clothes on!

Sitting up, having first made sure that the sheet was decorously clutched over her breasts, she turned a furious face to the manservant.

'Get out!' she yelled at him.

He paused in the act of settling a tray on a small table under the window.

'Begging your pardon, miss…madam, but I always bring the Captain's breakfast to—'

'Not any more you don't! Not while I am in his bed. If the Captain wants you, he can ring for you.'

Linney straightened up, his face blank. 'He did ring for me.'

She turned to look at her husband, who was regarding her with a look of barely concealed impatience.

Mortified, she slumped back on to the pillows, her only recourse to pull the covers completely over her head. Only once she had deduced, from the noises of crockery clattering, floorboards creaking, and the door squeaking open and shut, that Linney had left the room, did she emerge from under the covers.

'Good morning, to you too,' he growled.

'I don't know what kind of women you usually associate with,' she replied, resorting to frosty haughtiness to overcome her sense of humiliation, 'but I am not in the habit of displaying my naked body to anyone, let alone male servants!'

'Linney is more than just a servant to me,' he replied darkly.

Deborah gasped. He really put the dignity of his servant before her own discomfort. But then he added, 'Though, of course, I can see we cannot continue in quite the same habits we used to have. It's merely a question of logistics.'

'L-logistics?' she squeaked, increasingly outraged by the way he was treating her.

'Yes, you see, Linney and I have got into a routine that has worked for us both for several months now. It is not a simple matter to get me prepared to face the day. I warned you that you would have to get used to him being an integral part of our life. He is not just a valet, who lays out my clothes, pours my washing water and shaves me.' He speared his fingers through his fringe, pushing it out of his eyes. 'Damn it, Deborah, have you no sensitivity at all? Do I have to spell it out for you? I need help just to piss in the mornings! And if you don't get your carcass out of this bed, and ring for him to come back, you are going to have to be the one to hold the bottle to my…'

'I'm sorry, I'm sorry,' she stammered, sliding out of the bed and groping on the floor for her wrap. 'I'll ring for him to come back, and get out of your way.' Her cheeks flaming, she did as she had said, then hastily made for the door to her dressing room.

Once again, she had only looked at things from her own point of view. Her husband had told her he did not want her in the room while Linney undressed and put him to bed at night. She pressed her hands to her flaming cheeks, recalling the crude way he had spoken of having the man carry him back to his own bed, if she insisted on having her own room. Why had she not taken in the significance of what he had been trying to tell her? He could not get about with any ease, once he had removed his false leg, without the help of his burly serving man.

She sank to the floor by the washstand, bowing her head in her hands. She had not really comprehended just how awkward things that she took for granted were to him. And with her clumsy insistence on her own rights, she had forced him to speak of the weakness he managed to conceal from the rest of the world with such resounding success.

She felt thoroughly ashamed of herself.

And, worse, experienced a sinking feeling that she had given her rather touchy husband yet another reason to dislike her.

Captain Fawley lifted his eyes from the balance sheets, to see if Travers was trying to make fun of him.

There was nothing in the factor's pale eyes to show he was anything but a diligent employee.

'Are you quite sure?' he eventually brought himself to ask.

'Well, of course, the figures are only to the end of last quarter. Bound to be some fluctuations in the overall value since then. But not to any significant extent.'

'I had no idea.'

Travers smiled for the first time since he had walked into the office, as arranged, to go over the books with the new owner of The Dovecote.

'Nobody did, save Miss Lampton and myself,' said Travers, a gleam of enthusiasm lighting his formerly colourless demeanour. 'A very astute mind, had Miss Lampton. Invested very wisely.'

Captain Fawley suddenly found himself assailed by a wave of curiosity towards his benefactress.

'Explain,' he barked, inadvertently reverting to the attitude of commanding officer towards a subordinate up on a charge. Travers automatically sat a little straighter in his chair.

'Well, Miss Lampton, you see, sir, did have a little money of her own, when she initially came to live here. Her father had banished her from the parental home when she refused to enter the marriage he had arranged for her. But instead of begging his forgiveness, Miss Lampton found that his harshness had stiffened her resolve to become independent of any man. And so, secretly, she began to, umm, speculate in various ventures….'

'On your advice?'

'Oh, no, sir. She had her own ideas about how she wanted to invest her money. Very forceful, she was. Would have dealt with the city traders herself, but for the fact such activity is forbidden a lady. Disliked having to use me at all, to tell you the truth, at least at first. After a few years, though...' he smiled as though indulging in fond memories '...well, we got used to each other.'

'A very successful partnership, in effect.'

'Yes sir, as you can see.' Travers indicated the ledgers which lay open on the desk.

Almost every single venture Miss Lampton had decided to dabble in had paid huge dividends. The wealth she had bequeathed to Captain Fawley was stupendous. He could live like a lord for the rest of his days. He frowned. His own modest requirements would scarcely make a dent in such an enormous fortune. He was too disfigured to try to cut a dash in society. At one time, he would have been delighted at the prospect of being able to indulge in his love of horseflesh. Now he could scarcely control the gentle mare Lensborough had trained and sold to him on terms that were akin to giving the creature away.

'I cannot continue on the path she trod,' he admitted to his factor, after a moment or two of reflection. 'I have always been a soldier. I have no head for business.'

'She foresaw that eventuality,' Travers said just

a shade too quickly. 'She suggested you might like to simply sell up, invest in the funds and live a life of indolence.'

From the expression on his factor's face, Captain Fawley judged that Miss Lampton had not held very high expectations of his capabilities. Yet that had not prevented her from leaving everything she owned to him. He ran a rather shaky hand over the stack of ledgers on the desk.

He had a sudden vision of the woman who had lived in this house, scheming and plotting to make a fortune that she would leave to a complete stranger. She had not done it because she had any personal feelings for him. From what he had been able to tell so far, she disliked all males, on principle.

'Why me?' he grated. 'I am no relation to her at all.'

Travers stuck his chin out a little as he said, 'That was to your advantage, sir. Her family washed their hands of her when she became, as they termed it, difficult. Either of her brothers could have defended her when her father ousted her from the family home. Or even when the old man died. But they did nothing. The only person who tried to intercede on her behalf was your mother. She went to the old man and begged him to let Euphemia choose a husband she could love. It was perhaps inevitable that when Algernon became head of the family, he began to persecute your mother. He blamed her, you see, for encouraging his sister to defy their father. By the time Miss Lampton discovered what was afoot, there was nothing she could do for the unfortunate lady. But she felt she could partially redress the injustice by making you her heir. Shall I proceed with the sale for you, sir?' asked Travers, when Captain Fawley remained broodingly silent.

'I suppose that would be for the best,' he conceded. He could settle up his payment plan with Lensborough. It would be the first thing he would do. 'See to it, would you?'

Travers smiled as he got to his feet. 'With pleasure, sir. And may I say how glad I am you have fulfilled the terms necessary to inherit the fortune Miss Lampton worked all her life to bequeath to you. I would have been sorry to see that scapegrace nephew of hers get his hands on it.' His smile dimmed. 'Not once did he ever try to so much as visit her, when he thought she was just an eccentric old lady, eking out her existence in rural fastness!'

'To be fair, nor did I.'

'Ah, but you never even knew of her existence, did you, sir? It amused her, to think of herself as a sort of fairy godmother, weaving her magic behind the scenes...' He ground to a halt at the appalled look on Captain Fawley's features.

'Well, I don't deny she was a little eccentric,' he said uncomfortably. 'Just one more question,' said Captain Fawley. The factor schooled his face into that of bland servitor, awaiting his pleasure. 'If she disliked her brother, and her brother's son, so much, how did Percy Lampton manage to get himself a mention in her will at all?'

'A bad business, that.' Travers' face darkened. 'In her latter years, when she became less mobile, Algernon took to visiting her occasionally. He would stride about the place, assessing its value, assuming she must bequeath it to another member of the family. He wanted his younger son, Percy, to inherit it, since the major part of his own estate went to his own heir. When he discovered that not only had she already made a will, but that it was in your favour, he became...well, I think *vicious* is the only word to describe it. He bullied and hounded her until she made that codicil, for writing you out altogether, he could not make her do!' Pulling himself together, he finished, 'Will that be all?'

Captain Fawley felt faint stirrings of a strange sense of kinship with the woman he had never personally known. She seemed to have disliked her brother almost as much as he did. She must have done, to have taken such pains to make sure that the boy he had set out to oppress became wealthy.

When the factor had left, Captain Fawley remained seated at the desk, marvelling at the extent of his good fortune. A feeling of exaltation rose within his chest and burst from his lips in the form of laughter. He had hoped he would never have to worry about a bill again. Buy a fresh set of linen whenever he felt like it. Play a hand of cards without having to consider how much change he had in his pocket first. Not this!

He had to find Deborah and tell her. Striding to the chimneybreast, he rang for the housekeeper.

'Tell my wife I want a few words with her,' he barked.

Mrs Farrell raised her brows in an expression of disapproval, but said nothing as she turned to obey his command. It was only when, some minutes later, a very timid knock on the door presaged his wife's arrival that it occurred to him it might have seemed a little autocratic to send for her as though she was one of his subordinates.

The look of trepidation on her face as she approached the desk behind which he sat only confirmed his sense of having treated her with less than the respect due to a wife. He recalled the way she had fled from his fit of temper that morning. He had not seen her since. She looked as though she wished she was not seeing him now.

'I only asked you in here to share the news that the factor has just given me,' he said. 'Do sit down! You look like a nervous subaltern up on a charge!' he snapped, his conscience provoking him to lash out, quite unfairly, in completely the wrong direction. It was with himself he was annoyed. He felt even more angry with himself when she sank into the seat, her head down, hands clasped in her lap as though expecting a scold.

Rapidly reviewing the few words they had exchanged since making their vows, he could hardly blame her. With a heavy sigh, he said, 'It cannot have been easy for you, the last few days. I apologise.'

'You apologise?' She looked up at him with swift enquiry. Then shook her head. 'It has occurred to me, during this morning, that I have some things to apologise for too.'

'You do?' he sat bolt upright, completely astonished. 'Why, what have you done?'

'Well, I have been angry with you on more than one occasion…'

'Which I thoroughly deserved, I dare say. Look,' he said, when she opened her mouth as if she would have protested, 'it is clearly not such a simple task to merge two lives together as I had thought it would be. We will have to come to some accommodation regarding Linney's presence in our room. I cannot do without his aid, you know, but—'

'If you would just tell me before you sent for him, so that I could cover myself up. Or leave altogether if your need for help is of a delicate nature.'

Her cheeks went bright red. It reminded him how delightfully tousled she had looked that morning, after having spent some minutes hiding under the blankets. He made an effort to soften his voice as he said, 'I should not have used such coarse language this morning, Deborah. It was inexcusable.'

She smiled shyly up at him. 'As you say, we both have adjustments to make, being married. I dare say it will take us some time to get used to each other's ways.'

What a generous nature she had! And how reasonably she was dealing with their earlier quarrel. He recalled some of the scenes that had gone on in Walton House when his half-brother had first brought home his French wife. Doors slamming, crockery being thrown, sulks and tantrums. Heloise had gone about town, acting as outrageously as she dared, to try to punish her husband for his cold and autocratic treatment of her. They had settled down eventually, but for a while, they had made each other miserable.

Of course, he had known from the outset Deborah would never treat him to such tantrums. He had never seen her make a fuss about the difficulties life threw in her way. She just got on with whatever she had to do, with good grace.

'We have a lifetime.' He smiled, congratulating himself on choosing such a levelheaded girl to wife. 'And if we can both be as reasonable as you are being this morning, then it will be a pleasure to get used to your ways.'

'Oh,' she said, her smile growing broader. What a lovely thing it had been to say. Especially since she knew he meant it. Had he not promised never to offer her Spanish coin? She ducked her head, fidgeting with a stray thread that was working its way from her cuff.

Watching her nervous gesture, he suddenly knew what he wanted to spend his money on. It was not just that she had not brought many clothes with her. She had never had many clothes. She had worn the same ball gown, with different trimmings, for the entire Season, until the night of Lensborough's ball. She had only three or four bonnets, to his knowledge, and she had always worn her gloves until the seams started to split.

'When we go back to London, I want you to buy an entirely new wardrobe,' he said decisively.

She looked up at him in alarm. 'You do not like my clothes?'

'That is immaterial. You need new ones. I want you looking extremely fashionable.' He wanted to see her enjoying herself. Women enjoyed shopping for clothes. And then showing them off.

'We will have to get a barouche, so you can drive round Hyde Park in it.' He frowned. 'And a house, a fine house, in the very best address.'

Deborah's heart sank. She was not the kind of woman he should have married at all. While her head had been full of dreams of a house in the country, filled with children, it seemed that, all along, he had wanted to live in town and cut a fashionable figure. With a pang, she realised that they had never discussed what they wanted out of marriage. Robert had mentioned children, and security, but not any details of where or how he anticipated they might live out their lives.

She pasted a brave smile on her lips as she forced herself to say, 'That sounds lovely.'

He frowned. 'It cannot be done all at once. It may take Travers some time to raise the capital.' He indicated the pile of ledgers on the desk that separated them.

'Oh, I shan't mind staying here for a while,' she put in quickly. If he intended to return to London, she had best make the most of what little time she had here. From the window seat of an empty upstairs bedroom, where she had taken refuge that morning, she had noticed, not an oak tree, but a massive yew in the centre of a velvety smooth lawn. Beyond that was a walled garden, over which peeped the boughs of what looked like a productive orchard. The housewife in her wanted to explore the orchard, the vegetable gardens and the stillroom. The mother in her wanted to see if it would ever be possible to build a tree house in that yew. Or, if not, at least hang a swing from its lower branches. From her recollection of the journey, the house itself stood not far from the village. She wanted to walk to it, and explore it and find out if there were other walks in the area. She wanted to attend the church with its squat, Norman tower, and make friends with the local ladies. In short, she wanted to make The Dovecote her home.

She would not care all that much if she never set foot in London again. Life there had seemed shallow, and brittle and not the least bit comfortable.

'I am sorry I did not give you the chance to bring a change of clothing with you,' he broke into her reverie. 'But you won't be needing much anyway, for the next few days.'

No, he would not wish to entertain, she thought, entirely missing the wicked grin that lit his face.

'No, I suppose not,' she said, trying to be as amenable to his wishes as she could. He could barely tolerate having his own wife in the room while he was eating, let alone strangers. She could make this one gown do until her trunks arrived, since she would only be pottering about the gardens and house. She would put off visiting the neighbours until the next time they came down here. Whenever that might be.

'Then you agree?' he said, getting to his feet and coming round the desk.

'Agree?' She was not aware he had asked her a question. With a puzzled frown, she swiftly reviewed their conversation.

'That we should spend these next few days getting to know each other better,' he said, coming to stand over her. She looked up at him in bewilderment. He reached down and ran one finger along the curve of her cheekbone.

'I want to take you back to bed, Deborah. Now. In broad daylight. Does that shock you?' His face took on a shuttered expression. 'Disgust you?'

Her heart leapt at the look of longing she had read before the shutters came down. She had thought he could barely tolerate having her in bed, because she was not the woman he wanted. Now she saw that part of his insistence on complete darkness stemmed from his fear *she* would find *him* repulsive. She wanted to cry. How could he think she might feel disgust, just because he had a few scars?

Slowly, she got to her feet. Then reached out her own hand, mirroring the way he had just caressed her face. Deliberately, she ran one finger down the unblemished side of his face. Then she reached up on tiptoe, to kiss the cheek that was puckered, and reddened, before saying, 'Not disgusted. But perhaps more than a little shocked. Oh, not at your suggestion, but at my reaction to it. I find that when you speak of wanting to return to our bed, my heart has started to beat faster. I believe it is quite improper, and yet...'

He caught her hand to his cheek, on a ragged gasp, his eyes darkening. 'You want me,' he growled, before sliding his hand round to the nape of her neck, and kissing her soundly.

'Yes.' She sighed, when he finally broke the kiss. 'I should not, but—'

'Why not? We are married. There is no sin in this, Deborah.' Grabbing her hand, he made for the door.

Now her heart was really beating fast. The thought of retreating to the seclusion of their room, in broad daylight, was incredibly exciting.

'Damn it,' he cursed, coming to an abrupt halt. 'I am going to have to get Linney to get me out of this leg first.'

She made a little mew of disappointment as she pictured the scene. He would ring for his serving man, and go through all the rigmarole of getting ready for bed, having first ensured her absence from whatever ritual he was so unwilling for her to witness. Then he would send for her. And then, when he had finished with her, send her away so that Linney could help him wash and restore him to an appearance of wholeness. The whole procedure would be cumbersome, and awkward, and embarrassing for all concerned.

'It will not be very romantic,' she acknowledged ruefully.

'We agreed, when I proposed to you, we would not try to cozen each other with romantic nonsense,' he spat at her irritably.

'Romantic nonsense…' She sighed, recalling she had gone along with everything he had demanded, so thrilled had she been he was proposing at all. 'No, we would not want that.' She looked at her husband, tense, frustrated and growing angrier by the second, and wondered what she could do to help him.

'I know what I do want, though,' she said carefully, drawing his gaze from the door at which he had been glaring balefully for the past few seconds.

'What is that?'

'The same thing as you.' And then she blushed, though she managed to hold his gaze. 'When you spoke about returning to bed…well, do we really need a bed? I do not know very much about it, but it seems to me that, umm…' And then she lost the ability to look at anything other than her hands, which she found she was twisting at her waist.

Without saying a word, Robert reached past her,

and turned the key in the lock. Then, quite calmly, he went to the windows and very deliberately drew the curtains.

'Are you quite certain about this?' he husked, turning to look at her. Even in the shadowed room she could read intense hunger in his face. Her own blood was pounding through her veins. She could not speak. She only nodded.

'Then come here,' he urged her, holding out his hand.

She flew to him, and he caught her, claiming her mouth in a kiss that had nothing of tenderness in it. Yet her spirit still soared. She did not care how unseemly this was, she only knew she would let nothing stop her from expressing her love in the only way he seemed able to accept it from her.

'I wish we could be naked,' he growled against her neck, while his hand kneaded at her breast. 'I wish I had the agility to take you standing up, against the door, or that you were not a lady, and I could bend you over the desk…'

The images his words conjured up should have shocked her. Instead, she found that she was growing even more excited. And eager to accede to his every demand.

'Do it, then,' she heard herself say, in a voice roughened with need.

His head flew up in astonishment. 'Do what?'

'Whatever you want,' she said, reaching round his waist to yank his shirt from the waistband of his breeches. She sighed at the satin texture of his body under her fingers. 'I need to feel your skin too,' she confessed, looking up at him with trepidation at her boldness. 'I want you now. I don't want to leave this room.' Her breath hitched on a sob. 'I don't want to have to wait for Linney, and for it to become cold and businesslike.'

'I won't let it be cold then,' he husked, 'nor make you wait. But if you want it now,' he warned her, 'you are going to have to help me.'

'I know,' she whispered. 'Show me what to do.'

With a fierce growl, he sought her mouth again, kissing her greedily. For the first time, he flung his injured arm about her waist, holding her close to him. She could feel how strong it was, holding her to his chest. It felt a little strange, ending just below the elbow. But that was just a fleeting thought. It was what his other hand was doing that dominated her mind. He had bunched up the material of her skirts and reached underneath until he found the soft skin of her thighs above her stocking tops. He only paused there briefly. Soon she began to moan, clinging to his shoulders for support when her knees became so weak under the ministration of his clever fingers, she thought her legs would give way.

'The wall, the wall,' he grunted, pushing her backwards until she was leaning against a space between two glass fronted bookcases. 'Lift your skirts,' he ordered, as he let them go, to unbutton the fall of his breeches.

'This won't be very decorous,' he warned her, as she swiftly obeyed, granting him the access he sought.

No, she gasped. It wasn't in the least bit decorous. Nor was it cold or businesslike. It was frenzied, and exciting and…necessary. Oh, so necessary, for her to have this—this proof that he could not wait for the night, but needed her now.

'Robert,' she gasped, winding her arms about his neck. 'Robert, I…I…'

I love you, she wanted to cry.

His mouth found hers, and the words were never uttered. He kissed her as though his life depended on it, pounding into her while she clung to him, her anchor through the storm of passion that swept them away.

This time, they drifted to shore together, clinging to each other like survivors of a ship-wreck. Their limbs tangled, they sank to the floor, gasping and shaking with the force of what they had shared.

'My goodness,' Deborah panted, her face pressed into the worn cloth of his jacket.

'Goodness had nothing to do with it.' He chuckled, rolling on to his side to look down at her. Her cheeks were flushed, her eyelids still heavy with passion. He leaned down to kiss each one in turn.

She flung her arms about his neck, arching up against him. She wanted this interlude never to end. She had hated it when he rolled away from her at night, silent and brooding. If only she knew how to prolong this sense of closeness!

'Have mercy, woman,' he groaned, rolling over so that he was partially on top of her. 'At least wait until after luncheon, when I have had a chance to recover, and we may retreat to the privacy of our bedroom.'

'What?' She gazed up at him in bewilderment for a few seconds before the penny dropped. He thought she wanted more of what they had just been doing! There was no tenderness in his look, just a sort of smug pride. The sort of look she guessed a man would give a woman he had just thoroughly seduced in his office.

She felt confused, cheapened somehow by the realisation that as far as he was concerned, their joining had nothing to do with love.

She sat up, twitching her skirts down over her knees. He rolled on to his back, his arms splayed out at his sides.

'Look at what you have done to me, woman,' he groaned in mock despair. 'You will have to help me to my feet, tuck in my shirt, do up my breeches…'

She wanted to slap him. It had been as much his doing as hers. More, in fact. He was the one who had suggested going back to bed in the first place! Briskly, she knelt up, then bent to the task of tidying his clothing. He caught her hand.

'What have I done now to make you angry?'

'Nothing!' she snapped.

And all the light died from his eyes.

He rolled on to his side, and pushed himself up on to his good knee, supporting his weight on his hand.

'I can manage without you!' he said, when she went to help him to his feet. And then, with an agility she had not suspected, after the way he had gone on and on about needing Linney all the time, he got to a standing position, using the leg of the desk, the back of the chair and sheer determination.

'I will leave you alone, then,' she said, as he slumped into the chair behind the desk.

'Deborah, wait!' she heard him say as she whirled away to the door. It took her a few minutes tugging on the handle before she remembered he had locked it.

'Deborah, for God's sake…'

She did not hear whatever else he had to say. Flinging the door open, she dashed out into the hall, making blindly for the front door, which stood ajar. Once outside, she lifted her face to the sun that streamed down from a cloudless blue sky. It seemed all wrong. How could it be such a gloriously beautiful day, when she felt so churned up and…muddied inside?

It made no difference though. She had to put some distance between herself and the man who could make her melt into a puddle of surrender at one moment, then shatter her with his coldness the next.

Stepping off the porch, she made her way out into the grounds.

Chapter Nine

'Would you tell my husband I have gone to our room for a rest?' Deborah asked Mrs Farrell.

She had walked for what felt like hours. She was footsore, and heartsore, and had the beginnings of a headache nagging at the base of her skull. It was her own fault, for dashing off without a bonnet. She could not quite understand what had happened to the sensible, practical girl who had weathered so much in the wake of her father's death. The slightest thing had her flying off the handle these days.

She had not even got across the lawn before seeing that the scene in the office had not been Robert's fault at all. She had been feeling ashamed of her wanton behaviour, and, when he had teased her about it, had lashed out at him. Turning towards the orchard wall, she harboured the mutinous thought that if only he had whispered words of affection, and reassurance, she would have been able to carry off the whole thing with aplomb.

But her innate honesty soon had her rejecting that scenario. As she pushed open the door to the orchard, she realised that it was the fact that she loved him enough to abandon all her principles that had left her feeling so prickly. Whatever he had said would have been wrong. Even if he had murmured those lover-like words she so longed to hear, she would only have accused him of being dishonest.

No, none of this was Robert's fault. He had been scrupulously honest with her. She was the one who was living a lie, by letting him think she had married him for financial security.

Mrs Farrell gave her a strange look.

'Well, since you missed your lunch, would you like me to bring you a tray too?'

'Thank you, yes,' she said, fumbling for the handle to the door to her rooms. 'If you will excuse me?' She crossed the sitting room swiftly, but paused on the threshold to the bedroom. Somebody had already been in, and drawn the curtains, as if they had known she would return with a headache.

'Where the hell have you been?'

The voice, emanating from the bed, made her jump out of her skin. Through the gloom she could make out Robert, reclining on top of the quilt. He looked incongruously dark and menacing, lounging against the froth of lace pillows banked against the headboard.

Her hand flew to her throat. 'I have been walking about the grounds,' she gasped, her heart still pounding with shock at the hostility in his voice. Though why should she be surprised he was angry with her? She had behaved extremely badly.

'Robert,' she said, hastening to the foot of the bed before he had a chance to say another word, 'I am so sorry for the way I ran off, after we— after, umm, well, you know.'

'Had marital relations up against the wall of my study?' he said coldly.

'Please don't make this more difficult for me,' she begged, her fingers gripping the footboard until her knuckles went white. 'I don't want to fight with you all the time. But I cannot…quite cope with…'

'The practical reality of being married to a cripple?'

Her head flew up, a stunned expression on her face.

'It is not that! You must never think that!'

She had thought once before that Robert's wounds were not just physical. His hurts went deep, and, in typical male fashion, he lashed out at anyone who touched on them.

Ruefully, she reflected she was guilty of doing exactly the same thing. Every time she became aware of just how little he valued her, her wounded pride made her lash out at him.

If they were ever to get beyond this dreadful sniping at each other, one of them was going to have to be willing to abandon their pride, and simply absorb the hurts the other dealt them. She did not suppose for a minute that person would be Robert.

She went round to the side of the bed and perched on the edge of the mattress.

'The practical reality of just being married at all is quite enough for me to cope with,' she confessed, linking her hands in her lap, and regarding them solemnly. 'I had little idea of what went on in the marriage bed before our wedding night. It was such a revelation. And when you began to speak of it…' She faltered, searching in vain for the words to describe what she had felt. 'My heart began to pound,' she said, her cheeks flushing as she admitted, 'and it suddenly struck me that we could do *that* again, and I…well, I know I lost my head. And afterwards, when you began to make a joke of what we had just done, I…well, I felt humiliated, if you must know. I had done something of which I felt quite ash…shamed.' Her voice hitched on a suppressed sob. She paused, sucking in a breath, turning reproachful eyes on him as she said, 'And then you mocked me.'

'That was not my intent,' he grated, reaching out to place his hand over hers.

'No, I…I worked that out for myself, as I walked round the orchard. You were just trying to make light of the difficulties you would have getting up off the floor.' She shot him another look, this one full of trepidation.

'In future, I think it would be better if we restricted our activities of that nature to the bedroom,' he growled. 'You may remember it was my first choice. I just wanted to get you naked and into bed and keep you there until it is time to return to town.'

She had completely forgotten the earlier part of their conversation, until this reminder. Her mind flew back to his stated determination to get to know her, and his puzzling reference to not needing clothing. Why had she not understood at the time that he had meant in a carnal way?

At that moment, Mrs Farrell returned with the

promised tray. Deborah was glad of the interruption. She was feeling quite flustered by the blunt way Robert spoke of what she considered a very delicate topic.

'There, now,' said Mrs Farrell, placing the tea tray on the small table under the window, 'you have a nice cup of tea, and a bite to eat, and you'll soon be feeling much better.'

Smiling wanly, Deborah went to the table, allowing the housekeeper to pour for her.

'You too, sir, if you don't mind me saying so. Hardly touched his lunch,' she informed Deborah, with a sorrowful shake of her head. 'I can see the news Mr Travers brought you came as quite a shock.'

After only a moment's hesitation, Robert swung his legs off the bed and joined Deborah at the table.

She noticed that all the food which had been brought had been prepared so that her husband could eat it without assistance. Even the cold mutton pie had been cut into tiny squares. There would be no need to ring for Linney and have him hovering over them while they ate. She felt some of the tension ease from her shoulders.

Mrs Farrell only departed when she saw they were both making inroads into their light meal.

'She seems quite determined to mother us,'

said Robert, jerking his head in the direction of the doorway through which their housekeeper had just gone.

Instead of making the riposte that his own man-servant was not exactly a typical valet, she pondered over something Mrs Farrell had said, which had puzzled her.

'Did Mr Travers not bring the news you expected? Are you very disappointed?' She was not surprised the supposed fortune was not what Robert had hoped for. The house was modest in its dimensions. And from what she had seen, the grounds were only capable of providing the kitchen with the barest essentials. 'I beg your pardon,' she added hastily, at the stony expression on her husband's face. 'I did not mean to pry….'

'No, not at all,' he said, eyeing her keenly. It had not occurred to him, until this very moment, that she had no idea of the size of the fortune that would transform their lives for ever.

He could no longer attribute her enthusiastic participation in their sexual athletics in his study to a desire to pander to her suddenly wealthy husband, in anticipation of the rewards he would shower on her for showing him such generosity.

'I never did get round to telling you what Travers told me, did I?' he mused.

If he had been thinking logically, he would have known that if avarice had prompted her spectacular departure from propriety, she would not have flounced off in such a huff afterwards. He might have been able to eat his lunch, instead of pushing the food around the plate morosely, wondering why he was so disappointed at receiving further proof Deborah was no different from any other woman.

'When that was the whole purpose of asking you to join me in the office. We got…distracted, did we not?'

She looked away, quickly, rolling a piece of bread and butter between her fingers into a doughy ball.

He popped a piece of mutton pie into his mouth, recognising her action as a symptom of acute embarrassment.

Though she had shown no embarrassment in his office. She had been just as keen to lift her skirts as he had been to get underneath them.

Until that morning, he had always thought she was a rather shy, retiring girl. And her stammered confession earlier had confirmed his belief she was also rather naïve. What on earth had come over her, then? Not two days ago she had been a virgin. This morning, she had practically ripped off his shirt in her eagerness to press herself against his naked skin.

Had she truly enjoyed her first sexual experience so much that she could not wait to repeat it? She *had* admitted to losing her head. It was only afterwards that she had felt ashamed.

Having a vicar for a father, she was bound to have had a rigidly moralistic upbringing. Did she believe that enjoying sex was sinful? Was that what it had all been about? Not money, but morals? It certainly fit with his initial assessment of his wife's character.

'Deborah,' he said gently, 'there is nothing wrong with enjoying marital relations. Don't you remember the words of the marriage service? Yes, celibacy is an honourable estate, but there are some people who just have passionate natures. You are one of them.'

She dropped the sticky ball of dough on to her plate, wishing she had the courage to tell him how wrong he was. She did not have a passionate nature. Until she had met him, she had never hankered after male attention. She could have lived her whole life without ever marrying, and been content. It was meeting Robert that had changed everything. Because she had fallen in love with him!

When he was not with her, she had only to think of him to turn shivery with longing. When she saw him, she always yearned for his touch. And when he did touch her, she stopped thinking of herself as a practical, plain spinster, whom no man would look at twice. She became Captain Fawley's woman, her heart beating with such passion it swept everything away but her body's insistent clamour to merge completely with him.

But he did not want to hear her speak about anything to do with the emotions. No romantic nonsense for him! She turned to stare bleakly out of the bedroom window.

'You don't need to be ashamed of the way you are,' he persisted. 'I, for one, am very glad of it.'

She was shocked when a little dart of pleasure shot through her.

He reached across the table, capturing her chin in his hand, and turned her face towards his. Looking deep into her eyes, he said, 'Do you have any idea what it did for me, to have you clawing at my back, urging me on, while I pushed up your skirts?'

'Robert, please, don't…' How could he like the idea she could behave like that, without knowing it was because she loved him? She tried to avert her head, but his grip on her chin was too strong.

'No, Deborah, it is too late to pretend you don't enjoy my attentions. Why should you even wish to?' He relaxed his hold, so that his fingers only framed her face. 'We are man and wife, now. I never thought,' he said, his hand stroking her face gently, now that she had ceased trying to avert her gaze, 'that I could...' He halted, on the brink of confessing he had once feared he would never fully recover his manhood. He had accepted the fact that even if he ever did regain his natural urges, any encounters would be brutish, brief, and confined to the kind of dark dens where money exchanged hands. To have this lovely woman kissing his face as though there were nothing wrong with it, exploding into rapture while he took his pleasure in her, was more than he could ever have dreamed of. That, he suddenly saw, was why he had been so disappointed to think she had been motivated by avarice, had perhaps even faked her response.

He shook his head. He had met this woman only a few weeks ago, had been intimate with her for a matter of days. He was not about to bare his soul when he had not the least idea what motivated her.

So he leaned across the table and kissed her instead.

For a fleeting moment, she wondered if she ought to put up some resistance. But it was only the last dying gasp of her rapidly withering pride. He wanted her, and even if it was only in a physical sense, even if this was the only way he would ever want her, she would not deny him. Besides, she wanted him too. She would be a hypocrite to pretend otherwise when just the merest brush of his lips on hers reduced her to a quivering mass of longing.

She sighed into his mouth, winding her arms round his neck. It was all the encouragement he needed. Getting to his feet, he dragged her upright, and pulled her hard against him. He wondered, after what had happened this morning, if her conscience would make her fight her own inclinations. But far from struggling away, she pressed herself up against him, her breath coming in needy little gasps.

'Bed,' he said firmly, in between kisses. He did not break contact with her for more than the second necessary to grate that one word as he backed her away from the table.

She felt her knees hit the edge of the mattress,

and then they fell together in an ungainly tangle of limbs. Clinging to her resolve to concentrate on his needs, she asked, 'Don't you need Linney?'

'Not until later,' he growled, raising himself to tug at the laces to her gown. He pulled her bodice down, growled, 'Much later,' and lowered his head to suckle at her breasts through the material of her chemise.

'These buttons would not dig into you so if you were to undo them,' he said, a little later.

She felt a sense of jubilation at this invitation to remove his jacket. She knelt up on the bed beside him when he sat up to facilitate the procedure. It would not have been at all hard to push the sleeves down his arms, since he was not in the habit of wearing his false hand when they were at home, if he had not been kissing her neck all the while.

'Now your shirt?' she asked, still hesitant to proceed without his full agreement. Once she had bared his upper body, he would not be able to hide the scarring she had glimpsed down the left side of his chest. When he nodded, she felt honoured that he was permitting her to do something so intimate for him. It was a simple matter to unlace his shirt, and pull it over his head. But, terrified of shattering his trust at such a crucial moment, she kept her eyes averted from the stump of his left arm, bending swiftly to kiss his mouth, as soon as she had flung the shirt to the floor.

Freed of this barrier of clothing, Robert rolled her beneath him, taking back control. Gripping the neckline of her chemise between his teeth, he bunched the delicate fabric in his fingers, and ripped it away from her breasts. It may have been his inability to deal with tricky fastenings that had him tearing her clothing, but oh, it felt wickedly exciting! She writhed ecstatically beneath him as he licked, and nipped with his teeth, and suckled at her, her hands sweeping the breadth of his back.

Her legs felt trapped by her skirts. She wanted to be able to spread her thighs, so that he could settle between them. As though he had read her mind, he solved their mutual difficulty by reaching down and ripping the flimsy muslin from ankle to her waist. For a split second, she regretted the ruination of the one gown she had brought with her, but then she recalled his stated intention to keep her naked, in bed, for an unspecified amount of time, and a sensuous thrill swept all her practical concerns away.

He could not fully remove his breeches. He had been lying on the covers fully clothed when she had come in. His boots, she thought fleetingly, as between them they frantically tore away the last barriers of fabric, were going to ruin the quilt. But then they were one, and her capacity for rational thought ceased. She loved him, oh, how she loved him. And to feel him filling her, embracing her, needing her in this way, stoked her own need to fever pitch.

But afterwards, as they lay side by side, amidst the tangle of ruined clothing, the doubts and fears crept slowly back. He had only to kiss her, and she lost her head. How was she going to explain to Mrs Farrell just how they had managed to get boot blacking all over the beautiful white quilt? And it was all very well saying she did not need clothes, but that was nonsense. She supposed she could borrow one of her husband's shirts, she reflected, chewing at her lower lip. Or send a maid to fetch one of Miss Lampton's shapeless gowns for the moments when she simply would have to leave the bedroom….

'Stop it,' Robert growled.

'What? Stop what?'

'Thinking. You are growing as tense as a board.'

He tugged her up against his side, dropping a kiss on to the crown of her head.

Bother the quilt, she thought, snuggling into his side and draping her arm about his waist. And bother the servants too. They can think what they like. *So long as Robert wants me here in bed, he shall have me.*

And with a smile playing about her lips, she slipped into a deliciously restful sleep.

Robert shifted slightly, so that he could look down at her. Her head rested upon his scarred shoulder, her hair flowing over his mangled arm like a sheet of softest silk. Something stirred in his chest at the sight of her gleaming perfection curled up trustingly against his battered body.

It was not tenderness.

It was not!

It was the warm glow that sometimes came over a man after such a satisfying sexual encounter. And—naturally he felt particularly pleased at the way things were working out. He had feared he might never have a willing woman in his bed again. Not only was Deborah willing, but she could rouse him to a state where he could perform twice in one day!

Naturally he got a warm feeling when he looked down at her lying in his arms. She had given him much to be thankful for.

* * *

And over the next two weeks, he decided that asking Deborah to be his wife had been an inspired choice. She seemed to have taken on board his assurance that it was not a sin for married people to enjoy sex. Though she never instigated it, she always responded enthusiastically to his overtures. Once, she had even made him laugh, tilting her head to one side, tapping her finger thoughtfully against her chin, saying, 'It is as well I am of such a practical nature. And that I care little what becomes of my clothing.' For despite him saying they had best restrict any amorous interludes to the bedroom, he soon discovered there was nowhere they could not make love, in spite of his disability, if she put her mind to it.

She was a marvel.

He looked at her across the width of the dining table, admiring the way the candle-light brought out the rich chestnut tones in her hair, and wondered how he had ever existed before she came into his life.

The thought was like being doused with a bucket of cold water. He had only planned to spend a week at The Dovecote, at the most, just long enough to take possession and look over the place. His one driving ambition had been to return to London, and flaunt his wealth in Percy Lampton's face. But she had put all his plans out of his head. They had been here over a fortnight, and all he had done was establish that there was nowhere a disabled man could not have sex, if his partner was determined enough.

Laying down his wineglass with a snap, he glared at her.

'We have dallied here long enough. Tomorrow, we must return to London.'

His grim face and curt tone cut Deborah to the quick. She had, she suddenly saw, allowed herself to hope that his attentions over the past two weeks had meant he was growing fond of her. But that one word, dallied, was like a sharp frost, blighting tender shoots that had been fooled into premature growth by a few unseasonably warm days. Dallying was what a man did with a kitchen maid. Not their own May, of course, since any man foolish enough to try dallying with her would likely receive a frying pan to the skull for his temerity.

She bowed her head over her plate, forcing herself to continue cutting up her pigeon as though his remark had not just shrivelled her burgeoning happiness to a stalk.

Carefully wiping the meat through the sauce, she placed it in her mouth, chewing slowly while she tried to muster some response that would not sound as though she were a petulant child. Robert had never offered her affection. It would be foolish of her to distance him by complaining that he hurt her when he dismissed their physical intimacy as exactly that. Merely physical. She would always treasure the memory of the two weeks they had spent here. They had acted just like real lovers, unable to keep their hands off each other. Even if it had meant so little to her husband, to her it had been a real honeymoon. She would allow no cross words, no petty accusations to taint this magical time.

'I shall be glad to see my mother again,' she eventually managed. 'I have been a little concerned that she has not written to me. Nor has Susannah. They must have the address,' she continued, 'because they sent my trunk here.' Her brief fears that she would have to wander about the house clad in only her husband's shirt had proved groundless. The very day after they had ruined Miss Lampton's pristine white quilt, a carrier had turned up at the door with her possessions.

Captain Fawley's frown deepened. He suspected that if Lampton was running true to form, he would have ditched Miss Hullworthy the minute he heard about Deborah's wedding, leaving her prey to malicious gossip. Mrs Gillies would not wish to blight her daughter's honeymoon with that kind of news. He was only surprised Miss Hullworthy had not written to tell her supposed best friend of that misfortune herself.

'I expect they had their reasons.'

'Well, I shall be able to see them both, soon, and speak to them, which will be better than getting a letter, will it not?'

It comforted her to speak of her mother and her friend, she reflected. She really would be glad to see them both again. Perhaps her mother would be able to offer her some words of wisdom, even if all she did was listen while Deborah poured out her heart. It would help her to cope with this unequal marriage.

'I should like to make an early start,' said Robert, his eyes snapping a challenge.

He expected her to make a fuss, she could see. Complain that he had not given her enough notice, and that she needed time to pack. Laying her napkin down beside her plate, she rose to her feet with a sad smile.

'Then we should have an early night.'

Their last night in the house where she had been so blindly happy. Tomorrow, they would return to London, and she had the horrible feeling that it would be a return to real life. In London, she would discover what marriage to her really meant to her husband.

If it meant anything at all.

Their coach drew up outside the front steps of Walton House late the following afternoon.

'We will live in the rooms my brother set aside for my use to begin with,' Robert had explained on the journey up from Berkshire. 'Though I should like to begin searching for our own house at once. Do you have any preferences?'

'I?' Deborah had been startled when he had asked for her input. She had assumed he would just do as he pleased, and ride roughshod over any objections she might raise.

'Yes, you. It will be your home too. And don't forget, money is no longer an object. Miss Lampton left me an enormous fortune.' Then he frowned, remembering they had still not discussed anything that really mattered. Whenever they had been alone, talking had been the last thing on either of their minds. He had no more idea of what went on behind those languorous brown eyes than he had on their wedding day. She had fascinated him, dazzled and distracted him with her eagerness to participate in lovemaking. Physically, yes, they were as intimate as it was possible for two people to be.

But he did not really know her.

'My wealth exists in the form of shares in various enterprises. You may reside at as fashionable an address as you wish.'

'I…I had not given it any thought,' she admitted.

Robert had scowled at her, as though her remark displeased him. But all he had said was, 'Perhaps we should get an agent to scout about for us and let us know what is on the market before making any decisions.'

'Very well.'

'And in the meantime, you will open accounts at dressmakers, milliners and so forth. Lady Walton will be only too pleased to guide you, I dare say. She always looks bang up to the knocker.'

And I do not, she thought, battling yet another wave of hurt. He had told her once before that he wanted her to look fashionable. Like Lady Walton. His dear friend, she thought, her lips compressing in irritation. The woman he had confided so much in, when he did not trust her as far as he could throw her. He did not even trust her enough to purchase her own clothes. He wanted another woman to watch over her, and make sure she did not go about looking like a provincial dowdy any more.

An impressive-looking footman, in blue-and-silver livery, bowed them into the house when Linney knocked on the door. Robert just stalked across the hall, opened an inner door, and said, over his shoulder, 'If you have any complaints about the accommodations, I don't want to hear them. We will only be here until you choose our new address.' With that, he just disappeared through the doorway, leaving her floundering in the hall.

To her surprise, it was Linney who came to her rescue.

'Don't pay no attention, madam. He's always like this when his leg's giving him pain. And long journeys in a carriage near always jolt him up. I hope one of the first things you will persuade him to buy, now he's got so much money, is a really well-sprung coach. So he won't go hiring no more of them bone-rattlers no more.'

'Thank you, Linney,' she said, though she did not know why on earth he would think she might have any influence over her irascible spouse.

She trailed across the hall, pausing on the threshold to her husband's domain to see why he should think she might not like the rooms.

She was looking at a sitting room. A very masculine room, she had to admit, with large, leather sofas and chairs dotted about a floor that had not seen polish for some time. Robert was sprawled upon one of the sofas that flanked an empty fireplace, a crystal tumbler of spirits already clutched in his hand, leading her to suppose that Linney's assumption had been correct.

'Through here is the bedroom, madam,' Linney said, opening a door to the right of the fireplace. She peeped inside. Again, it was a very masculine room, with a solid-looking oak bed, heavy furniture and bare floorboards throughout. The washstand, she noted with some misgiving, was placed beside the wardrobe. She would have no privacy, unless she evicted her husband from his own bed every morning. The logistics, as Robert had once put it, would be somewhat tricky. There was a truckle bed just protruding from under the main bed, upon which she guessed Linney had used to sleep. Eyeing it, he leaned towards her, murmuring, 'I will move to rooms along with the rest of the staff here, madam. He won't be needing me the same, not now he's got you. And if he gets into any difficulties, you will only have to ring, and I can be down here in a trice.

'This here is the door that leads to the mews,' he continued, in a louder voice, indicating a door tucked into a far corner of the sitting room.

'My wife will use the front door of Walton House, not skulk in at the back as though she were some kind of miscreant,' Robert growled from the sofa.

'Do many miscreants come in at the back, then?' she asked, taking a seat on the sofa opposite her husband and pulling off her gloves. If she did not manage to lighten the atmosphere, she was afraid she might burst into tears.

'One or two,' he growled, draining the glass and letting his head fall against the sofa back, though he kept his eyes fixed on her.

'What a very interesting life you must have led before you married me. I hope I am not cramping your style?'

'We had best keep that door locked, now you are in residence,' he said, ignoring her attempt at humour. 'All the miscreants I know must come in through the front door, from now on. See to it, Linney, would you?'

She untied her bonnet, and laid it upon the cushion beside her.

'May I fetch you some refreshment?' said Linney.

While Linney played the host, her husband simply lay there glaring at her.

'Thank you. What is there?'

'Only strong liquor or ale down here. But I dare say that, if I was to ask, Lord Walton's staff could rustle you up some tea and such.'

'Thank you, Linney. That would be welcome.'

With a nod, and an affable smile, the manservant left the room.

She fiddled with the ribbons of her bonnet, wondering if there was any topic she might safely broach without getting her head bitten off.

'Well?' he snapped. 'Can you live in two rooms that have been set up for the purpose of making life easy for a cripple?'

And then it hit her why the floorboards were bare, and unpolished. No rugs, or slippery surfaces to trip him while he had been learning to walk first with a crutch, and, later, his false leg. No need to climb the front steps, should he wish to go out. The way to the mews was probably all on a level. No little tables, that he might bump into in here, either, she noticed for the first time.

Only a sturdy desk, under the window, with two upright chairs beside it that informed her it doubled as a dining table. She remembered the handrail beside the bed, where she would have expected a night table to stand. The extra-broad steps placed to make it easy to get into, and out of, that bed. Nothing in itself had been remarkable enough to draw notice, but, put together, they clearly spoke of his disability. And he hated her seeing it.

'It looks like any other set of bachelor's rooms, I would imagine,' she said, with a slight shrug. 'Why should I object to any of it? After all…' she shot him a look from under her lashes '…I never heard you complain about all those feminine frills that dominated the decorations at The Dovecote.'

'Hmm,' he said, looking at her through narrowed eyes. 'You have a knack of making the best of things, haven't you?' His lips twisted into a sneer. 'You would no doubt have resorted to quoting some uplifting portion of scripture to get you through the days if you had become a teacher.'

She flinched at the bitterness in his tone. And felt heartily relieved when Linney returned, saving her the necessity of having to make any reply.

'Lady Walton has heard you have returned, and

wonders if you would like to take refreshments in her sitting room? She wants to discuss the ball.'

'Ball?' said Deborah.

'Hell and damnation!' said Robert. 'I had forgotten all about the wretched ball.' Sitting up, he wearily rubbed his hand across his face. How could he have forgotten the ball he had arranged to hold here, in Walton House? It had all been part of his plan to flaunt his victory in Percy Lampton's face. And his brother had been equally as keen to do his part.

'It will be a public demonstration of our family solidarity,' Charles had said. 'A way of silencing the disgraceful rumours regarding your birth once and for all. Though how they got away with it for so long beats me. Anyone who has ever been in the portrait gallery at Wycke would see at once you are more of a Fawley than I am!'

'I suspect the circumstances surrounding my marriage will cause far more gossip than will be silenced by one ball,' he had countered.

The Earl had smiled coldly. 'But it will serve to separate the sheep from the goats.'

Society would be polarised between those who wished to retain the Earl's good graces, and those who supported the Lamptons. Lord Lensborough would stand buff, he was sure, and he was not without influence. His presence would assure his and his wife's acceptance amongst his own coterie. His true friends, comrades from his regiment, would stick by him no matter what. And as for what the rest of society thought, well, he did not give a rap! The Lamptons would no doubt spread tales of him being a usurper, who had gained his fortune by deceit and trickery. But he was used to their malice. So far as they were concerned, he had always been the cuckoo in the nest.

He had been looking forward to launching himself into the polite society that had always excluded him, thanks to the Lamptons' lies. Yet one night in Deborah's bed had put all thought of it clean out of his head.

He glared at her. 'The ball to celebrate our marriage is to be held two weeks' Friday. You had better go and find out what arrangements Lady Walton has made. And offer what belated help you can. She should not have to do all the work, not in her condition.'

She felt a peculiar shrinking sensation in her stomach. He was chastising her for not organising a ball she'd had no idea was being held.

'Well, get on with it!' Robert barked, when she

had sat frozen on the sofa staring at him in silence for several seconds. 'But don't expect tea up there. Heloise won't touch the stuff.'

'Are you not coming?'

'Absolutely not!' What did he know about arranging a ball? It was women's business. They would enjoy it, no doubt—women seemed to. And it would be a good opportunity for Deborah to get to know Heloise better. The countess had few close friends, but she had already taken to his wife, for some reason that eluded him.

'All I want is my bed. And some peace.' He needed to remove his false leg. He had been wearing it for longer and longer periods, and it was chafing almost unbearably. This was the price he had to pay for indulging in vanity. He had not wanted his wife to see him hobbling about the place on his crutches. And he had left off having Linney in each night, to rub on the ointment that might have soothed the stump, because Deborah did not like having a servant intrude in their bedroom.

Rather stiffly, Deborah got to her feet and stumbled to the door. He wanted some peace. In other words, she was irritating him. This was why he had suddenly decided to come back to London. Not only was he was tired of the dalliance, but he wanted his life to go back to the way it had been. He could not have told her more clearly that, if it had not been for the inheritance, he would as soon have not married her at all.

Chapter Ten

Susannah had been quite right. The Countess of Walton was a useful person to know. Modistes, milliners, haberdashers—they all fell over themselves to serve such an exalted personage. Even with the Season being in full swing, and all the best dressmakers working flat out to meet the demands of their fashionable customers, they assured the Countess that her friend would have a fabulous creation ready in time for her ball.

The Countess picked out an underskirt of pink. Since it suited Deborah's dark colouring, she saw no sense in raising any objections, especially since she was sure that, had she come alone, this particular modiste would have shown her the door. She did demur over the level of the neckline, but both the modiste and the Countess insisted she would not look fashionable if she had an extra inch of lace added to preserve her modesty. Since Robert had stipulated he wanted her to look fashionable, she ended up agreeing to purchase a garment that she felt was little more than a strip of ribbon bound round her nipples, from which quantities of spangled gauze cascaded as insubstantially as a waterfall.

While the seamstresses set to work on it, Robert accepted an invitation to an informal card party at the house of one Captain Samuels, and an evening at the opera with the Earl and Countess.

'My friends won't care what you look like,' he bluntly informed her. 'So it won't matter if none of your new gowns are ready. And I thought that sparkly thing you had on at Lensborough's ball would do nicely for the opera. Just be sure to get a cloak to wear over it. That should not be too difficult, should it?'

'Not at all,' she had replied, baring her teeth in a polite smile. Not even a clueless, provincial vicar's daughter could fail to get her hands on an opera cloak with two full days' warning. She could borrow Susannah's, at a pinch.

She managed to enjoy herself eventually, at Captain Samuels's party, though the angular, sandy-haired officer greeted her with a sort of bluff camaraderie that was quite outside her experience. It took her a little while to work out that all the gentlemen present now regarded her as a fellow officer's wife and accepted her into their midst as an extension of Robert.

The evening at the opera was more unsettling still. Whenever the Earl introduced her to anyone as his sister-in-law, they began looking at her as though she was someone worthy of respect. Not at all as people had looked on plain Miss Deborah Gillies. Of course, she was not Miss Gillies any more. Not now she was married. Though just who she was, she was not yet quite sure.

It dawned on her that it was a miracle she had ever met Robert at all. He moved in completely different social circles from what she was used to. In fact, if he had not been so doggedly determined in his pursuit of Susannah…

No, she would not allow her thoughts to stray in that direction. She would *not* allow jealousy to rear its ugly head.

Besides, nobody could feel jealous of poor Susannah at the moment. She was quite wretchedly miserable.

For Percy Lampton had not been near her since

the day the notice of Captain Fawley's marriage had appeared in the *Morning Post*.

'I was not unduly concerned at first,' Mrs Gillies had confided in her, when Deborah called, the morning after her return to London. 'Any number of matters could have prevented him from taking Susannah on those daily outings to Hyde Park. But then I began to hear whispers that he was actively avoiding any gatherings where he might run the risk of meeting her again. There is always someone malicious enough to relay that kind of rumour! I do not know what to do with her.' She sighed, then continued, 'If it was you, I could tell you to hold your head up, and weather it out. But Susannah does not have so much backbone. She will *droop* around the ballrooms once she discovers Mr Lampton is not there. Which, of course, is *fatal*.'

For a moment or two, Deborah had wondered if she should explain exactly what Percy Lampton had been up to. Only, she wasn't sure if knowing he had only toyed with her to lure her away from Robert because of their long-standing feud, would make everything worse. Believing he had just been indulging in a casual flirtation was hurting her badly enough. Oh, it made her blood boil to think of the way he had led her friend on!

'A lady should *never* wear her heart on her sleeve.' Her mother had shaken her head disapprovingly. 'Why, you would not let the world see your heart was broken, if you loved some man who did not return your regard, would you? She has ruined any chances she might have had amongst my own acquaintance. I do not know what to do with her. If she cannot pull herself together, I shall have to take her home. And then it will be even worse for her next Season. She will have destroyed any illusion that she could pass for a lady of quality! But anyway, enough of that.' She had folded her hands in her lap, as though closing the topic.

'I must say it is good to see you looking so well, my dear. The break in the country has done you the world of good.'

Deborah bade farewell to any hope of confiding in her mother then, for Susannah came drifting into the drawing room. With a determined smile, she launched into a description of The Dovecote. By the time she had recounted the peculiarities of the staffing, Susannah was beginning to look interested. Though she flinched the first time Deborah mentioned the name of Lampton, she did seem to find that lady's history and eccentricities quite diverting. Deborah felt that, on the whole, her visit had lifted her friend's spirits, though she wished she could have done more.

It had been several nights later that she realised there was one way, at least, in which she could help her friend. And it was Mrs Samuels who showed her the way.

'We are going on a picnic on Wednesday,' she said over her shoulder, while leaning over the edge of the box where they were taking supper at Vauxhall Gardens. 'The lads are going to row us upriver till we get to green fields. We will be taking two boats, at least. I expect it will degenerate into a race, with neither team wanting to concede until we end up at Windsor!' She laughed. 'Do say you will come. It will be tremendous fun. The Countess used to come on some of our jaunts, before that Friday-faced husband of hers put his foot down. She always used to enjoy herself immensely!'

Score one more point to the Countess of Walton, thought Deborah resentfully.

Mrs Samuels, seeing Deborah's reluctance, gave up trying to attract the attention of a particular friend she had seen disappearing down one of the dimly lit paths, and sat back down next to her.

'I realise you might find our set a little overwhelming at first, without your husband,' she said in a reassuring tone. 'Look, why don't you bring a friend along, to help you keep that pack of ruffians at bay?'

She tilted her head to where several of their party were frisking about a pair of strolling beauties across the lamplit lawn, like a pack of springer spaniels. She would have been mortified to have been the focus of such boisterous attention, but the beauties were lapping it up. And when one of them dropped her haughty pose of indifference to giggle, causing the young officers to set up a rousing chorus of cheers, it came to her in a flash that this was exactly the kind of diversion Susannah needed. Oh, not that she would get over Lampton's defection all at once. But receiving the adulation of a fresh set of admirers might at least halt her downward slide.

'Thank you,' she smiled. 'I should like that.'

It was only as she was on her way home that she wondered why the woman had assumed Robert would not come with her. Had he asked Mrs Samuels to take her off his hands? Though it was not as if they saw all that much of each other these days. Life in London was such a whirl. With her having a ball to organise, and Robert being tied up with all sorts of business men in connection with the settling of his new fortune, as well as visits to his tailors and so forth, they only seemed to meet up at mealtimes. Their conversation consisted of relaying their daily schedule, and discussing which invitations to accept.

'Though before long, I don't expect our social lives will coincide much at all,' he had once said, sending a chill down her spine.

Had that been his subtle way of saying he did not want her hanging on his sleeve in public all the time? Until Mrs Samuels's invitation, she had been trying to laugh off her ridiculous sense of foreboding. Why, Robert did not know how to be subtle. If he had anything to say, he would say it straight out!

Surely?

She shook her head. She knew she was unbearably sensitive where her husband's moods were concerned. She was probably reading too much into his words.

But as to this picnic…oh, she would love to get beyond the noisy, crowded city streets for one day, and breathe fresh country air for a while.

And she *would* invite Susannah to come along. Especially since Robert was not, apparently, going to form one of the party. She did not suppose for a minute that Susannah would find it awkward to run into Robert again, but he certainly would.

Her shoulders slumped as she climbed the front steps to Walton House. She couldn't help feeling that if it were Susannah who had married him, he would have escorted her everywhere, proudly showing her off. As it was, he stood stiffly beside Deborah, at the few events they had so far attended as a couple, snapping curt responses to the fulsome congratulations he had received from his military friends. While she did not expect him to look at her with pride, or affection, like some of the other officers did at their wives, could he not at the very least try to look as though he was content with her? That was not too much to ask, when in public, was it?

She went to the multi-purpose table under the window and pulled open a drawer to extract some writing paper. She would invite Susannah to the picnic, and send the letter via one of Lord Walton's footmen. Lady Walton had airily told her she must consider them all at her disposal, until Robert hired more servants of their own. She grinned, flicking the end of the quill under her chin as she envisioned Susannah's face lighting up when a liveried footman of a belted earl delivered a note to her door. And the vicarious thrill her parents would get, when she wrote to tell them that little snippet of news.

From the shadowy bed, where Robert had been reclining, he saw the mischievous smile that lit her face with a feeling of deep unease. She had looked dispirited on entering. He had always known marrying him would not be a sinecure for any woman. But Deborah normally bore it with the fortitude that carried her through whatever life threw in her path. That grin though, as she penned a letter…

He grimaced in pain, though for the first time since returning from Berkshire, it was not on account of his leg. He had paid a heavy price for the bliss he had known in Deborah's arms, for the first few days of his return to London. The devil of it was that it was usually his foot that hurt the most. It was an eerie feeling, to wake with the burning need to fling off the agonising weight of the bedcovers, only to remember that the foot which hurt so abominably was actually lying on some dung heap in Spain.

No, the spasm of pain that had him rearing up off the bed was not a physical one. It was jealousy. Raw and scalding. He felt its sting every time some fellow congratulated him on his marriage, running appreciative eyes over his lovely young bride. For she was lovely. She had a healthy glow about her that had been lacking when they first met. Two weeks in the country had put flesh on her bones, and brought colour to her cheeks.

But the sparkle in her eye, as she received the compliments of his fellow officers, chilled him. She would lower her head, and look up coyly through her lashes at men he had considered his friends, and blush receptively at their frankly lecherous looks. He wished he had not taken such pains to ensure her pleasure in the marriage bed. He wished he had been brutish, and swift and made it such an ordeal she would shudder with revulsion at the prospect of a man's touch. He had thought sexual pleasure was the one thing he could give her, in return for all she had given him. But it had been a grave error. Now he had awoken that side of her nature, there would evidently be no stopping her.

She must have heard him moving about in the bedroom, for she looked up from her missive, a troubled frown appearing on her face. It did not escape his notice that she shoved the half-finished letter furtively into a drawer.

He leaned against the doorjamb, feeling unutterably weary. What did a man do in such situations? Demand she tell him who she was writing to? Forbid her to have anything to do with any other man?

Why should it bother him, anyway? he thought, slouching across to the well-stocked sideboard. He had gone into marriage knowing no woman could stand him. Deborah had tried, he had to give her that. But when it came down to it, of course she would prefer the company of a man who was whole, and handsome and given to dishing out the kind of complimentary claptrap all females lapped up like cats at the cream.

She frowned when she saw him slump on to the sofa, a large tumbler of brandy in his hand.

'Is your leg giving you pain?'

'No,' he snarled, tossing back half the drink in one go.

From the way he was glaring at her, Deborah suspected he wanted to say that she was the one driving him to drink. Suddenly, she decided she would go and visit Susannah in person. Reaching into the drawer, she took the crumpled letter and stuffed it into her reticule. She did not want to leave it lying around for Robert to find.

'Where are you going?' Robert asked as she set her hand to the door.

She did not wish to hurt him any further, when he was already in such low spirits, by mentioning the woman he had wanted to marry.

'To visit a friend,' she replied, hastily escaping through the door.

A friend. He downed the rest of the drink in one great gulp, and tossed the empty glass among the cushions.

If he were a whole man, he could scotch her schemes by offering to escort her. Or maybe even follow her. Though what good would that do? If he prevented her from embarking on an affair now, it would only postpone the inevitable. Women were fickle creatures. No constancy in them. He had always known that.

So why did it hurt so damn much, knowing Deborah was just like all the rest?

Deborah had sent one of the footmen to procure a cab. She planned to go and collect Susannah in it, rather than have her come to Walton House, and risk her running into Robert. Then they would go down to the landing stage to join up with the rest of the party.

'You are looking decidedly fetching this morning,' Robert remarked gravely as she tied the ribbons of a new chip straw bonnet in a jaunty bow under her left ear.

'Why, thank you!' She felt ridiculously pleased by this compliment. He gave her so few. It made them all the more precious, because she knew that when he uttered one, he meant it, not like some men who spouted such stuff almost out of habit.

'Going somewhere special?'

'For a picnic, with Mrs Samuels, Captain Samuel's wife, and some of his friends. We are taking a couple of launches up the river.'

'It is a fine day for it,' he remarked, glancing out of the window. 'Perhaps I shall come with you.' There was no mistaking the consternation his statement created in Deborah's breast. And it decided him. He jolly well would go with her, and find out which one of his so-called friends was sniffing round her skirts. 'An outing with Sammy's crowd may be just what I need to shake off these blue-devils.'

Deborah's heart sank. But while she struggled to find a way to gently explain that he might rather not come, because of Susannah, he had turned on his heel, saying curtly, 'I shall fetch my hat.'

Linney sat bolt upright, a concerned expression on his face.

'Should I—?'

'No! No need for you to tag along,' he snapped. 'Take the day off. I shall be among friends.' He did not want Linney to know, quite yet, what Deborah was up to.

'If you are sure…?' he began doubtfully, glancing at Deborah.

Deborah gave him an encouraging nod, as her husband disappeared into his room to fetch his hat, and a brand-new ebony cane with a chased silver handle.

'For getting into and out of the boat,' he explained. 'I told you I would not need you, Linney. For even if I should slip and fall into the water, there will be half a dozen muscular young chaps ready to haul me out.'

Suddenly, Deborah understood why Mrs Samuels had assumed he would not be going on such an excursion. Why could she never remember he was not in top physical form?

It was not until they had got into the cab that she rather haltingly confessed she was going to collect Susannah.

He made no verbal response, but she could tell

by the tightening of his lips that he was not looking forward to coming face to face with the woman he had loved and lost.

'I will come in and pay my respects to your mother,' he said when the cab drew to a halt outside the rented house. 'It was remiss of me not to have performed that duty sooner.'

'I am sure she understands completely,' said Deborah sympathetically, when his frown deepened. Her mother had felt so sorry for him when Susannah had turned to Percy Lampton.

'She could have called on us,' he reflected, as he descended from the cab. 'Have you said anything to make her suspect she might not be welcome?'

Rather taken aback, Deborah said, 'Of course not! If you must know…' she took a deep breath, steeling herself to be the one to break it to him '…Susannah is taking Mr Lampton's defection extremely hard. She barely goes out, and, when she does, she *droops* apparently. And my mother does not like to leave her in the house on her own.'

Captain Fawley flinched. 'I should have thought she would think herself well rid of that toad.'

'Well, she does not. I think she really l—'

She could not tell her husband Susannah had

fallen in love with his worst enemy. He already had quite enough to contend with.

She tried to keep a smile pasted to her face while her husband paid the formalities to her mother. She wished now she had warned him exactly what her plans had been at the outset, so that he need not have come. He could hardly withdraw now.

She felt so guilty for having put him in such an awkward position. He was plainly so uncomfortable at being cooped up in the hired cab with both the woman he loved and the woman he had married, that her own insides began to churn in sympathy.

By the time they reached the wharf, though, it had become plain that he had mastered his own roiling emotions, and compressed them into an iron-hard resentment, which he aimed directly at her. And then, later, at the young officers who dared to flirt with Susannah.

Deborah had no defence against the piercingly sharp glances he continually darted in her direction. She did not even try. She felt she deserved his contempt for forcing him into this excruciatingly painful position. From the moment a pair of his robustly healthy comrades handed him into the

boat with the same tender concern they had shown
the ladies, she wanted to curl up and weep.

Susannah sat across the thwarts from him,
twirling her parasol, completely oblivious to the
pain that racked him every time one of the shirt-
sleeved oarsmen coaxed a smile to her lips, while
Deborah's conscience smote her afresh, every
time she glimpsed him moodily repelling all
attempts to draw him away from the fringes of the
rest of the day's activities.

She was relieved when at long last, they deposited Susannah back at her house, and his ordeal
was at an end. She was not surprised that he did
not speak a single word to her in the carriage
home. His embittered look said it all. By keeping
him in the dark about her plans to help Susannah
get over her heartbreak, she had caused more for
him. He had been obliged to watch her gradually
unfurl and blossom like a bud under the adulation
of his peers, while Susannah had not spared him
one glance.

He slammed the door of their rooms shut with
unnecessary force, striding across to where she
was removing her bonnet and spinning her round
by her upper arm.

'You are my wife, damn it!' he growled.

Oh, yes, and how he must wish she was not. Especially when he'd had all day to compare what he had wanted, with what he had ended up with. Tears sprang to her eyes, even though she knew the last thing he wanted from her was sympathy. Indeed, even as she opened her mouth to speak her heartfelt apology for making this day such hell for him, he brought his lips crashing down on hers, silencing her in a kiss that spoke of loss and anger.

Though she fully accepted he could not help being angry, at length she had to try to break away from his determined possession of her mouth. She could hardly breathe. Her head was beginning to spin.

It took him a moment or two to realise she was struggling, but as soon as he did, he broke away, to glare down at her with all the resentment that had been growing steadily throughout the day, blazing from his eyes.

'Oh, Robert,' she gasped, raising her hand to his cheek.

He caught it before it reached the puckered skin, his grip on her wrist bruising.

And before she knew it, he had tugged her into the bedroom and pulled her down on to the bed beside him.

Her heart soared as he kissed her more passionately than he had ever done before.

But then he closed his eyes as he pushed up her skirts. Buried his face in her neck as he freed himself from his breeches. And as he entered her with no further preliminaries, he gave a groan that reminded her it was not passion driving him, but pain. Pain that Susannah had caused. Oh, he might be seeking solace in her body, but *she* was not the one who had wrought him to this pitch.

A sob welled up and shook its passage through her throat as she did the only thing she could do for him. She wound her arms round his neck, her legs round his waist and let him pour all his grief and suffering into her, absorbing it with a shuddering desperation of her own. For even though she was convinced he was only using her, she could not stop her body responding to his wild mating as it always did. Need was soon driving them both, raw and agonising in its intensity. She pulsed around him the very second he emptied himself into her, tears flowing unchecked down her face and into her hair.

'I am not sorry,' he panted hoarsely into her ear. 'I do not care if I hurt you.'

'I know,' she whispered, letting her arms fall limp against her sides. 'But you did not hurt me.'

'No, you liked it, didn't you?' He raised himself up, looking down at her with searing contempt. 'You like it hard, and fast, like the cheap slut you are.'

He rolled off her then, flinging his arm over his face, as though he could not bear the sight of her.

She felt something inside her die. Hadn't he always assured her that he liked the fact she always responded to his advances with a passion to match? Now he was telling her it was no such thing. And it was too late to try to explain that she could not help it if she responded the way she did. He would think she was making up excuses to try to justify her behaviour, if she told him she loved him after what had just taken place.

He had taken her loving, free offering of herself, twisted it into something nasty and sordid, then flung it back in her face. She slid off the bed and staggered from the room.

But it was not far enough. She could not stay in the same house as him—no, not for one second longer.

Picking up her bonnet from the side table by the door, she let herself out quietly, and stood irresolutely on the front step for some minutes. A cab swept round the corner, disgorging its passengers outside a house three doors down.

She hurried along the pavement, intent on seeking the only sanctuary she could think of.

'Could you take me to Half Moon Street, please?' she asked the driver.

She needed her mother.

It was ridiculous to be holding this ball, thought Deborah some ten days later, to celebrate the marriage of two people who barely spoke to one another any more. She stood pale and trembling to receive her guests, beside Robert's stiff and taciturn form, though only Lady Walton seemed to have noticed anything was amiss. She had taken one look at their set faces at the dinner preceding the ball, and leaned across to whisper to her,

'The first few weeks of marriage are horrid, are they not? But once you get past all that silliness, I am sure you will be as happy as Charles and me.'

Deborah very much doubted it. Though given to extreme formality in his dealings with most people, the Earl of Walton was clearly very much in love with his wife. He revealed it in a dozen little ways. A touch of his hand to the back of her waist as he escorted her into a room, or a glance and a smile that spoke of shared thoughts.

Robert never smiled at her. Nor could he bear to

touch her any more. Not since the day of the picnic, when he had expressed his contempt for her in such a way that even she could no longer cling to any hope that he might one day grow fond of her.

He had even argued with his brother upon the subject of this ball. Though it was to be held in honour of his marriage, he saw no reason why he should be obliged to dance at it.

'Do you think I want to make a spectacle of myself capering about a slippery floor while the guests are laying side bets as to how long it will take for me to fall over?' he had snarled.

Deborah had wanted to curl up and die. He would not be raising any objection if he had married Susannah. He had begged and pleaded for a dance with her, pursuing her from one event to another. And he had not looked as though he cared in the least what Lord Lensborough's guests had said or thought, when she had finally capitulated.

'Why do you not open the ball with a waltz?' Heloise had suggested. 'Rather than a really long set of country dances?'

'Not exactly the traditional opening to a ball, but I think it would serve,' replied the Earl, looking proud of his wife's suggestion.

Robert had simmered down, his grudging agreement twisting the knife a little deeper. 'I will dance part of one waltz with my wife, and that is my limit.'

He would have walked across hot coals for Susannah, but he did not even want to perform one sedate waltz with his plain, despised wife.

Yet dancing a waltz required that she take hold of his left hand, the false hand, the very prospect of which had made Susannah squeal with disgust.

Saddened, she looked over his left shoulder as the musicians struck up the first chord, remembering the defiant tilt of his chin when Linney had buckled it on earlier before helping him on with his shirt. Like a knight, being armoured by his squire, ready to go into battle. She felt that it would have been an honour to take that hand now, and demonstrate to the world that nothing could ever come between them, if only he was not so reluctant to have her in his arms.

A fine sweat broke out on Robert's brow. Damn it, perhaps he should have just gone along with the set of country dances, and put up with the pain all that capering about would have brought to his severed limb. It could not have been worse than the agony of having so many people watching him stumbling about the floor with a woman whose face was rigid with distaste. He could hardly blame her. What they were doing was not so much dancing, as walking very carefully in time to the music. Once upon a time, he would have relished sweeping his dance partner into a spin turn at the corner of the dance floor, taking the opportunity to pull a pretty woman a little closer to his body than was strictly allowed. Now, he dreaded coming across any kind of obstacle that would require him to attempt anything more than the most basic step. Thankfully, after a few bars of excruciating embarrassment, the Earl led his wife on to the floor, Lord Lensborough followed with his, and soon, so many partners were twirling around him that he felt safe to abandon the pretext of dancing at all, and headed straight for the nearest open door.

'Thank God that's over with,' he said, letting go of Deborah's arm.

'I suppose you will be spending the rest of the evening in the card room?' she said stiffly, as he subsided on to the nearest chair. Since the picnic, this had become the pattern of the few events they had attended together. He had escorted her, introduced her to a few of his friends, then abandoned her to their care while he strolled off to watch the play.

He got to his feet, and gave her an icily polite bow before stalking away, leaving her entirely alone. On other evenings, it might have been excusable. But could he not have pretended just this once, on the night they were supposed to be celebrating their marriage, that he did not regret having done so, quite so much?

Was he deliberately trying to humiliate her?

She squared her shoulders, and raised her chin before stepping back into the ballroom. She would not let anyone know that she cared. She would not become the object of anyone's pity. And so she acted as though she was perfectly happy to dance with other gentlemen, and that she did not feel acutely distressed by the way her husband publicly shunned her. Her dance card was soon filled by Robert's friends, who jokingly commiserated with her for being shackled to such a dull dog of a husband. One or two of the Earl's political cronies, who would not have deigned to so much as nod to her when she had been Miss Gillies, seemed to feel it was appropriate to notice her at her own ball, as well.

At length, she calmed down enough to stop thinking only of herself. She knew she ought at least to make sure Susannah was coping. She had noticed her dancing with the Earl at one point, but not looking all that happy to be doing so. Now, she was nowhere in sight.

She went to the chaperons' benches, to ask her mother if she knew where she was.

'She went out on to the terrace to try to compose herself,' said her mother, ominously.

'Oh, dear. Perhaps I had better go after her, and keep her company for a while.'

'Oh, yes, dear, would you? I must confess, I am at my wits' end with her. Why, at one time, just being at an event like this would have…' She trailed away, shaking her head.

Deborah knew exactly what it would have meant, at one time, to her ambitious friend to be moving in such exalted circles and dancing with an earl.

She got right to the end of the terrace before she detected the faint sound of sobbing coming from beyond the flight of steps that led into a sunken garden. As she got further from the house, and the music from the ballroom grew fainter, she became increasingly concerned by the way her friend seemed to have finally broken under the strain, even hiccupping out the odd words between sobs. But when she finally found her, rather than hurrying to her side and wrapping her arms about her, she froze.

For Susannah was not alone.

And the man who was with her, who had just

pulled her into his arms so that her sobs were muffled against his chest, was Robert.

'Hush, now,' he said as Deborah skidded to a halt, not five feet away from them.

It was not seeing her husband put his arm about Susannah's shoulders that shocked her so much. It was the fact that *she* had overcome her revulsion enough to let him hold her. That she was clutching at his shirt front, raising her tear-stained face to his, and confessing,

'I have made such a terrible mistake!'

'Not so great a one as I have,' replied Robert, looking ruefully down into her beautiful face.

Chapter Eleven

Deborah walked back into the ballroom, feeling as though she was encased in ice. She never could remember the rest of that evening's events. She supposed she must have mechanically executed the steps of the dances she had promised to all those faceless men who came to claim her, but all she could see was her husband, telling the woman he loved that he had made a terrible mistake.

He meant in not asking Susannah to marry him, of course. If only he had gone to her, and explained that a great fortune could be hers, this ball could have been given in her honour. She would have become a member of the Earl of Walton's family, and gone shopping in Bond Street with a countess.

For such compensation, Susannah would have been well able to overcome her revulsion at Robert's injuries. She must be sorry now she had ever let that revulsion show. Yes, her mistake had been spurning Robert's devotion.

She did not like to think what the next step would be for the ill-fated lovers now they had reached an understanding. Whatever they chose to do, there would be an almighty scandal. Robert would come out of it none the worse, of course. He had married for convenience. Nobody would expect him to stay faithful to his wife. And if the most beautiful débutante of the Season chose to throw herself at him, who would blame him for taking what was on offer? Other men would just chuckle, and call him a sly dog, but all doors would remain open to him.

But Susannah would be ruined. Even if Robert did not go so far as to make her his mistress, there were enough beady eyes trained on Miss Hullworthy to ensure any clandestine encounters, such as the one Deborah had witnessed, would be shouted from the rooftops. Social ruin was as painful as ruination in fact, with none of the attendant pleasures.

Once all the guests had gone, she returned to their rooms on the ground floor. Deborah stood stock still in the sitting room when Robert stalked past her into the bedroom, finally realising that there was a point beyond which even the strength of her love could not take her. It would be like a knife thrusting into her heart every time he sneaked off for snatched moments of intimacy with Susannah, expecting her to turn a blind eye. And if he ever took her with his eyes shut again, slaking the lust that another woman had aroused, her very soul would shrivel away to dust.

She rather thought she might go back to The Dovecote, before the storm broke. If she left it until the affair became public knowledge, people would see how she felt. No lady, surely, could conceal that amount of anguish behind society manners? She knew such a feat was beyond her. She would feel humiliated every time she went out of doors, conscious of people eyeing her and talking about her. Eventually, it would prove too much for her, and she would have to flee from town.

She might as well get the fleeing part over with, then, right now, and avoid the humiliation.

She rose early the morning after the ball, having spent a sleepless night shivering on the sitting-room sofa. She had not been able to bring herself to enter the bedroom, not even to get herself a blanket. It was only when she realised she could not leave the house wearing her ball gown that she summoned up the courage to tiptoe in, and sneak a walking dress, coat and bonnet from the clothes press. She could not prevent herself from stealing one last look at her husband, who was, she discovered resentfully, sleeping soundly, with his arm flung out across the space where she usually lay.

She would go to her mother first, she decided, as she tossed the flimsy ball gown over the back of the sofa, and wriggled into her sensible, cambric walking dress. It would not be fair of her to leave London without warning her the affair was likely to commence as soon as she was out of the way.

A sleepy footman unbolted the front door for her, asking if she needed his escort.

'No, thank you. I plan to take a cab straight to my mother's. Oh, see! There is one just at the corner.'

Having given her address to the driver, she climbed inside, and sank gratefully on to the cushions. She hoped it was not too early to be making such a call. She was sure her mother would not mind getting up. Or perhaps she would just go straight up to her mother's room and speak to her there. What she had to relate was not for anyone else's ears.

She wondered that she had not yet felt the urge

to cry. She knew she loved Robert more than life itself. Yet, since the moment she had seen Susannah in his arms, she had felt strangely frozen.

She had heard people talking about being numb with grief. She supposed that was why she was outwardly maintaining an appearance of calm, whilst inside she felt so terribly cold. She had been just like this after her father had died, mechanically seeing to all the necessary details. It had only been after the funeral was over, when she had been folding away one of his coats, and caught his dear, familiar scent lingering about the cloth, that it had hit her that she would never see him again. That was when the tears had begun to flow.

She would mourn Robert when this chilling numbness wore off, she expected. Wearily, she turned to look out of the window. And sat up with a sharp frown upon seeing the cab was passing through a shabby street she was sure she had never been down before.

She pulled the window down, and shouted up to the driver, 'Excuse me, I think you may have mistook my direction. I asked you to take me to Half Moon Street.'

The driver pulled the cab to a halt at once. Another man, one who had been sitting on the box with the driver, got down, and came to the window from which she was leaning.

Instead of apologising for his error, to Deborah's complete astonishment, he opened the cab door.

'What do you think you're doing?' she squeaked as he pushed her roughly back into her seat, and got in, sitting down opposite her.

'Making sure you don't slip through our fingers,' he said laconically.

'Slip through…what are you saying?' Her heart began to pound against her breastbone. 'Stop this cab and let me out at once!' she demanded, in as authoritative tone as she could muster. 'Or you will be sorry!'

'Threats, is it, now?' He grinned. 'No, you should not be making any threats to me, Mrs Fawley. What you should be doing is begging for mercy.'

The dim hope that he must have mistaken her for someone else fled when he addressed her by name. Nevertheless, she put on a brave face, forcing herself to look directly into his puffy eyes, as she said, 'Begging for mercy? Oh, no. You are the one who should beg my forgiveness for being so ill mannered as to try to frighten me.'

The man chuckled as he dealt her an open-handed slap across the face. She could not believe it. He seemed to have hardly put any effort into the blow at all, and yet it had sent her reeling into the corner of the carriage. She pulled herself upright, her hand instinctively going to her stinging lip. The man's grin broadened, as though well pleased with his little demonstration of brute strength.

'That was just a hint, Mrs Fawley, to show you we mean business. If you have any sense, you won't try to argue with me again. Just behave yourself, and there'll be no need to give you another lesson, see?'

He spoke so calmly that Deborah could hardly believe he had just hit her. But then she looked down at her glove and saw a red stain upon it. The force of his blow had split her lip. The feeling of wetness on her chin was her own blood, trickling from the stinging wound.

The disbelief on her face seemed to amuse her captor, for he chuckled, before folding his arms across his chest and settling down to watch her with lazy contempt.

He thought he had cowed her. Well, she would show him how wrong he was. If he thought she was so feeble-spirited that she would meekly let him carry her off without putting up a struggle, he was fair and far out!

As soon as the cab stopped, and her captor leaned forward to open the door, Deborah sprang to the opposite door, flung it open and dived out into the street. She had no idea where she was, but if she ran, shouting for help, someone was bound to come to her aid.

Her feet had barely hit the muddy surface, when a large hand descended on her shoulder. The man who had hit her had lunged through the coach the moment she had leapt out and grabbed for her.

'Help!' cried Deborah, struggling against his grip. She felt her coat rip along the shoulder seam, as she pulled from him with all her might. But then the driver, about whom she had forgotten, came to his partner's aid, jumping down from the box and landing in the street before her. With a scowl, he put his open, gloved hand against her face, and shoved her, sending her sprawling backwards into the coach, where she landed on the floor at the other man's feet.

Her skirt tore as he dragged her, kicking and struggling, through the carriage and out the other side, where she landed on all fours in the mud. He grabbed the collar of her coat, yanking her roughly to her feet and, not content with having recaptured her, he swung her round, smashing her face into the side of the cab. She reeled back from the explosion of pain, half-stunned. As her knees buckled, her assailant grasped her round the waist and swung her over his shoulder, as though she weighed no more than a sack of hops.

A series of impressions flitted across Deborah's dazed mind. A weary-looking woman, her eyes sliding away as though the sight of a kidnap in broad daylight was none of her business. Blood dripping down the back of the man's coat from her own face and splashing on to a flight of rough-hewn steps. Increasing darkness, and with it a strong smell of damp as her captor carried her ever deeper into his lair.

Finally, he stooped to pass through a low arch, then dropped her on to a mattress stuffed with straw. He stood looking down at her prostrate form with complete composure, while her dazed state crystallized into ice-cold fear.

'I warned you to mind your manners,' her captor said coolly. He squatted down on his haunches beside her bed. 'You ain't going to make any more trouble now, are you, pretty lady?' For good measure, he laid one meaty paw upon her ankle, running his hand under her skirts a way.

Deborah had thought she was levelheaded

enough to cope with anything. But the slide of that man's hand filled her with such sick loathing, she couldn't prevent herself from uttering a shriek of terror and drawing her leg away. She was completely in his power. The violence he had used to subdue her had been meant as a demonstration of what she might expect should she offer any further resistance. He could do anything to her, and there was nobody who would stop him.

She felt as though she had stumbled into another world. A world where the rules that had governed her sheltered existence until that point no longer applied. In this world, men could strike women in the street, and anyone who saw it would pretend they had not, lest they suffer the same fate.

'Pity, almost, you've broke so soon,' he mused. 'I would have enjoyed making you mind me.' He reached out, as though intending to take hold of her again. And Deborah scuttled backwards along the bed until she was curled into a ball, pressed up against the wall. He leaned over her, his eyes boring into hers as he took firm hold of her arm. When he snapped the strings of her reticule, as he pulled it from her wrist, she almost fainted with relief. He tore it open, tipping the contents on to the rough brick floor.

'You don't carry much money for a woman as has married such a wealthy man,' he complained as he picked out the coins from amongst her clutter of personal effects. 'Still, it will pay for the cab fare, and your board for as long as you're with us.'

With that, he left the room, bolting the door behind him.

She was ashamed to find she was shaking like a leaf, little whimpers of distress escaping her lips with every ragged breath. She had not thought she was a coward, but that man's casual attitude to violence, his clear enjoyment of inflicting injury on her, had been inhuman. He had even indicated he wanted her to resist, so that he would have an excuse to hurt her even more. What kind of a monster was he?

And why had these men taken her? She simply could not understand why anyone should want to kidnap her. Though she was definitely their intended victim. They had called her by name.

Her face and hair felt sticky, her left eyebrow throbbing from where her kidnapper had slammed her face against the coach door. She knew she was bleeding, but had no way of attending to her hurt, other than pressing her already-stained glove to the cut, hoping pressure might stem the flow. There was nothing in her prison, save the mattress she cowered on and a bucket by the door, which she assumed was for her convenience.

The room itself she guessed must be a part of a cellar, since it was so dark. As her eyes became accustomed to the gloom, she saw that it was shaped in the form of an arch, made of brick. There was no window, and what little light there was filtered in through a small grille set into the stout oak door, which she had heard her captor bolt on the outside.

She did not know how long she crouched there. It seemed like a very long time, yet it was not long enough for her to stop shaking. But at length she heard footsteps approaching, and the sound of a chair scraping back. Was her captor sitting on the other side of the door then, guarding her? Though why should he, when there was no way she could escape such a secure prison?

She heard the bolts grate and then the door swung open.

She found she was panting with renewed fear. Why had they opened the door? What new cruelty did they mean to inflict on her? She felt so vulnerable, huddled on the floor, that she pushed herself shakily to her feet, leaning against the wall when her legs proved to have the consistency of jelly on a summer's day.

A neatly dressed, thin man walked in, and stood regarding her with his head tilted to one side for several minutes.

'I expect, Mrs Fawley,' he said eventually, 'you are wondering why I have had you brought here?'

She nodded, her mouth so dry with fear she was incapable of speech.

'I need to get your husband's attention. He owes me, you see, and needs to understand he must pay me back.'

'R…Robert does not have any debts!'

'Well, now, that is where we have to differ. When he cheated a man who does owe me, leaving him without the means to repay me, that man's debts became his.'

Robert would not cheat anyone!

The only person who could even come close to making such an accusation against him would be…Percy Lampton.

Had the fool borrowed against his expectations? From this man?

She looked upon the thin man with dawning comprehension. Lampton had no means of repaying anyone anything now. Robert had all the money he had assumed would be his.

'I see you know exactly what I mean,' the man sneered. 'So glad you have dropped the pretence of innocence. People like you need to learn you cannot get away with cheating men like me. You must pay. One way or another,' he said, taking a step towards her, 'I always make 'em pay.'

As he moved, she saw the dull gleam of a knife blade in his hand.

'No!' she cried, feeling the blood draining from her face.

'I would advise you to hold still, Mrs Fawley, if you don't want to get hurt any further,' the thin man said menacingly. 'It will all be over before you know it.'

Mad panic gripped her. She darted towards the open door, running full tilt into the burly man, who appeared out of nowhere. He flung her back into the cell so forcefully that the back of her head cracked against the rough brickwork on the wall opposite the door. He stalked in after her, closing one meaty great hand round her throat, whilst deftly untying the ribbons of her bonnet with the other. Deborah's senses swam. The stench of him filled her nostrils, choking her as effectively as the stranglehold he had round her neck. Spots danced before her eyes while pain blossomed and spread its tentacles from the initial point of impact at the back of her head. She only dimly registered him tossing her bonnet aside, for she had seen the thin man approaching, the knife stretched out towards her.

With one swift flick, he cut off a lock of her hair, the burly man left off his stranglehold, and Deborah fell to her knees on the floor between them.

'Tsk, tsk.' The thin man shook his head at her. 'Such a lot of fuss over one lock of hair. Anyone would think we meant to murder you.'

As she dragged in a painful breath through her bruised throat, she knew that was exactly what they had meant her to think. They wanted to keep her in a state of terrified submission. They both laughed mockingly as she cowered on the floor at her feet. And she felt a fresh wave of humiliation that they were succeeding so well. She *was* terrified.

'Now give me your hand,' the thin man ordered.

Well beyond the point of daring to display any defiance, Deborah held up her hand. At a nod from his master, the burly man knelt on the floor beside her, took her outstretched hand between his and slowly unbuttoned her glove. He then stroked it from her hand, finger by finger, his gloating, puffy eyes never leaving her face.

She felt violated.

She did not stop shivering, her stomach heaving, until long after the door had been shut on her again, leaving her in darkness.

But she would not cry. The burly man was out there, sitting on a chair, guarding her. He would hear if she began to cry. She would not give him the satisfaction!

It was quite late in the evening when Robert received the packet. He was in no mood to receive any kind of post. It was probably a sample from a tailor, he thought moodily. He was past caring about such trivialities, though once the prospect of having silk shirts and natty waistcoats had filled him with pleasurable anticipation.

'Here, deal with this, would you?' he said, tossing it to Linney.

Deborah had shunned him last night. She had finally given up the pretence she could bear sharing a bed with him. And this morning, before the rest of the household had begun to stir, she had run off to her mother's house. She had not returned since, not even to keep the various social engagements she had previously arranged.

'Captain!'

The tone of Linney's voice had him turning from the sideboard where he was pouring himself a brandy.

Linney's face was white.

'What is it?' Robert demanded sharply.

In reply, the man held out the contents of the package. A bloodstained glove and a lock of dark hair. He recognised that glove. He knew that hair.

'Deborah!'

In two strides he was taking the note that had come in the package from Linney's hand: *You stole from my client. I reckon his debts now belong to you, along with all the rest you took from him. Settle them if you want to see your wife again.*

There was no signature on the letter, and no direction on the packet.

He went cold inside. How could he pay a ransom, when he did not know who to pay it to?

'This will be the first of a series of notes, I expect,' said Linney darkly as Robert sank to the sofa, Deborah's bloodstained glove lying limply on his open palm. 'This was just to get your attention. He'll send instructions as to how to pay, and how much, once he's let you stew a while.'

'I cannot!' Robert lurched unsteadily to his feet. 'I cannot sit here and wait for further messages, while Deborah may be suffering God alone knows what!' He looked at the bloodstained glove, his cheeks going chalk white. 'They have already hurt her.'

'Might just have been done for effect. Might not be her blood, sir.'

'By heaven, it had better not be.' His expression hardened. 'This is Lampton's doing. There is no one else that could accuse me of stealing from him. Though I had every right to claim that inheritance! It is his lying tongue that has exposed Deborah to danger! It must be!'

'Sir, Captain sir, just think for a minute—'

'No, I've done with thinking, and behaving and pretending to be a gentleman! I am a soldier. And I will take a soldier's solution.'

Linney swore under his breath as his master pulled open the sideboard drawers and pulled out a pair of heavy military pistols.

While he clumsily loaded them, Linney fetched a wicked-looking blade, which he hid under the folds of his coat. He helped his master into his old army greatcoat, clapped a battered forage cap upon his head, then both men plunged out into the night, side by side.

The man who opened the doors of Lampton's rooms in Albany Chambers soon lost the haughty expression he habitually wore when denying access to unwelcome visitors. But then, nobody had ever requested entrance at gunpoint before.

'Is your master in?' said the scar-faced ruffian on the doorstep. 'Don't tell me any lies now.'

'I wouldn't dream of it, sir,' he replied, nervously swallowing as he caught sight of a second, broad-shouldered man standing on the step, his back to the building as he scanned the street.

'Show me to him, then!'

Any hope the valet had of summoning assistance for his master, who he was convinced was about to be murdered, faded when the second intruder bounded up the steps, slammed the front door behind him, and bore down upon him with grim purpose.

'He...he's in there,' said the valet, turning white as he indicated the sitting-room door. He could not stand the sight of blood. It had been bad enough the last time, but those men had not used pistols. He really would have to think about handing in his notice. Staving off criminals was not part of his job description. Though after tonight, he would probably not have a job any longer. Resentment swelled his emaciated chest. What kind of person would employ a valet whose former master had been brutally murdered? Only the kind who sought notoriety. He had no wish to work for that sort of person. With an affronted sniff, he sat down on a settle in the narrow hall, glaring waspishly up at the thickset man who stood, arms folded, with his back to the front door.

Captain Fawley strode into the sitting room, training one of his pistols on the young man who was sprawled on an armchair in front of the fire. He checked at the sight of Percy Lampton's face. It was covered with fading bruises and crusted scabs. The once elegant fop was bundled up in a disreputably shabby dressing gown, a bowl of what smelled like punch at his elbow, a great deal of which, judging by his heightened complexion, he had already imbibed.

'Come to finish me off, have you, Fawley?' Lampton drawled, eyeing the pistol with weary, bloodshot eyes. 'Don't suppose you want to hear it, but in fact, you would be doing me a favour.'

'It would be only what you deserve,' Robert bit

out coldly. 'But I am no murderer. It is answers I want, not your blood.'

'Just as well. Don't think there's all that much left,' Percy said, his fingers tracing over the patchwork of bruises. 'Though I don't know what kind of answers you might want from me.'

'I want to know who has taken my wife!'

'Taken your wife? In what way?' he sneered. 'Cuckolded you already, has she? Not that anyone could blame her.'

The pistol went off, shattering the punch bowl and showering shards of glass everywhere.

'Your aim is off,' Percy taunted, flicking rum punch nonchalantly from one elegant hand, though his lips had gone white.

'My aim is perfect,' Robert replied, pulling the second pistol from his pocket. 'The next ball will go straight through your black heart unless you tell me what I want to know.'

'I have no idea who your wife may have taken as her lover, nor why you should suppose it was me,' he protested. 'I am no adulterer!'

'No, just a seducer of innocent young girls!'

'I have never seduced an innocent young girl!'

'Have you forgotten Miss Hullworthy already, you rogue?'

'I did not seduce her! I just—'

'Led her to believe you would marry her. Toyed with her affections and broke her heart! You villain. Are there no depths to which you Lamptons will not sink? You would destroy a woman for sport—'

'Now hang on a minute!' Percy sat forward, his brow knotting angrily. 'A little light flirtation is hardly a crime. I gave Miss Hullworthy no assurances. If she imagined I would ever propose marriage to a woman of her class, that was entirely her own fault! And as for accusing any Lampton of acting dishonourably towards a female…'

'Your father did! Claiming I was not my father's child was tantamount to branding my mother a whore! It destroyed her! Can you deny it?'

'Th…that's ancient history,' Percy countered, his face darkening. 'I had no part in that.'

'But you are just like him! Claiming a woman is not fit to marry because of her background. No woman should be treated as you have treated Miss Hullworthy. Or as your father treated my mother. Women should be protected, cared for, not abused as though they are of no account!'

As he said it, Captain Fawley realised he meant every word. This was the creed by which he had grown up. When had he lost that belief? When had he begun to treat women with the cynical contempt that had made him ruthlessly exploit Deborah's vulnerability so that he could exact revenge on his enemies?

It was not just his body that had been crippled at Salamanca, he suddenly saw. His mind had been warped too.

Shakily, he sank into the chair opposite Percy, his fingers clutching convulsively on the grip of his pistol. When he had first seen his face in the mirror in that makeshift hospital outside Salamanca, he had been appalled. As a youth, he had been handsome. Nobody could have looked at the mass of blistered, suppurating skin and felt anything but disgust.

In the long months of his recovery, he had seen the way women reacted to the sight of his broken body and scarred face. Where once they had smiled at him, flirted with him, now they twitched their skirts away in disgust.

So he had branded them all shallow, calculating bitches when the truth was, he hurt so much, whenever one of them wrinkled up her pretty little nose, he could scarcely breathe.

Driven by a sense of the injustice done him, he

had used Deborah as ruthlessly as Lampton had treated Miss Hullworthy, as Lampton's father had treated his mother. He looked at Percy Lampton with growing horror. He had allowed bitterness and resentment to eat away at his soul until now there was nothing to choose between them.

'Somebody has kidnapped my wife,' he said bleakly. 'The note I received this evening, along with this…' he laid the pistol across his knee as he drew the bloodstained glove from his pocket '…led me to assume it was connected to our long-standing feud. It demanded repayment of debts that somebody seems to think I ought to pay, though I suspect it was you that racked them up.'

'Hincksey,' said Percy, his eyes fixed on the bloodied glove. 'My God, Fawley, I never meant it to come to this. I just thought he would send some of his men to dish out more of the same…' he fingered his bruised face '…to you.'

'You expect me to care what you think?'

Lampton's eyes narrowed. 'Look, I know your view of me is coloured by what my father did, but I am not like him. I would never deliberately put a woman in harm's way.'

'What of Miss Hullworthy? Or Lady Walton? Last year, you—'

'I did not cause that French woman any real harm! I just saw the opportunity to make Walton a little uncomfortable. And after the way he did me out of Aunt Euphemia's property, that was the least he deserved! And it wasn't as if she lost all that much money at cards. Chicken feed, to a man of his wealth!

'And as for Miss Hullworthy, she'll soon get over me when someone with a title decides to drop her the handkerchief, you mark my words! But that…' he pointed to the bloodied glove lying in Captain Fawley's lap '…that is not something I would ever wish to happen to a lady.' He grimaced. 'It's all Walton's fault anyway that I fell into Hincksey's clutches in the first place,' he whined. 'If he had not contested that will…if I'd had the money my father swore was coming to me…'

'That was not how it was at all!' Captain Fawley thundered. 'It was your family that contested the will. Your aunt left everything to me!'

'Well, she shouldn't have done! *You* ain't her nephew!'

'And you think that is justification for telling your money-lender he could apply to me for restitution of debts you had run up?'

'He was threatening to break my legs. Good

God, man, have you not seen the state of my face? Haven't been able to go anywhere for days. And I did not say he could apply to you. I just explained about the legacy—how I had thought it as good as mine, but that, in the end, you managed to snaffle it by marrying Miss Gillies.'

His eyes widened in horror. 'My God, I gave him her name. I might as well have handed her to him on a plate. I shall never forgive myself if…'

Captain Fawley could see his rival's remorse was genuine. While Percy Lampton was not the most honourable man he had ever known, the thought that any action of his might have exposed a lady to real danger clearly appalled him.

'Help me find her, then.'

'I shall.' Lampton sat up, looking Robert straight in the eye. 'And while we are about it, I want to say that I deplore what my father did. Even—' his face flushed '—the way he acted over my aunt's will. I wanted the money, I don't deny it. But not that much…' He eyed Deborah's bloodstained glove, his fists clenching. 'If there were anything I could do to settle this stupid feud, once and for all, then believe me, I would do it.'

'Would you, now?' replied Robert, eyeing him

with a cynical sneer. 'Forgive me for finding that hard to believe.'

'Try me!' said Percy, leaping to his feet, showering the hearthrug with shards of crystal punch bowl. 'I would do anything to atone for any harm that may have come to poor Miss Gillies through any careless word I may have spoken. Anything!'

Chapter Twelve

Deborah lost all sense of time in that uniformly dark prison. Three times after the thin man had cut off a lock of her hair, the door opened, and the burly man who had hit her came in with a plate of bread and cheese, and a mug of what looked and smelled like ale.

The first time, though her throat still ached from when he had half-choked her, she had disdained drinking the ale. The prospect of having to use that bucket later on, and either have him empty it with a smirk, or leave it to add its pungency to the already nasty smell of the place, were both too horrible to contemplate. She had torn a strip off her petticoat, dipped it in the ale jug, and pressed it against her brow, though, hoping the alcohol might cleanse the cut, which simply would not stop bleeding. It only made her feel worse. Not only did it sting rather badly, but now she stank of ale too.

Not long after that, she began to scratch. And she discovered that the mattress, upon which she had been sitting, was hopping with fleas. Horrified, she leapt to her feet, and made for the furthest corner of her cell. She could not stand still for ever, though. The blood seemed to pool in her feet, making her feel faint. She tried pacing up and down, which helped a little, but she could not keep going indefinitely. Eventually, when exhaustion overcame her, she crouched in a corner, as far from the verminous mattress as she could.

When, at length, the door opened, and the burly man brought in fresh food and ale, she felt too weary, her legs too stiff and her back too sore to wish to reach for it. And the darkness, which had seeped into her soul, as dampness soaked into her clothes, made her wonder whether it was worth trying to keep her strength up anyway. She dared not hope Robert would part with any money to rescue her. It was the money he cared about, not her. But her captors had said 'someone' would pay. It was increasingly obvious that 'someone' would be her.

A shudder racked her body. She would never be

strong enough to fight them. They would do what they wanted with her. They would make her suffer. Her only hope was that she might be too weak to survive her punishment for long. In a spurt of defiance, she kicked over the ale jug, and ground the stale piece of bread into the floor, the crumbs mingling with the mildewed mortar that held the bricks in place.

The last time her enemy had come in, she had felt too weak to even reach for the dishes he dropped on to the floor next to her. Her very frailty caused a brief flare of triumph to loosen the despair that had closed round her, like an iron fist, as the unremitting darkness had gone on, and on. It might not be so very much longer, she smiled to herself, before she was out of here.

She could hear her jailor moving about on the other side of her door. She heard another man join him. She heard the low murmur of male voices, a chair rasping across the brick floor, and then periods of quiet, interspersed with terse outbursts of profanities. From the occasional recognisable word that filtered in through the grille, she deduced that they were playing cards.

Then there came a clatter of booted feet on the cellar steps. The beginning of a shout was choked off into a grunt of pain, and then it sounded as though somebody was throwing furniture about.

There was a fight going on.

'Deborah!'

She lifted her head from where she had been resting it on her bent knees.

'Robert?'

She could hardly believe her ears.

'Deborah, where are you?'

From some hidden inner reserve, she gathered the last of her strength and crawled to the door. 'In here!' she croaked hoarsely, straining upwards to try and reach the grille. 'Robert!' Her voice was rusty from disuse. He would never be able to hear her. In desperation, she raised her fists, and pounded ineffectually against the stout door.

She heard the sound of the bolts being drawn; before she could get out of the way, the door swung inwards, pushing her aside so that she sprawled inelegantly in the middle of the floor.

And Robert stood there, a dark silhouette against the dim light from the outer cellar.

Her arms shook with the effort it took to raise herself to a sitting position. She felt as though she had expended the last of her strength in making him hear her. But he just stood there, in stony silence, and somehow she knew she was going to have to get up on her own.

He did not want to be here. He could not have made it more obvious if he had shouted it. The very way he drew to one side, as she finally managed to stagger towards the open door, spoke of his reluctance to so much as touch her.

But he had come. She would live.

And that knowledge gave her the strength to reach the doorway, where she leaned for a moment or two, her head spinning.

In the outer room four men were fighting like demons. Her jaw dropped at recognising one of them was the Marquis of Lensborough. The first time she had met him, she had thought he was an ugly customer, and he certainly had an ugly expression on his face now. But it was magnificent to behold, for the man he was pounding, as though he were a punch bag in a boxing school, was the man who had taken such pleasure in hurting her.

Her hand flew to her mouth as the other villain, the one who had been driving the cab, raised a chair to smash over her other rescuer's head. To her shock, she recognised the gleaming golden brown hair of the Earl of Walton. But the Earl surprised both her and his assailant with the agility of his next manoeuvre. He sprang aside, dodging the chair and simultaneously raising his knee to jam it into his assailant's stomach. As the cab driver doubled over, the chair somehow ended up in the Earl's capable hands. He brought it smashing down over the kidnapper's head, a split second after the Marquis dealt a massive knockout punch to the burly villain's jaw.

The kidnappers lay sprawled amongst the smashed furniture. The Earl and the Marquis stood there panting, then grinned at each other like a pair of mischievous schoolboys as they reached over the bodies to shake one another's hands.

'This way,' said Robert, extending his arm to indicate a stairway, snaking up out of the cellar. 'And be quick about it.'

Flinching at the curtness of his tone, Deborah tottered towards the stairs. She had not gone more than a few steps, before the Marquis took one arm, the Earl her other, and they half-dragged, half-carried her up the stairs, while Robert followed behind. The four of them emerged into a dank courtyard in which stood a plain black cab. Linney was sitting on the box, a brace of pistols sweeping the few people who dared to poke their noses out of the doorways or windows.

'How did you find me?' asked Deborah, once they had all got into the cab. 'Did you have to pay a ransom? That man said you owed him money—'

'Lampton owed him money,' said Robert curtly as the Earl and the Marquis settled on the seats opposite them. 'And it was Lampton who told me where I might find you.'

The coach set off with a jolt that flung Deborah back into the cushions. Robert steadied her, then moved away swiftly. So swiftly that she had to turn her head away from him to hide her hurt.

'Your man may be handy to have about in a tight spot, but he is no coachman,' observed the Marquis, grabbing hold of the strap.

'You are a handy man to have in a tight spot too,' said Deborah, turning wide eyes upon his saturnine features. 'I must thank you for what you have done today. Both of you,' she added, addressing the Earl.

'I am merely returning a favour Captain Fawley did, not so very long ago, for my own wife,' the Marquis replied coolly.

'Think nothing of it,' added the Earl. Then, turning to Robert, he drawled, 'I had no idea taking you into my home would provide me with such adventures.'

They kept up a constant barrage of inane obser-
vations, reminding her again of a pair of naughty
schoolboys who had just got away with some
prank. It didn't take her long to work out that
much of the badinage was intended to distract her,
for which she was grateful. The last thing she
wanted to do was break down in front of two such
aristocratic males and, judging from the way
neither of them could quite meet her eye, the sight
of a female in tears would make them extremely
uncomfortable too. And she had felt very inclined
to burst into tears when the cab had set off, sig-
nalling her ordeal was at an end.

The Earl and the Marquis helped her out of the
cab when it stopped in an alley at the back of
Walton House. Contrary to her expectations, there
was a flight of steps leading to Robert's back door,
which they reached by crossing a paved yard.
There was even a sign on the door, bearing his
name, and a doorknocker in the shape of a lion's
head, as though this were a private, rented apart-
ment, rather than an integral part of Walton House.

The Countess was waiting for them. The
moment she saw them, she leapt to her feet, her
eyes widening in horror at Deborah's appearance.
Her next action was to snatch up a blanket from

the sofa on which she had been sitting, hurry to her side, and drape it round her, shooting just one reproachful look at Robert as she did so.

'Nobody must see her looking like this,' she exclaimed. 'What were you thinking?'

'Of getting her out of that place, primarily,' Robert snapped back. 'But at least I took the precaution of smuggling her in by the back door. Nobody knows about this dreadful business,' he said to Deborah. 'We have managed to hush it up. I was sure you would not want to distress your mother. So whenever enquiries were made as to your whereabouts, I said either you were indisposed, or out shopping, depending on who was doing the asking. Now I suggest you go upstairs with Lady Walton, who will see to your immediate needs.'

It was as if he could not wait to be rid of her, she thought, glancing at his set features.

Strangely, her earlier desire to weep had frozen solid under the blast of his coldness. She could feel it, a tangible presence, just under her breastbone, as though she had swallowed a lump of ice. It was amazing, she reflected as Lady Walton led her up the stairs, just how much strength pride could lend to legs that she had thought too weak to carry her one step further.

'You will feel better for a bath and something to eat,' said the Countess, ushering her into her pretty, feminine sitting room.

'Will I?' She shook her head, wearily. She had not been able to forget for one second, even through all her other terrors, that her husband was about to embark on an affair with another woman. So far as he was concerned, she could not have got herself kidnapped at a more inconvenient moment. He must have had to go to a great deal of trouble to effect her rescue, when he would much rather have been planning…

Feeling a wave of faintness overcome her, Deborah dropped on to the nearest sofa, bowing her head over her knees.

'Here, here!' The Countess knelt at her feet, holding up a teacup and saucer.

'I thought you never took tea,' Deborah attempted to joke weakly, as she gratefully took the hot, sweet drink.

'Oh, no, I hate it. But you English love it, and say it is restorative, and you look as though you need to be restored. Did they not feed you? Oh, pardon! I am not supposed to pester you with questions. Robert said you would not want to talk about it.'

Getting to her feet, the Countess went to the fireplace and tugged on the bell rope.

'Please to come into my bedroom, Deborah. The maids will bring up water for a bath, but I am sure you will not want them to see you…' She trailed off, her eyes darting to her face, and then flinching away.

For the first time, Deborah wondered what her face looked like. It ached all over, so she supposed it must be bruised. Draining her cup to the dregs, she followed the Countess through into an opulent bedchamber. The bed was hung with velvet curtains, the carpet was a soft swathe of blue that invited a woman to sink her bare feet into it, and there were bowls of fresh flowers upon several of the little tables that dotted the room. She could smell them, above the stench of imprisonment that clung to her clothes. Everything looked so clean, and so delicately feminine, that Deborah felt as though she were polluting the place just by standing there in all her grime and disorder.

The Countess darted out, upon hearing the maids clanking about with cans of water in the dressing room, and Deborah took a moment to go to the dressing table and peer at her reflection in the mirror. Her face was swollen almost out of recognition. She had a black eye that would not have looked out of place on a professional boxer, and a crusted scab over her eyebrow. Her hair on that side of her face was matted with blood from that cut, and her mouth… She touched it gingerly with the tips of her fingers. Her lower lip was puffy and scabbed from that initial, casual cuff.

Absently, she reached under the sleeve of her dress, to scratch at one of the fleabites on her wrist, then suddenly she was tearing off her filthy clothes. By the time the Countess returned to tell her the bath was ready, Deborah was crouching naked before the fire, holding her petticoat in the flames with a poker.

'It has to be burned,' she explained, when Lady Walton looked at her in amazement. 'All of it. Right down to my shoes.' It was the only way to stop the fleas from getting into the carpets and curtains. When the Countess made an involuntary movement towards her, she held up her hand to ward her off. 'No, I must do this myself!' She did not think she carried any fleas on her person, but she did not want to take the chance of passing them on, if she had.

As she stood up, she noticed that her knees were badly grazed, though she could not remember exactly when that had happened. It could have been when she had fallen to the cobbles, when the burly man hauled her out of the cab. Or later, when she had been forced to her knees in the cell after they cut off her hair. By the way the Countess had been glancing at her back, then looking hastily away, as though something distressed her, she guessed she had bruises all over her.

The Countess proffered a large towel. 'Your bath is ready,' she said, her eyes full of tears.

'Oh, yes, how I need one,' Deborah agreed. She had been in the same clothes for she knew not how many hours. Fear had made her sweat profusely during several thoroughly unpleasant incidents. That cell had been filthy, the men who had man-handled her had left their rank odour in her nostrils… Was she just imagining it, or was it really there? And then, of course, she had attempted to wash her cut in ale. She must smell like something out of a tavern.

Though a bath in water, no matter how deliciously scented, would never erase the imprint of ugliness and evil from her mind. She had seen another face of human nature these past few days, and she already sensed the experience had left an indelible stain on her soul. As she sank gratefully into the perfumed water, she murmured, 'I wonder if I will ever feel completely clean again.' Then, concerned lest any of the fleas should have taken up lodging in her hair, she slid beneath the surface of the water, immersing herself in the hope she might drown them.

Robert sat on the sofa, an untouched tumbler of brandy in his hand, staring blindly at the floor between his boots. He did not think he would ever get the image of Deborah, cowering on that filthy straw mattress, her face all over bruises, her dress soiled and torn, out of his mind. He had wanted to go to her and carry her out of that foul cell, wrap her in his arms and tell her he would never let anyone hurt her ever again.

Instead, he had to endure the humiliation of letting others fight for her freedom, and accept that he would never be able to lift her in his arms and carry her anywhere. When she had got into the coach, and he had seen the bruises on her neck, it had been all he could do to restrain himself from marching straight back into that warehouse and shooting the brutes where they lay on the floor.

He had been angry enough at the thought of Deborah being taken, imprisoned, and perhaps frightened. But to see what they had done to her…blacked her eye, split her lip, half-strangled her…to have left such marks on her body attested to a level of violence that told its own story. There was only one reason why men held a woman by the throat, punched her in the face and tore her gown.

How many of them had raped her? How often? She had been in their clutches for a night and the best part of two days. He groaned, leaning his forehead on his hand to hide the tears, which were stinging his eyes, from Linney's notice.

It was all his fault. He had never considered what repercussions might rebound upon her when he had been making his plans to best Percy Lampton. Not that he could have foreseen she might have suffered this level of brutality. But nor had he taken any steps to ensure her safety, when he should have known… He thumped his thigh with his clenched fist.

It had all got completely out of hand. This feud with the Lamptons had gone too far! Because of his obsession with them, Deborah had suffered the most terrible fate that could befall a woman.

It was not the men who had raped her that should be shot, it was he. He had brought her to this.

He had crept in to her bedroom, and stood over her, just filling his eyes with the sight of her, once Heloise had come to tell him she had fallen asleep.

'She must have been exhausted,' Heloise had said, as they had climbed the stairs, side by side. 'I wondered, after all she had suffered, and considering the pain she must feel, if I would need to give her something to help her sleep, but almost before she had finished her bath, she was struggling to keep her eyes open. And she told me she had hardly slept at all…nor does she seem to know what day it is, for it was so dark in the cell….'

He had not been surprised to hear she had fallen asleep so quickly. She had obviously exhausted her meagre reserves of strength trying to fight off those men. Her whole body had been trembling with the effort it had taken her just to get up off that filthy floor.

Heloise had gone on to tell him how Deborah had burned her clothes, saying she would never feel clean again, and his heart had sunk to his boots.

She had begun to tactfully withdraw from the bedroom, intending to leave him alone with his wife. But he prevented her. Their marriage had faltered to the degree where the last thing she would want, if she should wake, was to see him looming over her. It would be like waking from one nightmare into another. He stood, ramrod straight, cursing himself as he looked down at her battered face.

She had not bothered to plait her hair neatly for bed. It spread in damp tendrils all over her pillow, making her look very young and vulnerable.

He longed to reach down and take one of those locks of damp hair in his fingers, raise it to his lips and kiss it. He had dreamed of her hair, the night she had been away from him, the few times he had managed to doze off. He had dreamed he was running his fingers through it, as she lay beside him, smiling up at him with the sleepy satisfaction he had sometimes had the privilege of imparting to her face. But then her image had shimmered, and dissipated like mist on a breeze. He had leapt out of bed, run to the door, and, shouting her name, run out into the street to search for her. But that mist closed in, blinding him, and as he batted it from his face with his hands, he would wake, sweating and shaking, to the harsh reality of his life. He had lost the hand, the one he had dreamed was filled with the silken texture of his wife's hair, in a makeshift hospital tent outside Salamanca. Nor would he ever leap, or run anywhere, ever again. But that loss was as nothing compared with the pain of knowing his Deborah was gone, and he did not know how to get her back.

She should have a decent husband, one who

could protect her, not a useless cripple, who drew danger down on himself and those around him!

Most of all, she should have someone she could turn to, someone who could hold her in his arms and comfort her, not a man whose touch could only add to her distress.

He ached for her isolation. Yet he knew there was nobody she could talk to about her ordeal. It would be like living it all over again. As a soldier, he had encountered women who had been brutalised by French troops, and the last thing any of them had wanted was to have anyone so much as mention their violation.

Eventually he had retreated to his rooms, though he knew he would not sleep tonight. Knowing she was upstairs, and safe, should have brought relief. Instead his agony was redoubled by the knowledge that, if she had not hated him before this, she surely would do now. She was more lost to him than ever.

Bone weary, he sank on to a sofa with a glass of brandy. It had taken hours of painstaking searching through Hincksey's known haunts before a handful of guineas had brought them the information he needed.

'Want to know where Hincksey would hold a woman?' the denizen of Tothill Fields had leered.

'Same place as he always takes them, to break them in, I'd wager.'

When Robert had seen her in that place, he had wanted to howl with rage and pain. His Deborah, his beautiful wife, defiled by those brutes! And all he could do was stand there, and look at her, knowing that if he once knelt down on that floor, and took her in his arms, he would have broken down completely. But there was no time for such self-indulgence. Hincksey had left only two men to guard her, but he was the head of a criminal gang, whose members ruled the area they had in-filtrated. All they had on their side was the element of surprise. They had to swoop in and get her out, fast.

Walton and Lensborough had both agreed, having seen the state of her, that there should be no trial. Though kidnapping alone was a hanging offence, bringing the villains to trial would mean Deborah would have to give evidence. She would have to relate all that had happened.

All of it.

And though if ever two men deserved to hang, it was those brutes, he could not expose Deborah to the shame of having all society knowing what they had done to her.

Once she had recovered enough to travel, he would send her out of London.

She was too straightforward a person to want to have to make up some tale about how she had come by her facial injuries. So she could not go to The Dovecote, where the servants, who had no idea how they ought to behave towards their betters, would all expect some kind of explanation. No, it was better that she stay among people who knew what had happened, and could help her to come to terms with it.

He knew Walton wanted Heloise to travel down to Wycke for the birth of their child. Nobody would question it if Deborah went with them. What could be more natural than for a lady to want her sister-in-law to be with her for the lying-in? Everyone knew Heloise had no other female relatives in England.

Deborah could avoid having to answer any questions that might arise from her inability to go out of doors until the bruises healed. He had his own suite of rooms at Wycke, to which she could retreat should she wish for privacy. And female company, in the form of Lady Walton, should she need to confide in someone.

It was the best he could do for her.

* * *

'How are you feeling today?' Heloise chirruped brightly, coming in behind the maid who bore her breakfast tray.

Numb. She felt numb. She just could not dredge up any sort of emotion at all. It was as if all her capacity to feel had frozen solid.

She assayed a polite smile and replied, 'Oh, much better, thank you. I slept so well.'

It had seemed unreal, when she had woken earlier, to find herself in this beautifully soft bed, with its crisp, clean sheets and velvet hangings, in a room that smelled of flowers. And to be wearing another of the Countess's scandalous nightgowns.

She had reached out for Robert, during the night, but of course, he wasn't there. And then she remembered that she would never wake up next to him again. For a while, she had found it hard to breathe. It felt as though a great weight was crushing her. But slowly, slowly, as she had lain on her back, gazing up at the pleated velvet canopy, listening to her breath going in and out, in and out, the numbness returned. And she welcomed it.

She endured the day as well as she could, replying with politeness to all the Countess's attempts to draw her into conversation, meekly eating what food was set before her and then getting dressed, when a selection of clothing was brought upstairs for her from Robert's rooms. She refused the offer of a visit from a doctor. She was sure her physical injuries were only superficial. Bruises always faded in a day or so.

The Countess finally left her alone when she claimed she still felt exhausted, but, though she lay down on the bed, sleep was far from her.

Why had Robert not come? She knew he did not care for her, but could he not at least have pretended? Just this once?

Though why should he, when he had warned her, from the very start, that he would not pretend anything he did not feel, or use soft words when blunt ones would serve his purpose much better?

The day dragged interminably on, the one maid who had been granted the task of caring for her tiptoeing around her, wide-eyed, as though she was some sort of bomb that might explode upon the least provocation.

And Robert did not come to see how she was.

She ate, and slept another night, in her own nightgown this time. One that she'd brought up to

London with her, which had remained among her things during the moves from The Dovecote to Robert's rooms. It had worn almost transparent from washing, and had a patch near the hem where she'd put her foot through.

As she lay in the solitary comfort of the Countess of Walton's bed, it seemed symbolic of her state. Once, she had slept naked in her husband's arms. Now, she slept alone, in the nightgown she had worn as a single woman.

Single.

Alone.

She found it harder to rouse herself from bed the next morning. She had tossed and turned all night, replaying every single minute of her relationship with Robert, trying to see if there was anything she could have done differently, any way she could have made him love her, just a little.

And the harder she thought about it, the more she began to see that she had made excuses for him every time he had been rude or unkind. She had built him up in her imagination into something he was not, then clung to this image of him, when all the evidence was to the contrary.

The imaginary Captain Fawley, the hero of the Peninsula War with whom she had fallen in love, would have come to her, sat with her holding her hand lest she have nightmares, kissed her bruises and told her she was beautiful in his eyes, not flinched from her appearance as though it turned his stomach.

The real Captain Fawley was a hypocrite. He knew what it felt like to have people turn their eyes from his injuries, and yet he had done just that, to her!

He had only married her to spite Percy Lampton. He had wanted to hurt the other man, and did not care whom he used to achieve his aims. He had urges, and had used her to satisfy them. And because she had been a romantic fool, and had responded with love, he had called her a slut. And had then carried on pursuing Susannah.

She had been such a fool! She had fallen headlong in love with a schoolgirl's vision of a wounded hero, not the real man at all.

By the time he did come up to the Countess's sitting room, after dinner on the second day, she was having trouble remembering what she had ever seen in him. And it was all she could do to keep her resentment reined back when he walked in. How could he have done this to her? Made her love him, then made her fall out of love just as fast?

She could feel the ice round her heart melting under a scorching blast of anger. Which was swiftly followed by the most agonising pain. Oh, how she wished she were still frozen in shock. Falling out of love hurt far, far worse than falling into it. For when she had fallen, she had at least had hope. Now there was none.

'What do you want?' she shot at him, as he hesitated upon the threshold.

'I have only come to inform you that arrangements have been made for you to accompany Lord and Lady Walton to Wycke, when they remove there at the end of the week. I will not be going with you. I thought it would be for the best.'

Yes, he would want to stay in London with Susannah while the Season lasted. Sending her to the family estate, to be a companion to the Countess during her lying-in, would cause no undue comment in society at all. He would be rid of her, well rid of her.

And she of him!

Lifting her chin a notch, she said, 'I could not agree more. Is that all?'

'No. I thought you would wish to know there will not be a trial, as a result of your…ordeal. Nobody need know if you do not tell them.'

So, he did not think it worth prosecuting the men who had dragged her off the street, beaten and starved her and held her captive? What further proof did she need of his total lack of compassion? He just wanted the whole incident swept under the carpet.

Just as he wanted her to disappear from his life.

She was only surprised he had bothered to come and rescue her at all. If he had left her, he would probably be without a wife at all now. The will only said he had to marry, after all, not that he had to stay married for any specific length of time. As a widower, he would have been free....

No, she could not pursue that line of thought. It was one thing to accept his nature for what it was, quite another to think he would connive at her death. Shakily she raised one hand to her brow, waving the other towards him in a dismissive gesture. She was not thinking clearly. She was still overwrought, that was what her mother would say.

When she raised her head, to give him some kind of reply, she found she was alone in the room once more.

Well, what had she expected?

He had come to tell her what his plans were for her future. He had no reason to stay once he had delivered that message.

No reason at all.

Quite suddenly, it felt as though a black pit had opened up before her. She was falling, falling into it, and there was nobody to help her, nothing to cling to. She reached out and grabbed at the arms of the chair, reminding herself that she was in a pretty sitting room, on a comfortably upholstered chair, and soon she would be travelling into the country to stay at what was, by all accounts, a magnificent estate.

Her world was not really coming to an end.

So why did she start to weep? Why did the sobs rack her body, driving her to her knees on that soft, blue carpet? Why did she curl up into a tight ball, her fists clenched?

She did not know.

She did not love Robert any more, so it was foolish to cry because they were going their separate ways.

She thanked God she had fallen out of love with him, she really did.

Or being sent away from him would have broken her heart.

Chapter Thirteen

They were going to travel to Wycke on Friday. She would be glad to go. She was beginning to feel as much a prisoner in this pretty suite of rooms in Walton House as she had been in that filthy cell. After the first couple of days, when she had felt too weak and battered to do more than eat and sleep by turns, she spent longer and longer pacing up and down like a caged tiger she had once seen in the Tower menagerie.

At least at Wycke, she could take long walks in the grounds and burn off some of her anger in the exercise. Or ride. The Earl had come in, and spoken to her quite kindly one evening, telling her he would make sure there would be a suitable horse for her use in his stables.

But Robert had not come with him.

She'd had enough! Turning on her heel, she marched to the fireplace, and tugged on the bell pull.

When Sukey came in answer to her summons, she said, 'Can you please send one of the footmen to summon a cab for me?' She wished she had taken that precaution the last time she had decided to go out. Those men, she had realised, a shiver sliding down her spine, must have been watching her movements for some time, looking for an opportunity to take her. She had frequently hailed cabs to take her to visit her mother. She would never be so careless again.

If Lord Walton did not mind, she thought she might even take one of the footmen with her.

She went to the armoire Lady Walton had given over to her use, and took out her blue merino spencer and the bonnet that went with it. It took a matter of seconds to attach a veil to its brim. For some reason, Robert did not want anyone to see her face, though she did not see why he was making such a fuss. Her bruises were fading now, and much of the swelling had gone down. Arnica was wonderfully soothing—much more effective than ale, she grimaced as she twitched the veil into position.

A few minutes later, Sukey came to tell her a cab

was waiting. She had got part way down the stairs, before noticing Robert bristling at the foot of them.

'Where are you going?'

She lifted her chin.

'To visit my mother.'

'That would be ill advised.' The expression on his face was forbidding.

But she had had enough of his high-handed edicts. 'I am not going to leave town without bidding her farewell. She will think it most odd.' Deborah descended the last stair and made as though she would have stalked past him. But he reached out, taking her arm, saying,

'If you insist on going, I will go with you.'

'There is no need.'

'There is every need!'

She locked glares with him for a few seconds, puzzled as to why he would want to go with her, when he had made it so plain that he was sick and tired of the very thought of her. It only took a few moments' reflection to work it out. He would not want her to say anything that might upset his precious Susannah, who was still living with her mother. The only reason he was insisting on going with her was to make sure she behaved herself.

She felt the insult keenly.

'If you insist, I suppose I cannot stop you.' She sighed, turning her head away from him, to gaze longingly at the open door.

It took him only a minute or two to fetch his own hat and coat. Then they walked to the cab together, he handing her in as correctly as though they were any normal married couple, going visiting together.

But his face was grim, and neither of them spoke for the duration of the short journey.

Mrs Gillies was delighted to see them. She rose to embrace her daughter as the butler showed them into the sitting room, where she had been writing some letters. Though her face puckered with concern the moment Deborah lifted her veil to return her kiss.

'Oh, my word! Whatever has happened to your face?'

'I…'

She had not thought of an excuse. She had not thought beyond getting out and seeing her mother. All she had wanted was to kneel at her feet, lay her head in her lap and sob her heart out.

But at that moment, Susannah bounced into the room.

'Debs!' she cried, going to hug her. 'I have

missed you so much these last few days. I am so glad you are come, for I have such news! Oh, good morning, Captain Fawley,' she checked herself, dropping a polite curtsy, before turning back to Deborah.

Robert glowered at her before crossing the room to take a seat beside Mrs Gillies, who had subsided on to a sofa, anxiously plucking at the strings to her lace cap.

It was then that Susannah looked at Deborah properly.

'Whatever has happened?' Impulsively, she reached out to touch the bruises that were leaking from Deborah's eyebrow, down the left side of her face.

'I fell out of a coach,' Deborah said. It was almost the truth—the only part that she felt ready to share on this occasion. 'So silly of me,' she said, settling on to a chair by the fireplace and smoothing down her skirts. 'I would really rather not speak of it.' She raised her head to look directly at Susannah. 'Let me hear your news, instead.'

While Susannah went to her favourite chair by the window, Deborah caught her mother's eye, and gave a tiny shake of her head. Then she shot a meaningful look towards Susannah, who was positioning her chair in the exact spot where the early morning sun would paint highlights in her hair.

'I can quite see why you have claimed to be indisposed for the last few days,' her mother said.

She cleared her throat. 'Naturally, I could not go out while the bruises were at their worst. And I was a little shaken up, to be honest. I would not have come today, were it not for the fact that I shall be travelling down to Wycke tomorrow, and wished to take my leave of you both. I will write, of course, from there.'

Mrs Gillies relaxed immediately, understanding the silent message that her daughter would tell her everything in due course.

'Well, I am glad you came in person. For I should not have liked you to find out my news by means of a letter. I am engaged to be married!' Susannah beamed. 'To Mr Percy Lampton!'

Deborah felt the world tilt on its axis. She dared not look in her husband's direction. What a blow it must be to him, just when he had believed he was on the verge of winning his heart's desire.

'H-how came this about? I thought you had quite despaired of him.'

'Yes, I had,' she admitted, her eyes growing soulful. 'And despair...yes, yes, that is exactly what

I suffered. I did not know how I could bear it. But only yesterday he came here, begging leave to speak with me in private. I did not know that I should receive him, but in the end, your mother persuaded me to take a turn about the garden with him.'

Deborah's heart jolted. Could he have proposed, in the garden, in the very spot where Robert had proposed to her?

'Firstly, he begged that I would forgive him for neglecting me for such a long time, after having paid me such particular attention. He explained that, at first, he had only meant to pass some time flirting with the prettiest débutante of the Season. But as time went on, his attraction to me grew so strong that he felt impelled to break off all contact with me, before things went too far. For his family would never agree to him marrying a woman from my background. He knew that he would have to choose between me and his family, should he propose marriage. But in the end, he could stay away no longer. He cannot live without me. There!' she finished, her hands clasped together, her eyes bright with wonder. 'Is that not wonderful?'

'Amazing,' said Deborah weakly, finally darting a concerned look in her husband's direction. His face expressed all the contempt she had known he must feel on hearing such an ingenuous declaration. They both knew why Lampton had begun to flirt with Susannah. And could both guess what he was playing at now.

Hincksey was a dangerous man to cross. He was obviously not going to rest until he recouped Lampton's debts one way or another. He must have realised he had made a grave error in supposing Robert would be a soft target, and decided to lean on Lampton again.

Desperate to find the money to pay the villain off, Lampton must have seen he had no choice but to take advantage of Susannah's infatuation with him. It might mean breaking with his family, but, by the sound of it, the threats Hincksey had used on him had made him fear for his very life. He probably believed he would not live if he could not persuade Susannah to marry him, and thereby gain control of her dowry. It would have given his lying words the very ring of sincerity needed to convince Susannah he was in earnest, especially when he was telling her exactly what she most wanted to hear.

'I do hope you will be happy,' she managed to say, when she could not in all conscience offer very fulsome congratulations.

'Oh, I shall be…' she sighed, a faraway look in her eyes '…for I love Percy so much! We will be married as soon as the banns can be called,' she went on, sitting forward. 'I do hope you will be my maid of honour. Even though you never asked me to be yours,' she added with a touch of reproof.

'I am sure Deborah would be delighted,' Robert put in, rather shocking her. 'You must let us know when and where the wedding is to take place, and she will attend you.'

The rest of the visit was taken up in discussing Susannah's bride clothes, how delighted her parents would be that she had made such a satisfactory match in her very first Season, and whether she should marry in the fashionable St George's Chapel, or in their own parish church at Lower Wakering.

Robert, unsurprisingly, had made no contribution to the conversation. When the time came for them to leave, he could not disguise his relief.

He sank into the seat opposite her in the cab that they hired to take them back to Walton House, looking drained.

In spite of the fact that Deborah had decided she no longer loved him, he looked such a picture of abject misery that her tender heart went out to him.

'I am so sorry,' she said softly, barely restraining herself from reaching out to touch him comfortingly upon his sleeve.

His eyes flew open, catching her in the very act of withdrawing her hand and curling it in her lap.

'What have you to be sorry for?'

'That Percy Lampton is going to marry Susannah after all.'

He frowned at her for a few seconds before saying slowly, 'I do not know why you should think I might be sorry Lampton is marrying her. It was at my suggestion, after all!'

'Y-your suggestion? But you could not want him to…not any man to…' She faltered to a close, completely bewildered by his statement.

'Of course I wanted Lampton to marry Susannah. They deserve each other!' he snapped. 'She is a silly, selfish, shallow creature who only looks upon the outward man, and all he wants is enough money to live in style. He does not care how he acquires it, even to marrying a girl he feels is so far beneath him on the social scale that she is fit only to be his mistress.'

Deborah shook her head. 'I cannot believe…' but suddenly, she saw what had happened. He had fallen out of love with Susannah, just as painfully as she had fallen out of love with him. It seemed that unrequited love was doomed to wither away. It certainly explained the bitterness of the words he had chosen to describe Susannah's character. Had she not cursed him soundly, during her long, lonely, sleepless nights? And as she turned to look out of the window she noticed how many people's faces, as they hurried along the streets, looked strained or downcast. Life, she decided, was a depressing business.

'Can you not believe that I would do anything to keep you safe, Deborah?' he said urgently, leaning towards her.

She turned to him with a start. This was the very last thing she would have expected him to say. Her astonishment must have shown on her face, because he sat back, his own face taking on a sardonic cast.

'No, you cannot believe anything good of me. I do not blame you, I suppose, but this I will tell you. I warned Lampton that if he did not marry Susannah, I would make him pay for putting your life in danger. I only had to discharge my pistol the once, to make him see that it was high time he swallowed his pride. He soon decided he could marry a girl whose money comes from trade, once he understood he had to pay Hincksey what he owed, else face my vengeance. Why should I care how miserable either of them are, so long as I know Hincksey will never have cause to go near you again?'

'Y-you threatened him with a pistol?' Her heart had begun to beat in a strange and irregular rhythm.

'I took Linney with me, naturally,' he sneered. 'I am not up to doing much in the way of intimidation on my own. Even with a brace of pistols. But then, Lampton is not much of a match,' he said bitterly. 'He is only up to bullying and cheating women. Faced with a man, even half a man like myself, he soon showed his true colours.'

'Why, Robert? Why did you insist he marry Susannah? When you could have… Oh!' It would be easier to conduct an affair with a married woman. If they were discreet, Susannah's reputation would not suffer.

'Robert, I am sorry, but I do not think it will work out for you. Susannah loves Lampton. And she never…that is, she could not…' She shook her head again, unable to tell him, even now, that her friend found him physically repulsive.

Though she had turned to him that night by the fountain. Perhaps that one incident had given him hope that, once she had seen through Lampton, Susannah might be desperate enough to turn to him again.

The cab drew up outside Walton House and a footman hurried to open the door and help her, and her husband, to alight.

They went inside, side by side, to all appearances as though they were any married couple, returning from paying a morning call. Though he looked as though his world was coming to an end, and she felt as though she was bleeding inside.

When they reached the foot of the stairs, he cleared his throat.

'Would you spare me a few moments before you return to your rooms?' he said in a clipped voice. 'There is a matter we need to discuss.'

Her heart sank. There could surely not be anything more to say, could there? Their marriage was over. Did he really think she could sit and discuss it, rationally? Yes, she thought, turning to him with a resigned expression on her face. He still thought this had been just a business arrangement on her part. He still had no idea how she had felt when she had agreed to be his convenient wife.

'Please?'

Her eyes came to rest on his face, flinching at

the look that struck such a chord with her own misery. There was nobody who could understand, better than she, what he was suffering right now at the thought of his beloved giving her heart and her life to another. With a sigh, she nodded her acquiescence.

She took her place on one of the sofas before the empty fireplace, mechanically removing her bonnet and veil, laying them on the cushions beside her, while Robert took the sofa opposite. For some while, he said nothing, though he never took his eyes off her. She had the peculiar impression that he was memorising every facet of her, from the tips of her pale blue kid half-boots to the crown of her head.

When Linney came to ask if she would like some tea, Robert's expression turned downright ferocious.

'I have no wish to discuss the breakdown of my marriage over the teacups as though it was a mere formality!' he roared. 'Make yourself scarce!'

Deborah clasped her hands in her lap, focusing on them through a film of tears as Linney beat a hasty retreat.

Funny, but though she had known he wanted an end to their marriage for days, accepted that it was for the best, because she hated him anyway, she really did....

She sniffed, appalled to find the mist clearing as a single tear brimmed over and rolled down her cheek.

Angrily, she wiped it away with her gloved hand. She was not going to cry in front of him! He was not worth it! If he could toss her aside, and still hanker after Susannah...

To her shock, Robert got up and came to sit beside her. He pressed a handkerchief into her hand.

'Please, do not cry, Deborah. You will be free of me soon, I swear.'

He got up then, and moved away abruptly. 'Forgive me. I know you would not wish to have me anywhere near you.' He paused before the sideboard, pulling the stopper from one of the decanters and twirling it between his fingers, before turning to her with a grave expression on his face.

'You must see that we have things to discuss, before you leave me for ever.'

Deborah put her hand to her temple, where a dull throbbing had begun. Was he talking nonsense, or was she in too much of a state to understand what he was saying?

'I don't see,' she admitted, shaking her head in confusion. 'What are you talking about, Robert? What things must we discuss?'

'Have you not thought that you might be with

child?' he blurted out, his face going so pale she thought he might pass out. Indeed, having said the words, he came back to the sofa opposite hers, and sat down rather heavily.

Deborah felt as though he had struck her. He had used her, lied to her, thrown her love back in her face and trampled it underfoot, and now he was turning white about the mouth at the prospect he might have accidentally impregnated her?

She had always borne whatever life had thrown at her with the grace she had been taught a lady should always display. On the very few occasions she had felt her self-control waver, she had walked away from the prospect of confrontation.

But now she felt something inside her snap. She surged to her feet, crossed the narrow space between the two sofas and slapped him hard across the face. Tears were streaming unchecked down her face now, but she was past caring. She stood over him, breathing hard as she struggled to find words to tell him what she thought.

But there were none sufficiently strong to express the scope of her anger, or the depths of her anguish.

She watched as the marks of her fingers blossomed red across his pale features, a stunningly satisfying testament to her physical outburst. And she drew back her arm to hit him again.

This time, he caught her hand in mid-air, the crystal stopper flying from his fingers and shattering against the marble lip of the hearthstone.

So she raised her other hand, clenched it into a fist and flailed out at him wildly. He raised his injured left arm to ward off the blows she rained down on his face and shoulders. But all the while, he was twisting her other arm until he managed to bring her whole body down beside his on the sofa. She slithered across the leather seat in her effort to pull herself away, but he was too strong for her. Catching her round the waist with his left arm, he hauled her up against his chest, and somehow she found she was sitting on his lap, sobbing into his neck, while he held her tightly against his body, her arms clamped to her sides.

Eventually she stopped struggling, and just let the tempest of tears flood out. When the storm passed, she sagged into him, her eyes closed, waiting for his hold on her to slacken, for him to put her away from him.

But he just kept on holding her tightly, his own face pressed to the crown of her head.

Finally, though she kept her eyes closed, her face

pressed into his neck, she drew enough strength from some source deep within herself to say, in a voice that quivered with defiance, 'If I am with child, I at least, shall love it. Even if you won't want to have anything to do with it, or with me….'

'No!' He sat up, and, taking her chin in his hand, so that she had to look into his eyes, said, 'If you are with child, I shall support you through the ordeal of bearing it. In any way I can! You only have to send me word, and I swear, I will do whatever you request of me!'

She frowned, once more puzzled by his words. But she seized on the tiny grain of hope she had gleaned from them.

'If I find out I am pregnant, would you come down to Wycke, then?'

'Of course, if you are sure that is what you want.'

Before she had time to think, she blurted, 'Oh, then I hope I am pregnant.'

He reeled back, an expression of horror on his face.

'You cannot wish that! Deborah, you cannot mean it.'

'Why not?' She sat up straight on his lap, glaring at him. 'What is so bad about wanting to have a baby? Even though you don't love me, surely you want to have children? When you proposed, you promised me—'

'This has nothing to do with love!'

'I know…' she sighed '…I know you only married me to get the money. I have always known that you are in love with Susannah. And, indeed, I—'

'In love with Susannah? Have you run mad? Where on earth did you get such a ridiculous notion?'

Her heart was beating very fast. 'B-but you pursued her. You kept on begging her to dance with you. You even got her an invitation to Lord Lensborough's ball so she would finally agree….'

His face darkened. 'That was what Lampton assumed too. That was what started this whole cursed train of events. Oh my God,' he breathed, shutting his eyes, and letting his head fall against the back of the sofa. 'How I wish I had not been such a damned fool. Though if I had not…' He stilled, opened his eyes and looked at her with such sorrow she wanted to weep for him.

'I know,' she said, disentangling her hand from his so that she could run her fingers over the weals she had raised on his face, 'you would not have had to watch her fall in love with Lampton….'

He drew in a sharp breath, catching her hand in his own and holding it so tightly it almost hurt.

'I can see the only way I am going to make you believe I care nothing for Miss Hullworthy is to confess the whole. Though it makes me ashamed to admit how low I sank.' He bowed his head, pressing his mouth to her palm, the slightest quiver going through his shoulders as he breathed in deeply.

'Though what have I got to lose?' he said bitterly, lowering her hand to her lap. 'You already hate me.'

She halted on the verge of agreeing with him. Could she really sit on the lap of a man she hated, her arm about his neck, hoping and praying he would not tell her to get to her own sofa, and leave him in peace? She had told herself she hated him, had even physically attacked him, and yet, when she had glimpsed one way of avoiding a separation, she had begged him to go to Wycke with her. That was not hatred. Her stomach seemed to turn over. It was very far from being hatred.

'I first ran across Miss Hullworthy when I was searching for a man who was causing trouble for Lensborough's fiancée. I had picked up his trail, and was looking for someone who could help me run him to ground. The first time she caught sight of me, she…' he grimaced '…shuddered. By that time, I thought I had grown hardened to causing pretty women to feel nauseous. Indeed, Heloise had assured me that my scarring was so much less than when she had first met me…but then Miss Hullworthy turned up her pretty little nose at me, and I…I am ashamed to admit this, I decided to teach her a lesson.'

Deborah cast her mind back to the way he had behaved in those days, her brow furrowing in perplexity.

'I could see how uncomfortable my presence made her feel. And so I made it my business to leap out at her, at every event I could find out she attended, just to spoil her evening! She sank even lower in my esteem when I perceived that if I had a title, or money, she would have overcome her disgust at my appearance, and positively fawned over me.'

Deborah could not argue with that statement. It was an aspect to Susannah's character she had disliked very much herself.

'So I held out the lure of an invitation to the most exclusive event of the season thus far. Lensborough's ball. And she behaved exactly as I had known she would. With the soul of a whore, she put aside her natural inclination and sold herself to me for the space of a half an hour.'

'No…you have misjudged her!' She could perhaps understand why Robert felt so bitter, but he was wrong about Susannah. 'She is just a bit spoilt, and rather silly, that is all. She got carried away with the idea of marrying well, at first, but she soon saw it was wrong to pursue a man only for his title. Lampton has no title. And she has agreed to marry him. She loves him!'

Robert made a sound that expressed his disgust at that statement. 'She does not know the meaning of the word. She is just dazzled by his looks and superficial charm. She knows nothing of him at all. But that is beside the point.' He shifted, taking her firmly round the hips and pushing her off his lap, though she derived some comfort from the fact that he placed her on the cushions beside him, rather than tossing her on to the floor, as she had half-expected he might wish to do at one point.

'It gets worse,' he said grimly, looking down at his boots, rather than at her. 'I made her the object of a wager. I bet Lensborough that I could get the prettiest débutante of the Season to grovel to me, though the very sight of me made her feel ill…' He ran his fingers through his hair, an expression of contempt on his face.

'I never cared for Susannah,' he confessed rawly.

'Not in the least. But because of that wager, Lampton set out in pursuit of her, thinking I was about to propose!' He laughed bitterly then, shaking his head at the absurdity of it all. 'I never had any intention of marrying her.'

He raised his head to look at her, as he said, 'The only woman I have ever wanted to marry is you.'

He got to his feet then, and paced away from her.

'God, what a mess.'

Deborah looked at the stiff set of his shoulders, the misery that had been a constant burden for so long lifting somewhat as she repeated, 'You wanted to marry me?' But she would not jump to conclusions. 'To get the money Miss Lampton had left you in her will. And to get revenge on Lampton for stealing Susannah from you....'

He whirled round, his expression so fierce it would have scared her had he looked at her like that earlier in the day, when she had still believed he was in love with Susannah.

'I did not consider he had stolen Susannah from me! It had nothing to do with her! Or, at least, very little. It was my past! My childhood. My God, Deborah, have you no idea how much I hate the Lamptons? Once I learned I could do him a bad turn, I did not care who I had to use, I wanted to hurt him! To avenge my mother, if nothing else! The Lamptons killed her, do you know that? Turning her out of her home, insinuating I was not my father's child, refusing to let her see Charles, who she thought of as a son...' His whole body was quivering with rage. 'And so I used you. I bullied you into marrying me, promising you a secure financial future, and children, without sparing one thought for what it would do to you.'

He marched back to the sofa, leaning on the back and gripping it tightly, his face a mask of grief as he said, 'And because of my selfishness, my desire for revenge, you got caught up in the feud, and those men took you, and hurt you...' With a hand that shook, he traced the fading bruises on her cheek, the scar on her lip.

'Raped you. And might have got you with child....'

She gasped. 'Nobody raped me!'

'But the bruises on your neck...your dress was torn...'

'You thought I had been raped?' she asked, shaking her head in disbelief. Instead of trying to comfort her, he had kept as far from her as possible. Had even decided to banish her to the country.

'You were wrong,' she informed him in a flat

voice. 'My dress got torn when they hauled me out of the cab. They split my lip to teach me a lesson for trying to think I could escape. And my neck got bruised when they held me down to cut off a lock of my hair to send to you.'

'But Heloise said you burnt all your clothes. She said you would never feel clean again. I thought—'

'Yes, you have told me what you thought,' she said bitterly. 'I burnt my clothes because I was afraid I might have brought fleas into the house. And you would feel dirty if you had spent a couple of days sleeping in your clothes, in a filthy cell, with nothing but ale to wash in! I stank like a brewery!'

He came round the sofa then, intent on taking her hand. 'They did not rape you. Thank God....'

But she leapt to her feet, backing away from him. 'What kind of man are you? You can hold my hand now, when you know I have not been defiled, but when I needed you, when I woke in the night shivering with fear, where were you then, Robert?'

She was shaking with the force of her anger and disappointment. Every time she felt as though there might be a chance for them, he slammed the door on her hope yet again.

'I thought you would not want me near!' he protested. 'Not after that last time, when you ran out on me. Not that I blame you, but don't you think I noticed how you flinched every time I got anywhere near you, after that?'

She realised she was standing with her fists clenched at her sides, slightly crouching as though she was preparing to spring at him. She made herself straighten up, and uncurl her hands, before hissing, 'After you called me a slut, you mean?'

He took a deep breath. 'I was so angry with you, Deborah, after the picnic. I had been watching you all day, trying to see which of my so-called friends it was you were planning on cuckolding me with!'

Hope flickered and died. Wearily, she went to pick up her bonnet.

'You do not know me at all, do you, Robert? From the very first time you asked me to marry you, you have done nothing but insult me.'

'I know.' He drew himself upright, standing ramrod straight as she made her way towards the door. 'You deserve better. It is why I am letting you go.'

'Letting me go?' She let go of the door handle, and turned to him with renewed anger. 'You are sending me away. You have decided, for whatever reason, you can no longer bother with the pretence of wishing to be my husband, and so you hide behind all these pathetic excuses!'

She marched back to him, her eyes blazing with a fury that she no longer had any intention of trying to control.

'For once in your life, Robert, why don't you admit the truth!'

'The truth?' he said. 'The truth is that once you have left me, I shall feel as though my heart has been ripped out. I don't know how I will survive it, but for your sake, I know I must. It is the only thing I can do for you....'

His heart would be ripped out? Her own heart gave a lurch as one or two of the comments he had made earlier, which had so confused her, came to mind. He had spoken of threatening Lampton with a pistol, so that she would be safe from Hincksey. He had denied loving Susannah, vehemently, declaring she was the only woman he had ever wanted to marry. She remembered the almost defiant nature of that proposal, his certainty that any sane woman would refuse it. And suddenly, everything seemed to fall into place.

'You really are the stupidest, most self-absorbed man I have ever met,' she said rather shakily.

'Yes,' he admitted bleakly. 'I have done everything wrong where you are concerned.'

'I, too, have been remiss,' she said thoughtfully. She should have told him she loved him right from the start. And then shown him, day by day, that she meant it. It would have saved them both so much pain. 'In not telling you that I love you.'

'You cannot!'

'That is what I have been trying to tell myself, but, sadly, it is the truth.'

He made an angry, slashing gesture at himself. 'No woman could look at this and love this!'

'Do you know,' she said, placing her bonnet carefully on the table, 'the first time I saw you, at Mrs Moulton's card party, you never even noticed me? You walked in through the door, and immediately, all the other people there seemed to me like actors upon a stage. You were the only real person in the room. You were so vibrant, so alive, in your uniform, standing there, scanning the room like a man on a mission. I think I lost my heart to you in that moment.'

'Mrs Moulton's card party?' He looked bewildered.

She began to draw off her gloves, noting with feminine satisfaction that his eyes were riveted upon her actions, 'Your eyes slid straight over me as though I did not exist, but they snagged on

Susannah, and stayed there. You looked at her the way all men do. Up and down her body, and then up to her face again, and then you sort of half-smiled.' She reached up to caress his face. 'Just a half-smile, the way you do. And that was when I noticed you had a few scars.'

'A few scars!' He flinched away from her hand. 'My face is a ruin!'

She nodded. 'A ruin of what it once was, perhaps. You must have been excessively handsome before you got burned. Probably too handsome for your own good.'

He stared at her as though she was out of her mind.

'I saw you on three more occasions before you spoke to me. At the theatre, at the Farringdons', and once, riding in the park, one morning, very early. It was not until you began to pursue Susannah, and got right up close, that I realised just how badly injured you were. And by then, all I could do was marvel at how well you concealed the fact.' She tilted her head to one side, running her eyes over his whole frame. 'When you wear your uniform, with those boots, it is almost impossible to tell that you have lost your left foot. You know, you are far more aware of your injuries than other people are. Certainly all I saw, in those days, whenever you came up to ask Susannah to dance, was the most attractive man I had ever met.'

'You…found me attractive?' He was leaning back against the arm of the sofa now, his breathing laboured. 'You lost your heart to me?' he said, as though her earlier declaration had finally sunk in.

'Why are you saying this?' His face flushed an angry red. He shook his head. 'You cannot have done. It is impossible.'

She shrugged. 'That was what I kept trying to tell myself. I knew a man as experienced, as sophisticated, as you would never look twice at a drab little provincial girl, scarcely out of the schoolroom, and that I must not let the infatuation grow any deeper. But I could not stop myself. And when you proposed…' her eyes were shining as she thought back to that day '…it was as though all my dreams had come true.'

'I am no woman's dream,' he persisted. 'More like a nightmare. Deborah, I do not understand why you persist in saying these things—?'

'Because it is the truth, you idiot,' she said rather sharply. 'Though heaven alone knows why I still love you. When you have been at such pains, right from the very first, to let me know how very little you think of me.'

'That is not true! At least, I may have led you to believe it, with the abominable way I have treated you, but it is not because I have no regard for you. I hold you in the very highest esteem. I have always known you are much too good for me, Deborah. You always looked so wholesome, so untouched, when my life has been tainted from the very start.'

'So you fought any tender feelings you began to have, and went out of your way to demonstrate you could do very well without me.'

'Yes,' he confessed, looking rather stunned. 'That is exactly what I did.'

'When did you…?' She cleared her throat, turned red, and looked down at her hands, which she clasped at her waist. 'When did you realise you loved me, Robert?'

Her voice was barely more than a whisper.

He pushed himself off the sofa, and gently took a lock of her hair in his fingers. 'When Linney opened that package Hincksey sent me, and your bloodstained glove tumbled out. I knew that then if I could not get you back, my life would no longer be worth living. I would gladly have given my entire fortune to ensure your release.'

She heaved a tremulous sigh of relief. It had

been a gamble to try to goad him into confessing to a love she had still not been entirely convinced he felt. But he had confirmed it.

'So, why did you come and rescue me instead,' she asked, gazing up at him shyly, 'and make Lampton marry Susannah so he could pay himself?'

'Damn Lampton. It has nothing to do with Lampton. I just could not bear to think of you alone, afraid and possibly injured. I could not sit back and wait to receive a ransom note. I had to find you and bring you home. Deborah,' he breathed, pulling her into his arms at last, 'Deborah, do you really think you love me? Even after all I have done?'

She nodded, flinging her arms about his waist and hugging him back for all she was worth.

'I still do not understand how you can. It is not just the way I look. The man I am inside is as scarred and crippled as what the world can see of me.' He put her from him so that he could look down into her upraised face. 'I was weaned on hatred. I have drawn strength from bitterness for so long that it has made me cruel….'

'But you will not be cruel to me, ever again, will you? Not now you have finally let love into your heart.'

'You think my loving you will somehow make me a better man?' He smiled sadly. 'Deborah, you are so naïve, so innocent....'

'Not so innocent as when I first met you,' she declared. 'Loving you has changed me. And if love can change me, it can change you too.' She took his face between her hands and, looking deeply into his eyes, said, 'Robert, I am never going to back down again, or let your foolish pride stand between us. I am going to love you with every fibre of my being, until you believe you are worthy of being loved. And you are going to stop being afraid loving me will somehow make you weak. You will love me back, and the combined force of our love will wash clean all the bitterness that has eaten away at your soul—'

'Deborah,' he groaned, stopping her mouth with a kiss. 'If any woman could work such a miracle, that woman would be you. But what have I to give you, in return for all your self-sacrifice?'

'Children,' she replied without a moment's hesitation, deciding to ignore his reference to self-sacrifice. It would take time to rid his mind of such nonsensical notions, not arguments. With a determined expression on her face, she unbuttoned his jacket.

'I want your children,' she said, going to work on his waistcoat buttons. 'At least two boys and two girls.'

'I was thinking more in terms of jewels or carriages,' he riposted faintly, as she ruthlessly dealt with his neckcloth.

She shook her head. 'I want a tree house and a swing.'

'Tree house it is,' he gulped, as her hands descended to the fall of his breeches. 'For those sons you want so badly,' he groaned, a sheen of perspiration breaking out on his brow.

'For our daughters!' she protested, tipping him back on to the sofa. As he fell, he just managed to summon the presence of mind to pull her down with him.

'Ah, yes, for a minute I forgot.' And for another minute, no more was said, as they found another, and entirely more pleasurable, way of occupying their mouths.

'Their education,' he gasped, as Deborah reached down to tug her skirts out of the way, 'is to be of an exceedingly liberal nature, as I recall.'

'Equality,' she stated firmly, as he, too, reached down between their bodies. 'It is very important between the sexes. Females have as much right to…education and…tree houses… and… Oh…and…'

'Pleasure?' he groaned, as he finally slid into her.

'Oh, yes,' she agreed. 'Yes!' Though she had completely forgotten what they had been talking about. 'Oh, Robert, I do love you so,' she cried, exulting in the freedom to be able to say it aloud at last. 'I love you!'

'I love you too,' he admitted, looking up into her gloriously flushed face. And discovered that surrendering was not an admission of weakness. Not in this case. This merging of two bodies, two hearts, two lives, was forging something stronger.

He was not alone any more, fighting for his place in the world.

As a couple, they would be strong enough to take on the whole world, should it prove necessary.

He had someone, at last, to whom he belonged as completely as she belonged to him.

His woman.

* * * * *